TERRORS
OF THE
FOREST

Books by Mark Cheverton

The Gameknight999 Series
Invasion of the Overworld
Battle for the Nether
Confronting the Dragon

The Mystery of Herobrine Series: A Gameknight999 Adventure
Trouble in Zombie-town
The Jungle Temple Oracle
Last Stand on the Ocean Shore

Herobrine Reborn Series: A Gameknight999 Adventure
Saving Crafter
The Destruction of the Overworld
Gameknight999 vs. Herobrine

Herobrine's Revenge Series: A Gameknight999 Adventure
The Phantom Virus
Overworld in Flames
System Overload

The Birth of Herobrine: A Gameknight999 Adventure
The Great Zombie Invasion
Attack of the Shadow-Crafters
Herobrine's War

The Mystery of Entity303: A Gameknight999 Adventure
Terrors of the Forest
Monsters in the Mist (Coming Soon!)
Mission to the Moon (Coming Soon!)

The Gameknight999 Box Set
The Gameknight999 vs. Herobrine Box Set

The Algae Voices of Azule Series
Algae Voices of Azule
Finding Home
Finding the Lost

AN UNOFFICIAL NOVEL

TERRORS OF THE FOREST

THE MYSTERY OF ENTITY303
BOOK ONE
<<< A GAMEKNIGHT999 ADVENTURE >>>

AN UNOFFICIAL MINECRAFTER'S ADVENTURE

MARK CHEVERTON

SKY PONY PRESS
NEW YORK

Copyright © 2017 by Mark Cheverton

Minecraft® is a registered trademark of Notch Development AB

The Minecraft game is copyright © Mojang AB

Sky Pony Press books may be purchased in bulk at special discounts for sales promotion, corporate gifts, fund-raising, or educational purposes. Special editions can also be created to specifications. For details, contact the Special Sales Department, Sky Pony Press, 307 West 36th Street, 11th Floor, New York, NY 10018 or info@ skyhorsepublishing.com.

Sky Pony® is a registered trademark of Skyhorse Publishing, Inc.®, a Delaware corporation.

Visit our website at www.skyponypress.com.

10 9 8 7 6 5 4 3 2 1

Library of Congress Cataloging-in-Publication Data is available on file.

Cover design by Owen Corrigan
Cover artwork by Thomas Frick
Technical consultant: Gameknight999

Print ISBN: 978-1-5107-1886-9
Ebook ISBN: 978-1-5107-1889-0

Printed in Canada

ACKNOWLEDGMENTS

As always, my family has been incredible through the past months of writing this book. My wife, my son, and Gramma GG have been supportive and understanding of my late-night writing binges and countless weekend writing marathons. Without their help, creating these novels would be a million times more difficult.

I'd also like to thank all of you, my readers. Your countless emails and letters telling me how you've embraced my characters and brought them into your lives have been heartwarming and motivating. Thank you for believing in me, and for continuing to believe in and follow Gameknight999 and his friends.

NOTE FROM THE AUTHOR

I had a lot of fun writing this book. However, because it was about modded Minecraft, that raised some challenges, as I hadn't played much of the Twilight Forest mod. So it gave me an excuse to do "research," which, lucky for me, meant playing the mod . . . a lot. So in this case, playing the Twilight Forest mod was technically working . . . can it get any better than that?

In my opinion, the Twilight Forest mod is, without a doubt, one of the coolest Minecraft mods out there. There are so many incredible things in it, such as the Labyrinth and the Snow Queen and the Dark Forest Dungeon, that I couldn't fit everything in this book. So you'll have to watch some videos to see everything in the Twilight Forest. I recommend Direwolf20's videos on YouTube; they are fantastic.

In case you aren't familiar with modded Minecraft, I'll try to explain it. "Modded" means someone has created their own modifications to Minecraft, changing the game to create something new. These mods are always free, but you never know how well they will run; making mods is not easy. You need to really know programming to create your own mods and have them work well.

Installing the mods to your computer can be challenging, and most of the times when I've tried it, Minecraft did not behave very well afterward. There are countless videos on YouTube to help you, but I've learned to just use the specialized installers like Feed-the-Beast and Curse. These make it much easier to play modded Minecraft. There are some notes at the end of this book, in the Minecraft Seeds section, to help you try these installers out.

Recently, I've been receiving a lot of stories from many of my readers; that is fantastic! You can see them if you go to the BLOG page on www.markcheverton.com. From that site, you can email me your story and I'll post it on my site. Some kids have even gotten so excited about writing that they've self-published their own books online, which is super cool. If you go to http://markcheverton.com/published-kids/ you can see the kids like you who have already self-published their own stories online. Watch the video on that page to see how easy it is to do.

If you're interested in writing, but need a little help, go to http://markcheverton.com/resources-for-teach-ers/. You'll find writing tutorials that I've developed based on everything I've learned from writing sixteen novels. Check them out; I think they'll help. You could even show the writing tutorials to your teacher at school, and then maybe you can use them in class . . . wouldn't that be cool?

If you want to talk with me, have any questions, or just want to say hi, you can go onto the Gameknight999 Minecraft server. You can find information about the server at http://gameknight999.com/. There, you can find the new overhead map for the survival server, where you can see what people are building and can even zoom in on them like you're viewing it from outer space. (Hey, a book about Minecraft in outer space . . . that's a great idea.) Anyway, the IP address for the server is mc.gameknight999.com, and if you join, maybe you'll bump into me, Monkeypants_271, or my son, Gameknight999. We'd love to play the game with you.

Please feel free to send me an email from my website, whether it's about something I've mentioned here, or just a general question or comment. I try to answer every email, but please be careful when you type in your own email address. If you do it incorrectly, I cannot reply. I'm on Twitter (@MarkC_Author) and on Facebook (@Invasionoftheoverworld). With your parent's permission, you can reach out to me and say hello!

> Keep reading, and keep writing,
> and watch out for creepers.
> Mark

You can only be what you *believe* you can be.

CHAPTER 1

WEAVER

The battle, long past, wrapped around him like an ice-cold serpent, the silent screams of the fallen jabbing at him with the venomous fangs of guilt. Tommy knew he was dreaming, but the feelings of terrible loss and sadness washed over him anyway, as if he were there again. This battle was the last one he'd fought in Minecraft, when he'd faced the terrible artificial-intelligence virus, Herobrine. They'd had their final conflict at the end of the Great Zombie Invasion, the outcome determined on the burning netherrack plains of the Nether with the Great Lava Ocean at their feet.

Right in front of him, in his dream, Carver slashed at a group of monsters with his great iron axe, cleaving through zombies and skeletons with ease. Next to him, Baker danced a graceful dance of death, her steel blade a blur as she parried the attacks of spiders and zombies and countered with deadly effect. Fighting back to back, the duo was unstoppable, each watching for threats to the other; it was magnificent to see. Those two NPCs (non-playable characters) were historical figures from Minecraft's distant past, as were the rest of the villagers around them. In fact, the entire scene was from hundreds of years ago in Minecraft time, even though Tommy had just lived it three days earlier. A glitch caused by a lightning strike had caused his father's invention, the Digitizer, to inadvertently send Tommy back in time to the Awakening, when Herobrine had first entered the worlds of Minecraft and brought all the creatures within the game, villagers and monsters alike, to life.

Now, that adventure was over and he was safely back home . . . but it didn't feel so safe. That final battle had replayed itself in his dreams every night, the scenes the same, the outcome always the same, and every time he watched the battle, Tommy felt as if something critical had transpired, but he'd missed it at the time. Every night, he searched for that thing, even though he didn't know what he was looking for. But this time, Tommy imagined himself soaring across the battlefield like an ethereal spirit. Since it was a dream, whatever he imagined, happened. As he flew across the conflict, Tommy was able to look at different aspects of the battle, rather than staying tethered to his body as it moved through the historic struggle.

He turned and watched as his digital self, Gameknight999, battled with Herobrine in a PVP contest that would decide the future of Minecraft. Herobrine attacked and Gameknight parried, his two swords meeting the unpredictable teleportation powers that the evil virus possessed. And then, suddenly, Gameknight999, the User-that-is-not-a-user, was on his back, Herobrine standing over him, the final blow in motion, when a shining iron sword flew through the air and smashed into Herobrine, forcing his retreat.

Something important was here . . . but what was it?

Now, howls filled his dream as a wave of wolves descended upon the monsters, their white fur standing out in stark contrast to the rusty red landscape. Tommy watched as the monsters were routed, the wolves adding the extra bit of strength that was needed to tip the battle in their favor.

As the fight progressed, Tommy floated through the battlefield. He saw Weaver fighting with some skeletons, slashing at their pale white bones with the expertise of a seasoned warrior, his skill far beyond his young age.

A pang of guilt stabbed at Tommy. He didn't get a chance to say goodbye to his friend before getting taken back into the physical world. In the last seconds, before the Digitizer had pulled him back to his own world, he'd looked for Weaver, but couldn't find him. Was that what he was missing? Was it Weaver?

"I wonder what happened to Weaver at the end of the battle," his subconscious mind said.

In his dream, Tommy reversed the battle, then moved it forward again. It showed Weaver using his skill with TNT, placing the red and white cubes in traps to catch the unwary monsters in their explosive embrace. He could remember seeing Weaver destroy countless monsters with his TNT during the battle. After all, Weaver was known for his experience with TNT and fireworks, and he would go on to teach his skills to many in Minecraft's more recent history, including Tommy's friend, Crafter.

The battle sped forward, then slowed and played at normal speed as Tommy altered the rate of the dream with his mind. He saw the monsters in retreat, the villagers charging after the horde, destroying those they could catch and chasing away those they could not. It was a complete victory, even though they didn't catch Herobrine.

Now, the conflict paused in Tommy's mind as he floated across the dreamy battle scene. Near the shore of the Great Lava Ocean, Tommy found Weaver standing alone, his iron sword in his hand. The light from the molten stone made his iron armor glow with an orange hue. Farther down the shoreline was another warrior, dressed in some kind of green-dyed armor. Tommy didn't remember seeing that soldier before, but there were a lot of villagers in the NPC army, so this person could have easily gone unnoticed until now.

Turning back to the center of the netherrack plain, he watched as a blindingly white shaft of light struck the ground. The intensity of the event had momentarily blinded most of them, Gameknight included. Even now, Tommy had trouble viewing the scene, as the bright bolt of lightning, or whatever it was, obscured his view.

He turned to look for Weaver. The last time Gameknight had seen the young boy was on the shore of the lava ocean.

Oh no—what if he fell in, *he thought.* No, Weaver would never be that careless.

He moved through the dreamscape, heading toward the edge of the bubbling mass of lava. But as he flew across the battlefield and neared the shore, he saw a diamond portal standing next to the boiling ocean, a silvery membrane stretching across the shimmering blue rectangle of the passageway. And there, again, was that strange soldier. He was wearing some kind of green armor. It looked as if it were made from leaves somehow . . . that's strange, *thought Tommy. And then he saw Weaver. The stranger dragged him to his feet, a rope tied around the young boy's body. Then, the strange soldier pulled him toward the undulating silver membrane of the portal, which was pulsing and writhing as if it were alive. The green-clad soldier smiled and pushed Weaver through the portal, then stepped through himself and was gone.*

He took Weaver! *Tommy's mind screamed.*

Suddenly, he sat up in bed, instantly awake. Beads of sweat dripped off his forehead and down his arms and back, yet somehow he was freezing cold at the same time.

That dream had felt so real, and for Tommy it had been . . . in the past. Everything that had happened in that dream had actually happened during the battle. Tommy knew it—he could feel it. He had watched himself, as Gameknight999, battling against Herobrine, and had seen all the events from the battle play out again. That wasn't just a dream; it was an exact replay of history. And every time he'd lived out that dream and watched the battle repeat itself, there had been something that felt wrong. Now he knew what it was.

"That stranger kidnapped Weaver," Tommy said to himself as he sat in the darkness.

Bark! his dog added from the floor. Suddenly, the animal jumped up onto his bed and licked his face. Barky the Physics Dog was just an ordinary mutt of no special talent, other than the fact that he could always tell when Tommy was worried, and right now he was terrified.

"What happened to Weaver, Barky?" Tommy said. He'd learned long ago that talking through a problem always helped him figure it out. Of course, it also got him in trouble at school sometimes. "And why would someone want to kidnap him? He was just a kid."

He threw off the covers and stood, his feet making a slapping sound on the cold hardwood floor as he paced back and forth, thinking.

"Weaver wasn't critical to the battle at that point," Tommy said, glancing at Barky. The spotted dog laid his head on his front paws and listened, his shaggy tail beating rhythmically on the bed. "The battle was already won. Taking Weaver wouldn't affect the outcome of the Great Zombie Invasion, unless . . ."

An icy chill moved down his spine, and Tommy stopped and shivered for an instant as waves of fear crashed down upon him.

"If that stranger takes Weaver, then he can't teach the other villagers about TNT," Tommy said. "And that means Crafter will never know anything about TNT or fireworks. TNT has always been our main weapon against Herobrine, and if Weaver is removed from the past, and we don't know how to utilize TNT, then who knows how the rest of Minecraft's history will have unfolded."

He looked down at Barky and patted the dog nervously on the head. His tail thumped a renewed rhythm on the bed. Barky, at least, was calm.

"I know I haven't been back into Minecraft since finishing that battle at the end of the Great Zombie Invasion, but I just assumed everything would be okay." He sighed. "I should have checked and made sure . . . I'm an idiot.

"Without Weaver teaching all the villagers about TNT, then the whole war with Herobrine—and not just the battles in the distant past, but also in the recent wars with his monster kings: Erebus, Malacoda, Xa-Tul and all the others—could come out completely differently. Maybe Herobrine would have won those wars and hurt my friends, or even. . ." He had trouble saying the words. Tommy looked down at Barky and scratched a floppy ear. "If the villagers weren't able to stop Herobrine, he might have escaped from the server."

Tommy's breathing came in short, rapid gasps as he imagined that terrible virus getting out of Minecraft and invading the whole Internet. Herobrine would destroy everything if left unchecked, and without Weaver, who knows what would happen, or had already happened, in Minecraft.

"Barky, I have to get back into Minecraft, now! I have to see what's happened to my friends," Tommy exclaimed. "It may not be too late to help make things right."

Pulling on clothes, he darted out of his bedroom and to the basement with Barky the Physics Dog following close behind, his tail wagging excitedly as if this were some kind of game. But Tommy knew it was not a game; Minecraft had stopped being just a game a long time ago. Now, it was turning into a nightmare.

CHAPTER 2

INTO MINECRAFT

Tommy adjusted his office chair to the correct height, then locked the wheels so it couldn't move while he was in the world of Minecraft. The basement was musty and damp, and it smelled of old magazines and decomposing cardboard boxes. They'd gotten a little flooded after the last rainstorm, and many of the failed inventions on the floor had been completely ruined. No great loss there; after all, they didn't really work as planned, except for the Digitizer. It was the one thing Tommy's father had made that actually worked. His dad had mentioned that a company had bought one of the Digitizers, but he wouldn't say who it had been . . . something about an NDA, whatever that meant.

Grabbing an overstuffed pillow, Tommy positioned it on the desk so he could rest his head when the Digitizer took him into the game. The many bruises he'd received on his forehead had taught him to have something soft to catch him when the Digitizer took over his mind, or being, or whatever it did. He didn't really understand it, and he wasn't sure if his dad did either, but it worked, and that was all that mattered right now.

"I hope you're all right in there, friends," Tommy said to the screen.

An image of blocky terrain showed on the computer monitor. A tall, rocky outcropping extended out over a wide basin, a waterfall cascading from the overhang of stone and dirt and falling into a pool underneath. This was where he always spawned when he went into Minecraft, and he knew the area well.

With his right hand, he grabbed a bottle of water and drained it. He'd also learned to be well hydrated so he didn't get too thirsty while he was in Minecraft. Setting the empty bottle aside (he'd learned not to throw it into the trash, since that was how all this started) and wiped his sweaty brow.

Tommy's breathing was shallow and fast. He was very nervous—no, he was scared. Setting his head on the pillow, he reached out and flipped the power button on the Digitizer to the *START* position. Instantly, a buzzing sound began to fill the air. At first, it sounded like a group of flies zipping past his ears, then it grew louder, morphing from flies to bees. The sound grew more intense, changing from a handful of bees to an entire hive. Lights flashed on and off as the power grew. The bees turned into angry hornets as the buzzing filled the basement.

I hope my parents don't hear, he thought. *If they do, then they'll* . . .

Suddenly, Tommy was enveloped in bright white light. He closed his eyes, but the light was still there, as if it were coming from within him. Waves of heat and cold smashed down upon him. Beads of sweat rolled down his forehead even though he shivered from the chill. The room felt as if it were beginning to spin around him, slowly at first, then faster and faster, as if he were being sucked down a bathtub drain. And then . . .

. . . as quickly as it had started, it was over. The brilliant white light that had blazed from within was gone. He opened his eyes slowly. A cow mooed nearby, followed by the bleats of a sheep. The landscape around him had changed from piles of boxes, stacks of books, heaps of failed inventions, and old jet engine parts, to a blocky landscape of grass-covered cubes, boxy trees, and large rectangular clouds floating in a blue sky.

He was back! He was in Minecraft again!

Getting to his feet, he glanced up at the tall hill before him. At the top, there was a tall column of stone that stretched high into the air, with burning torches adorning its sides.

He smiled. In the real world, he was Tommy, but here in Minecraft, he was Gameknight999.

He moved to the pool into which the water fell from far overhead. A spray of mist floated in the air, coating his face with cool moisture. Gameknight smiled. That waterfall had saved his life the first time he'd come into Minecraft, by capturing a giant spider in its flowing embrace, so he always thought fondly of it. Glancing down into the water, Gameknight saw his own reflection staring back at him. His dark blue eyes looked back at him from a blocky head and square face, and his short-cropped brown hair seemed, as always, disheveled. The blue shirt he wore almost matched his eyes, but the green pants certainly didn't. It was the skin he'd chosen for his Minecraft account long ago, and he would never change it now; this was what his friends in Minecraft expected.

Moving away from the water, he walked to a nearby oak tree. Gameknight quickly started to break the leaves, hoping to find an apple; it was always prudent to have food on hand in case he was injured. A sapling fell from the leaves and moved into his inventory, but no apples followed.

Gameknight sighed, disappointed, then ran to the side of the hill and punched two cubes of dirt until they shattered and fell into his inventory. The flickering light of torches spilled out of the opening; this was his hidey-hole. He moved into the tiny cave and was happy to see a chest, furnace, and crafting bench. This was the shelter he'd built when he was first pulled into Minecraft by his father's Digitizer. It seemed so long ago. The villagers had agreed to keep the cave stocked with supplies, just for this reason. He hoped they were still doing that.

Stepping to the chest, he opened it, and then breathed a sigh of relief. Inside were his armor, weapons, and supplies. Gameknight pulled out the diamond armor and put it on, then grabbed food and torches. He reached for his enchanted sword and bow, and put both into his inventory along with a single arrow. The bow had the *Infinity* enchantment on it; he only needed one arrow, and the magical spell would take care of the rest.

Stepping out of his hidey-hole, he sealed the opening again with the blocks of dirt, then started to run toward a place that he'd been to a hundred times: Crafter's village. It wasn't clear if he'd be able to make it to the village before dark, but Gameknight wasn't concerned. He was fully armored and heavily armed; there was nothing in Minecraft that would surprise him now.

He ran across the rolling, grass-covered hills, past groups of cows and chickens and pigs. The animals watched him with their dark eyes, their pleasant moos and clucks and oinks filling the air. Carefully watching for holes in the ground, Gameknight sprinted for as long as he could, then slowed to a walk, and then ran again when he caught his breath. He streaked across the grasslands like a shimmering diamond missile, speeding across the land with his enchanted bow in his hand, arrow notched. Ahead was a forest biome, but there seemed to be something different about it. The color of the trees seemed . . . wrong, somehow. Some trees were bigger than others. In fact, they seemed too tall, twice the size of a normal oak. *That's strange*, he thought.

Colorful flowers dotted the forest floor like scattered dabs of paint on an artist's canvas. It added a rich and beautiful touch to the normally mundane biome. As soon as he crossed over into the new landscape, his senses were filled with the peaceful nature of the environment. A banquet of aromas wafted into his nose, as the flowers made their presence known to more than his eyes. Gameknight stopped for a moment to take it all in; the smells, the colors, the rustling of the leaves, the buzzing of the bees . . . it was all so fantastic, so unusual.

"Bees?!" he said aloud.

Gameknight heard bees buzzing; he'd never heard that before. Bees didn't exist in Minecraft, did they? Off to the right, a white beehive, just a little smaller than a single block, sat on the ground, a dark entrance in its side. Bees moved in and out of the hive, flying to the many flowers nearby, then returning home. Gameknight moved away from the hive, since he wasn't sure if they were hostile or not.

As he moved through the forest, the User-that-is-not-a-user realized the trees were all the wrong color. Some were a dark red, some orange, some yellow . . . they were fall colors, not the usual deep green he'd come to expect.

"How is this possible?" Gameknight said to himself as he looked around at the forest.

Now he was getting a little scared. Something was wrong. Images of his friends, Crafter, Digger, Hunter, Stitcher, and Herder popped into his head. He had to make sure they were safe.

Sprinting again, he dashed through the forest, this time ignoring the colorful plants and focusing on the task at hand: getting to Crafter's village. Ignoring his fatigue, he pushed his body as hard as he could. When he reached the end of the forest, Gameknight stopped for a moment to eat a loaf of bread, then continued to run across the next grassy plain, which he knew led to the village.

Ahead was a large grass-covered hill with bright red and yellow flowers dotting its surface. Gameknight999 darted up the side, knowing he'd be able to see the village from the summit. But when he reached the top of the hill, he was shocked by what he saw.

Crafter's village was there, but it was twice the size he expected, and the fortifications were massive. Instead of a cobblestone wall that was only one block wide, the village now had a wall that was easily half a dozen blocks wide. Tall towers with multiple NPCs in each rose up over the village. Instead of the surrounding wall being built in the shape of a square, this new wall had bends and angles to it that extended outward in places, but also jutted inward toward the collection of homes it protected. The fortification created a complex shape that must have been difficult to build, and defend. It made no sense.

Just then, someone yelled from atop the watchtower; they'd seen him.

Gameknight ran toward the village. He glanced to the sun. It was nearing the horizon, getting ready to set and turn the Overworld from a place of relative safety to one where monsters ruled.

As he approached, the gate burst open and a group of villagers came out, with his friend, Crafter, at the front. He wore his normal clothing, a black smock with a gray stripe running down the center. The rest of the villagers wore iron armor and helmets, with the exception of two girls, both of whom had streaming red hair flowing down their backs, their curls bouncing with every step.

"Gameknight, you're back," Crafter exclaimed as he approached.

But the young NPC's blue eyes were not as bright and hopeful as Gameknight remembered. Usually, Crafter was a fountain of hope and positive affirmation, but now, he seemed sad and tired.

Hunter moved to Gameknight's side and punched him in the arm. "I knew you couldn't stay away for long."

"Well, I had to come back and check on something," Gameknight replied.

He glanced at Stitcher, Hunter's younger sister. She was scowling as if she was angry. With her bow out and an arrow drawn back, she scanned the terrain, looking for monsters.

"Stitcher, aren't you gonna say hello?" the User-that-is-not-a-user asked.

"Whatever . . . hi," she grumbled.

Usually she would have smiled at him and given him a big hug, her positive attitude just a notch below Crafter's; this was strange.

"Stitcher, what's wrong?" he asked.

She didn't reply, just continued to scan the horizon.

"What are you doing?" Hunter whispered. "Don't get her mad. You know how she gets when people pester her."

It was almost as if Hunter was afraid of her sister's temper . . . which wasn't like her at all. What's going on here?

"Crafter, I came back because I was thinking about your great uncle, Weaver," Gameknight999 said. "When you were young, did he . . ."

"Great uncle Weaver? I don't have a relative by that name," Crafter said.

"Of course you do. He taught you about TNT and fireworks. Weaver even told you the famous saying, 'Many problems with monsters can be solved with a little creativity and a lot of TNT.' Don't you remember that?"

"That's a great saying, I guess," Crafter said, a frown on his face. "But I've never heard it before."

"And why would you use TNT on monsters?" Hunter said. "I don't think that's ever been done. TNT is just used for mining and that's all."

"Crafter, are you saying you don't remember Weaver?" Gameknight asked. A chill settled across his body; he was afraid to hear the answer.

"I've met some Weavers before, but I never had a great uncle by that name," Crafter said. "I'm sure of it."

The User-that-is-not-a-user sighed as waves of guilt crashed down up on him.

Weaver, I failed to protect you, but I'll get you back . . . if I can, he thought.

Doubts and fears circled around him like moths to a flame. If Crafter had never heard of Weaver, then that meant the kidnapping had actually happened. But why?

He glanced across the grasslands to the distant forest. The unusually tall trees that shouldn't have existed in Minecraft stood high above the oaks and birches; their presence caused alarm bells to go off in his head.

"Something's changed in Minecraft," Gameknight said. "Something's wrong."

"As long as there are monsters to destroy, who cares what's changed," Stitcher growled.

Gameknight looked at his friend in shock. A thirst for violence wrapped around the younger sister like a thorny shroud. The Stitcher he knew was the kindest person in all of Minecraft. She always wanted to find a solution that avoided violence, but here she was, talking as if she wanted to destroy every monster in the Overworld.

Something's definitely changed, he though. *And it's not good.*

Somehow, this was all linked to Weaver, but how? The dangerous expression in Stitcher's eyes, and the way in which the other villagers talked around her made it seem they were all afraid . . . of Stitcher. It made Gameknight sad.

If Weaver's absence caused this, what else might be wrong with Minecraft?

The possibilities circled Gameknight like vultures around a wounded animal. He had to save Weaver, but what if he couldn't? What if he wasn't smart enough or strong enough or . . . all the possible ways he could fail piled up within his mind, each one just another brick in a growing wall of doubt.

A square tear trickled out of his eye and tumbled down his cheek. He was overwhelmed with guilt, but also filled with anger at the mysterious person in the green leafy armor he'd seen in his dream, the one responsible for taking Weaver away. Unconsciously, he reached into his inventory and pulled out his diamond sword, then drew his iron blade with his left hand. He gripped the handles of the weapons tight, squeezing them with every bit of rage that now flowed through his body.

Suddenly, a voice shouted from the edge of the forest. "Smithy! HELP!"

Gameknight turned toward the sound and was shocked at what he saw. There was Weaver! He was sitting on the back of a white horse, a rope tied around his body, pinning his arms to his sides. He was wearing his normal dented and scratched armor, his familiar bright yellow smock peeking out at the neckline. Holding the other end of the rope was the strange figure in the green, leafy armor. He sat on a horse that was as black as midnight.

The sun had finally reached the western horizon and was casting a crimson hue on the scene, giving it an almost magical appearance. Stars began to sparkle overhead as they emerged through the blue veil of the daytime sky.

"There's Weaver!" Gameknight exclaimed, pointing at the pair in the distance.

"Who?" Crafter asked.

Gameknight ignored the question. "Do any of you know the one in green armor?"

"I've never seen him before," Hunter said.

"He has letters like you," Digger said.

The big NPC had been hiding in the back of the crowd and had only now come forward. Gameknight instantly noticed there was something different about him; he didn't stand as tall, or look people in the eye the way he had. It was as if he was afraid of something.

"What do you mean, 'He has letters'?" Gameknight asked.

"He's a user, like you," the stocky NPC replied. "His name is floating over his head; it says E . . . N . . . T . . . I . . . T . . . Y . . . 3 . . ."

"Entity303," Gameknight growled. "I've heard of him."

"But there's no server thread," Hunter whispered.

"What?" the User-that-is-not-a-user asked.

"I have your friend, Gameknight999," Entity303 shouted, a scowl painted on his square face. "If you want your little villager here, you'll have to come take him. But first, you'll have to catch us . . . if you can. Ha ha ha ha."

The user spun his horse around and rode off into the darkening forest, Weaver in tow.

"What's going on?" Crafter asked.

"That was your great uncle, Weaver," Gameknight explained.

"But I told you, I don't have a great uncle Weaver."

"That's because that user, Entity303, somehow took him from the past and brought him here, into this time. He changed the past, and now the present is different."

"What are you going on about?" Stitcher growled.

"Look, I know it sounds crazy . . ."

"It always does," Stitcher added.

"Stitcher . . . shhh," Hunter chided.

"Anyway," Gameknight continued, "I know this sounds crazy, but the last time I came into Minecraft, I was transported into the distant past just after the Awakening, at the beginning of the Great Zombie Invasion. I helped stop Herobrine back then, with the help of your great uncle, Weaver and a bunch of your other ancient relatives. But right at the end of the war, that user, Entity303, somehow kidnapped Weaver, took him out of the past, and brought him here, into the present. I don't understand how, but that has changed everything in Minecraft."

"What do you mean it has changed everything?" Crafter asked.

"Those super tall trees, they shouldn't exist," Gameknight said, pointing at the forest. "And all those different colored leaves . . . that's not right either." And then he pointed at Stitcher.

"What?" she growled.

"She's different too," he said. "There's too much violence in her. The Stitcher I know is the kindest and most understanding person in Minecraft."

"Well, you might be a little aggressive too, if you'd been held prisoner in a Nether fortress for a year," she explained.

"What?" Gameknight asked, then turned to Crafter. "You see, that never happened in my timeline. Stitcher was rescued from the Nether fortress right away in my version of Minecraft. This version is all messed up. Everything is different, and I don't think different is good. Who knows what kind of damage this Entity303 has done to Minecraft. We have to catch him and save Weaver, now!"

They stared at him as if he was insane.

"You know I wouldn't just make this stuff up," Gameknight insisted. "Something is wrong and I'm afraid it's only gonna get worse if we don't do something about it."

Fear boiled up within Gameknight999. He knew he could go off and chase Entity303 on his own, but with everything having changed in Minecraft, who knew what dangers he'd face?

I don't know if I can do this on my own, he thought.

After almost being killed by Herobrine at the end of the Great Zombie Invasion, Gameknight felt as if there was some kind of monster hiding within him, and that inner beast was made of pure fear and was waiting to devour him. If he tried to do this on his own, he was sure he'd fail, and Weaver would be lost forever.

"I need your help to catch Entity303 . . . please."

"I can catch that user," Stitcher said. "Just give me one clear shot and I'll take him down for you."

"Stitcher, I think it best we tried to help Weaver without violence, if possible," Crafter said. "Gameknight, we'll do whatever is necessary to help."

"First, let's just get inside before the monsters come out," Hunter said. "If we're going after that user, we need supplies and horses."

Hunter moved toward the massive village gates with the rest of the NPCs following her. But Gameknight couldn't move. He'd seen Weaver, and the expression of confusion and fear on the boy's face had stabbed at his heart.

"Don't worry, Weaver, we're coming for you," Gameknight said, then raised his voice until he was shouting as loud as he could. "YOU HEAR THAT, ENTITY303? I'M COMING FOR YOU AND NOTHING'S GONNA STOP ME!"

A distant laugh echoed out of the forest, which just made Gameknight999 that much more determined. With an angry scowl on his face, he headed into the village.

CHAPTER 3

THE BAIT

Entity303 kicked his horse in the ribs, making it gallop. He yanked on the rope that led to his prisoner.

"Hurry up!" the user growled. "If you slow us down, villager, you'll be made to suffer."

Weaver urged his horse to a gallop, matching speed with his captor.

"You know, they're gonna come after us," Weaver said, his iron armor clanking as the metallic plates banged together with every hoofbeat.

The NPC could have adjusted his riding posture and moved with more fluidity on the horse's back, but he obviously chose not to. That insignificant bit of defiance made Entity303 smile.

"Good; I want them to come after us, especially your friend with the two swords. Now why don't you just shut up, like a good little program, and ride that horse quietly."

"When he catches you, he's gonna make you suffer," Weaver said.

The user laughed.

Reaching into his inventory, he pulled out a black cloth sack. Moving his horse next to Weaver's, Entity303 pulled the bag over the boy's head.

"Not this bag again, it stinks," Weaver complained. "Besides, I need to see where we're going."

"You only need to see what I allow you to see," the user said. "Now shut up or you'll be seeing the edge of my sword."

He drew his sword and held it up before his eyes. The edge of the blade glowed a bright yellow, as if powered by some kind of mechanism from within. Entity303 smiled, then swung the sword, slapping Weaver in the back with the flat side of the blade. The NPC grunted.

"Just remember, if you do as you are told, you might just survive this, villager."

An angry growl came from beneath the cloth. It made Entity303 laugh.

They rode in silence through the colorful forest. Each tree was a different autumn color: some were bright orange, some yellow, some a deep red. Quickly, they reached the edge of the forest, then turned northward into a new biome. All around them were trees with leaves in every shade of pink imaginable. Entity303 glanced at Weaver and smiled as the boy took in all the sounds and smells, even from under the black cloth bag.

"This is a Cherry Blossom Grove," he said to the NPC.

Weaver just grunted in reply.

Entity303 marveled at the smell of the landscape; the aroma of the fresh cherry blossoms was captivating. It was like being buried in rose petals, but with the added sweet taste of cherries dripped on top; it was just incredible. He reached into his inventory, pulled out a brown egg with green spots, and threw it to the ground. Instantly, a monster shaped like a tree appeared, its face looking ancient and wise.

"Those that follow me seek to destroy the forest," Entity303 said.

"Grrrr," the creature growled.

"Protect the forest," the user commanded.

The monster pulled in its arms and became still, merging into the forest as if it were just another tree. The user laughed.

He was sure Gameknight999 hadn't figured it out yet, but Entity303 was *inside* the game, too. After hacking into the computer Gameknight's father used for his invention business, he had found the company that first Digitizer had been sold to. Then, it was easy enough to break into that company and steal the device; their security system had been childlike. Now, Entity303 was *inside* the game, with his name floating over his head like every other user, but with no server thread connecting him to the Minecraft servers. He was just like Gameknight999, a user, but not a user: he was also a User-that-is-not-a-user. But Entity303 rejected that name; it was for his enemy, not him. He was Entity303, and he wanted everyone to remember his name after he'd destroyed every Minecraft server in existence. Then, all those foolish programmers who made Minecraft would truly regret the day they fired him from his job as a programmer there.

"Entity303 *will* have his revenge," he said under his breath.

Kicking his horse so it would move faster, he galloped through the Cherry Blossom Grove, heading due north. He yanked on the rope.

"Hurry up back there," he yelled at Weaver.

When they reached the end of the colorful pink forest, Entity303 headed to the west, into the next biome; it was a bamboo forest biome. Tall, thin shafts of bamboo stretched high into the air, the closely spaced trees making it difficult to pass at times. Starting about six to eight blocks off the ground, the narrow green trunks were covered with clusters of pale green leaves, making the bamboo seem top-heavy, even though it stood straight and tall. Entity303 had to slow his horse to a walk as he guided it through the forest so that he could find places their horses could pass between the trees. At times, he even had to pull out an iron axe and cut down a tree or two so they could get through. Eventually, as they moved deeper into the forest, he had to dismount and walk the horse forward, cutting through the bamboo trees as he went. It was frustrating, but he knew it was necessary, because he needed to bring Gameknight999 to the next biome.

Once they passed through the forest of skinny but tough bamboo stalks, Entity303 mounted up again, then drove the horses hard, turning again to the north.

"I can tell you're taking some kind of zigzag path. Why are you doing that, to confuse me?" Weaver asked. "You know they're probably already chasing us."

"I'm just giving your little friends a view of what I've done to Minecraft after snatching you up," Entity303 explained. "You see, you're just a program, so I don't expect you to understand, but . . ."

"I'm not just a program! My name is Weaver!"

"Oh, how cute, a program with a temper who wants a name. That is adorable. As I was saying, villager . . ."

"I said, my name is Weaver!"

"Whatever, *villager*, as I was saying, when I pulled you out of that battle with my virus, Herobrine, I was able to use some new software that I inserted into Minecraft. If that fool, Gameknight999 hadn't gone into the past, it would have never been possible. But his blundering intrusion in the past made it all possible: I just followed the signal from his PC and let it lead me to Minecraft's past. And then, when we stepped through that diamond portal, my software code followed the same path out of the past and into the present. So everyone in the past— all your friends and family—thinks you died in that legendary battle with Herobrine."

Weaver growled, but stayed silent.

"I've been watching Gameknight and his adventures in Minecraft for a long time. I know TNT was his weapon of choice against the mobs. When I took you, the great Weaver—the only NPC who really knows how to use TNT in battle—out of the past, I knew it would disrupt everything, changing the entire timeline for Minecraft. Things progressed differently than before, which enabled my wonderful little virus, Herobrine, to unlock the mods folder. I've made many modifications to Minecraft, just to make life more difficult for everyone. And so this zigzag path is to teach those who pursue us just how severe the damage to their precious world has been. Now, be quiet so I can concentrate."

They rode hard through the next landscape. The user knew it to be called the Mystic Grove Biome, and it was appropriately named: Everything took on a mystical appearance, from the sky to the ground. Overhead, the sparkling stars had a pink hue, as if a sheet of rosy glass had been pulled across the heavens. Even the moon showed the blushing color. Trees stood tall along the banks of the many rivers that crisscrossed the landscape. The waters in the tributaries were colored a deep purple, and looked inviting, almost as if they were beckoning them to jump in. Entity303 wasn't sure if that was even safe; maybe the water was poison, as he knew it to be in the Ominous Woods, the next biome.

Suddenly, Weaver fell from the saddle of his horse, landing with a thud in the thick grassy carpet, ferns and shrubs cushioning his fall and the musty hood falling from his head. Entity303 pulled his horse around and brought it up next to the boy. He then jumped out of the saddle and lifted Weaver to his feet.

"I don't know what happened. I must have fallen asleep."

"I know exactly what happened," Entity303 said. He helped the boy back into the saddle, then pulled out an arrow, the tip covered with some kind of thick green coating. "You know what this is?"

Weaver glanced down at it, then shook his head.

He poked the boy with the arrow. Instantly, green spirals appeared around Weaver's head, swirling in the air as his skin color became pale, then a sickly green.

"This is a poison arrow," the user explained. "If you try that trick of falling off your horse again to slow us down, I'll give you more than just a taste of this poison.

This stuff will make you so sick, you'll beg for death."
He poked him again, causing more of the green swirls
to appear. "Let me be clear. I need you so those fools
behind us will follow. But if you won't cooperate, and
make things difficult for me, then I'll just feed you to
some spiders and dress a zombie up in your clothes
instead. I'd rather not do that, because zombies stink so
much, but if you become a problem, you *will* be eliminated. Do we understand each other?"

Weaver nodded his head, then leaned down, resting
his chest against the horse's neck, struggling to stay
mounted.

"I'm glad we have an understanding," Entity303 said.

"Smithy is going to make you suffer when he catches
you," Weaver moaned.

"Smithy, eh?" Entity303 laughed. "Villager, you have
quite a surprise in store for you. Now you be good and
I'll keep that hood off you . . . agreed?"

Weaver grunted, but reluctantly nodded his head.

"Good."

They rode through the Mystic Grove in silence for
hours. Gradually, the moon began to touch the western
horizon as the sun rose in the east. The sky, instead
of fading to its normal deep blue, grew bright and
pink. That was how it worked in this biome. Normally,
Entity303 would have reveled in the beauty of it, but his
hatred for the programmers of Minecraft was so deep,
he wouldn't allow himself to think anything positive of
their creations.

With the landscape growing brighter, he glanced
back along their trail, hoping to see his pursuers, but
there was nothing. They were likely still too far behind
to be seen.

Reaching into his inventory, the user pulled out a
piece of rope and dropped it conspicuously on a small
bush.

"They should be able to find that if they aren't too
stupid," the failed programmer said. He glanced at

Weaver disdainfully. "I think you're going to enjoy what I have planned for your friends. It's a pity not all of them will survive this little adventure. But, since they're only lines of code inside a computer chip, what do I care?"

He smiled an evil, toothy smile, then guided the horses to the left, toward a gigantic tree that stretched high into the air, easily three to four times the height of the tallest oak. Its trunk was massive, at least six blocks across, with multiple levels of branches extending outward. It could almost hold a city in its canopy of branches.

As they passed beneath the massive plant, Entity303 could see the end of the Mystic Grove, the colorful trees, purple waters and pink sky ending abruptly. A gray, diseased-looking biome butted up against the colorful Grove, extending off into the distance.

"What's that smell?" Weaver asked.

Entity303 sensed it as well. There was an acidic, putrid aroma that battled with the aromatic flowers and fragrant trees. The scent assaulted his nose and he felt as if he could almost taste the air. Entity303 knew this was the Ominous Woods, and it was a dangerous place. Plants here tended to be poisonous, as were the rivers and streams. Everything was gray and devoid of color, even the sky. The entire forest seemed lifeless, as if some kind of lethal spell had been cast upon the biome.

"This will do nicely," said Entity303 as he stopped the horses, then dismounted. "Get off."

Weaver slid off the horse's back. "What are we doing here?"

"Shut up!" The user drew his sword, the sound of the blade leaving his inventory stilling any further questions.

"I can't wait to face you, Gameknight999," he muttered to himself. "We have much to discuss. But I'm sure you'll have far too many companions with you. It's unfortunate I'll have to destroy some of them."

He grinned an evil grin, like that of a snake after catching an unsuspecting mouse. Moving to an open area, Entity303 used a shovel and dug a two-block by two-block hole in the ground, then filled it with water. Reaching into his inventory, he withdrew a handful of flowers and planted them carefully around the edge of the pool.

"Are you ready to go someplace you've never been?" Entity303 asked.

"What are you talking about?" Weaver replied, confused.

The former programmer didn't reply. He grabbed a diamond from his inventory and threw it into the calm pool of water. Suddenly, a bolt of lightning shot down from the gray sky, the following thunder almost deafening. When the bright flash of light faded, the water had changed to a deep, sparkling purple.

"Here we go, villager. The adventure starts for real, right now."

He yanked on the rope, drawing Weaver next to him. He grabbed the villager's well-known yellow shirt and tore off a piece, then threw it to the ground. The user smiled as he glanced at the young boy, and Weaver scowled in return.

"That's just to make sure that idiotic, Gameknight999 follows us," Entity303 said with a chuckle.

Entity303 smiled, then shoved Weaver into the portal. Instantly, he disappeared. "I'll be waiting for you, Gameknight999," Entity303 said, and then he too stepped into the portal and disappeared from the Overworld.

CHAPTER 4

THE CHASE

With Herder at his side, Gameknight999 rode at the head of a formation of villagers, all of whom were ready for a fight. Herder leaned down to say something to his wolves. He'd brought a dozen of the furry animals with him, and their sensitive noses were proving very useful at finding Weaver's trail. After whispering something to the animals, they barked, then three of them ran to the back of the formation.

"What did you tell them to do?" Gameknight asked.

Herder was the only person with the gift of being able to speak with the wolves and get them to do what was needed. Many of the villagers called him Wolf-man, as a sign of respect for his gift. His wolves had proven truly helpful to the villagers many times in their past wars against Herobrine.

"I thought a rear guard might be smart," the lanky villager said with a smile, his long black hair hanging in tangles across his face. Then, with a suspicious tone to his voice, he added, "You never know who's following?"

Gameknight nodded, though he scowled a bit. Herder was not usually the suspicious type. He was always searching for the best in people, and expecting someone to be following them was out of character for the young boy. At least, it was out of character for the Herder he'd known before all this had happened.

"Do the wolves still have the scent?"

"They lost it, so they're searching the forest for it," Herder replied.

"Perhaps we should just continue in the direction they were heading," Crafter suggested. His tiny form seemed almost comical on his gigantic horse. Even though he was probably the oldest living villager in Minecraft, he currently inhabited the body of a young boy. "When the wolves find the scent, I'm sure we'll hear them. It seems reasonable that they were still heading in this direction."

"I agree; let's keep going this way for now," Hunter added. "Digger, what do you think?"

The stocky NPC just shrugged his shoulders and glanced down at the ground. Gameknight was accustomed to Digger being a leader, his booming voice filling others with confidence, but here in this timeline Digger was not a tower of strength. Instead, he seemed consumed by sadness and fear.

What happened to you, my friend? Gameknight thought. *How could Weaver's abduction in the distant past have done this to you?*

Gameknight wanted to ask Digger, but felt it wasn't the right time. Besides, Digger wouldn't have known anything was different with him, right? Because he'd never known anything different, his life in this timeline would seem normal to him, even though it was clearly different to the User-that-is-not-a-user. Gameknight glanced up at the square face of the sun. It had now cleared the horizon and was slowly creeping its way upward, the blue sky covered with boxy white clouds.

"Let's just get moving," Stitcher complained. "If we're gonna save that villager, we should find him quickly."

They rode through a forest that Gameknight couldn't believe actually existed. Countless plants sparkled, with shining particles rising from their multi-colored leaves and petals, the magic within the plants slowly leaking out. There were trees capped with purple leaves, and others with leaves of blue or green or silver. Vines covered with tiny white flowers hung down from the leafy canopy. Even the water in the streams was the richest color of purple he'd ever seen. It was incredible to behold.

"What kind of biome is this?" Gameknight asked.

"It's a Mystic Grove," Hunter said. "You should know that. We've been here a hundred times."

"Not in my timeline," said the User-that-is-not-a-user. "This is all new to me."

"Well, if you're surprised by this." she added. "Wait until you see . . ."

Suddenly, Hunter grew quiet, her eyes darting back and forth. She drew an arrow from her inventory and notched it to her bowstring. The smell of smoke wafted through the air, followed by what Gameknight could only describe as a distant giggling sound.

"Fire imp," Fletcher exclaimed. "Everyone watch your backs."

The short, chubby villager pulled his bow out and notched an arrow. Gameknight had never met this NPC before, but Crafter had assured him that Fletcher was a trusted companion, and that they'd been in many battles together. The User-that-is-not-a-user couldn't remember the villager at all; that was yet another stark example of how the timeline had changed with Weaver's kidnapping. Things had happened differently in this modified version of Minecraft, and Gameknight couldn't remember them because he was still part of the unchanged and undamaged timeline.

Fletcher jumped off his horse and crouched behind some tall grass. He moved much faster than Gameknight would have expected for a villager of his size.

"Stitcher, draw them out," Fletcher said. "You know what to do."

The young girl dismounted and ran to a nearby clearing, then pulled out two ingots of gold and banged them together. Gameknight moved to the girl's side.

"What are you doing?" he asked.

"I'm luring the fire imps to us. They love gold." She banged the ingots together again. "You should know this, you taught it to us. Now get your bow out and quit acting like a fool."

Suddenly, a ball of purple fire streaked toward them.

"Get down!" Gameknight said.

He grabbed Stitcher and pulled her down into the tall grass. Off to the right he saw Fletcher stand and fire his bow. He shot four times, drawing and releasing his arrows faster than Gameknight had ever seen before.

"Behind you," Stitcher said.

Now he saw the creature. It resembled a tiny demon with splotchy brown skin and glowing red eyes. Two sharp white horns stuck out of the creature's head, and a pair of stubby white teeth protruded from its snarling mouth. A pair of orange wings, like those of a bat, stuck out from its back. If not for its diminutive size, the creature would have been terrifying.

"What is that thing?!" Gameknight exclaimed. He was so shocked by the sight of the little demon, he couldn't move.

"That's a fire imp, of course," Stitcher said, as if it were completely obvious.

Suddenly, Woodcutter appeared with his iron axe. He hit the creature, making it flash red as it took damage. The monster turned and began to summon a ball of magical purple flames to retaliate, but just then Stitcher fired her bow.

"Ha ha," she exclaimed, then fired again. "Take that!" Then she fired one last time, and the demonic-looking monster disappeared with a pop.

Woodcutter smiled and waved at Stitcher.

"That was fun," she said as she helped Gameknight to his feet.

"Stitcher, killing should never be fun," the User-that-is-not-a-user said. "It should only be done when absolutely necessary."

"And that was necessary . . . and fun," she said with a smile.

Gameknight shook his head.

What happened to you, Stitcher? Gameknight thought. *The Stitcher I knew would never take joy in killing. What has happened here? How can so much have changed so deeply?*

Suddenly, the wolves began to howl in the distance, their proud voices echoing through the Mystic Grove.

"They found the trail," Herder said excitedly.

Woodcutter grinned and slapped the lanky boy on the back, his strong arm almost knocking the skinny NPC over.

"Everyone mount up," Hunter said. "We need to make up for lost time."

They gathered their horses and galloped off toward the howling animals. Gameknight moved his horse next to Digger's and rode at his friend's side. They moved quickly through the forest, all riding in silence.

When they reached the wolf pack, the white furry animals took off running, continuing to follow the trail. They passed out of the Mystic Grove and into a different biome. Here, bright pink leaves decorated all of the trees in every shade possible, with clusters of dark pink mixed in with groups of light; they reminded Gameknight999 of massive cotton candy trees, but Woodcutter told him they were actually cherry blossom trees. Delicate white, yellow and blue flowers decorated the grassy landscape between the trees. Gameknight was surprised to see iridescent particles floating up from the blue flowers as if there were some kind of magical effect on them. Butterflies flittered about. They sought out the sparkling blue petals and landed on them, somehow absorbing the glowing particles. It was a beautiful scene.

Suddenly, a growling sort of noise filled the air. But it didn't sound like some kind of enraged beast; it was more like wood creaking and groaning just before breaking.

The User-that-is-not-a-user drew his enchanted diamond sword and looked nervously around, wondering what new creature was stalking them now. And then, when he saw it, Gameknight couldn't believe his eyes.

One of the trees before him had just come to life. Its eyes opened, revealing a face in the gnarled bark, and then, before he could process what he was seeing, the tree's long arms were reaching for him and its muscular legs were pushing the massive creature forward—toward him.

"ENT!" Crafter yelled.

"You shall not *grrrrrr* be allowed to *grrrrrr* hurt my forest," the creature grumbled.

"Everyone scatter!" Fletcher shouted.

The companions kicked their horses into action, each galloping in a different direction. Gameknight wasn't sure what do to do. This monster—this ent—was far bigger than anything he'd ever battled.

How can I defeat this? he thought. *I'm not strong enough to destroy this giant monster.*

Gameknight reached for his iron sword, but his fingers brushed against something soft and fragile. And that gave him an idea.

Dismounting, he put away his weapons and held his hands out to show they were empty, and he was not a threat.

The monster came closer, its massive root-covered feet smashing into the ground, making the entire grove shake.

Gameknight stopped and pulled out the sapling that he'd picked up when he first came into Minecraft. Carefully, he planted it into the ground, then stepped back and sprinkled some bone meal onto the tiny tree. Instantly, it burst upward into a full-grown oak.

Moving around the trunk of the new tree, he walked to the ent, which now stood still, and stared up into its dark, woody face.

"I am a friend of Treebrin, and I have replanted forests destroyed by the blazes," Gameknight said in a loud voice. "I am a friend of the trees and am not your enemy."

"The one before *grrrrr* said you were here to *grrrrrr* destroy the forest."

"Did he have another with him, tied up with rope?"

The ent nodded its head slowly. The wood creaked and cracked as its neck bent, a shower of leaves falling to the ground.

"That was Entity303, and he seeks to destroy all of Minecraft," Gameknight said. "The fact that he takes an innocent villager as a prisoner shows the truth in my words. We are not your enemies, we are friends."

Crafter rode his horse near the ent, then dismounted and moved to Gameknight's side.

"You are *grrrr* a crafter?" the ent asked as it looked him over.

"Yes, and you can trust the words you heard," Crafter said. "We are friends and we pursue that user. He is an enemy to Minecraft."

The ent glared down at the pair, considering their words, then turned and glanced at the others in their party. "*Grrrrr* you may pass, but make sure *grrrr* that one keep his *grrrrr* axe still." The ent pointed a leafy branch toward Woodcutter.

"He will not use his axe on a tree," Gameknight said. "You have my word."

"Very well," the ent replied, then walked off toward the Mystic Grove, its natural habitat.

"Everyone mount up! We're losing too much time," Gameknight said, his voice now filled with the firm tone of command.

"Herder, get the wolves following the trail," the User-that-is-not-a-user ordered. "From now on, we ride hard!"

CHAPTER 5

THE PECH

The hooves of the horses were thunderous as the party galloped through the pink Cherry Blossom Forest. At times the wolves had trouble following the scent amidst the many aromatic flowers that covered the landscape. Herder chastised the animals, yelling at them with a fury that the User-that-is-not-a-user was shocked to see. He didn't know Herder had such anger boiling within his lanky frame. In Gameknight's timeline, Herder was the kindest, most compassionate and sensitive individual you could possibly meet. But here, in this modified reality, the Wolf-man had a dark side that Gameknight didn't like.

Soon, they came to the end of the pink forest and entered a terrain that appeared as if it was dying. At the boundary between the biomes, the lush grass from the Cherry Blossom Forest instantly turned a dull charcoal color, as if the vibrancy and life had been sucked out of it. All around them were tall trees, some reaching twenty to thirty blocks high. Their bark was as gray as the ground, and their barren branches reached up to the sky as if asking why they must suffer. Lifeless-looking vines hung down from the empty branches, their leaves also the pitiful gray of the surroundings.

The hanging vegetation made the trees appear as if they were actually weeping . . . it was a sad spectacle.

But worse of all was the smell. This forest had a putrid, decaying sort of smell, with an acidic bite to it that left a terrible taste in all their mouths.

"This is terrible," Gameknight said. "What happened here?"

"Nothing happened here," Crafter replied. "This is just an Ominous Woods Biome."

"*Just* an Ominous Woods Biome?" the User-that-is-not-a-user asked. "There is nothing *just* about this. The land here suffers. This is not acceptable."

"This is just how . . . ummm . . . this is how this biome was made," Crafter explained. "We can't do anything about it. Besides, you've been here countless times."

"Not in my timeline," Gameknight replied.

"You're still sticking with that weird time travel story?" Stitcher asked.

"It's not a story," Gameknight snapped. "It all happened, I promise. I was there when Two-sword Pass got its name. I was there when the Abyss was formed. I was there at Midnight Bridge, and I saw the Dragon's Teeth with my own eyes. The Great Zombie Invasion may have happened a hundred years ago for all of you, but it happened last week for me." His horse kicked a gray bush, and it collapsed into dust. "I remember what Minecraft used to be like, and now, with Weaver taken out of the timeline, I see what it has done to the Overworld and to all of you, and I'm telling you, this is all wrong. We *must* rescue that boy and put him back into the past, so everything can go back to normal again.

"Look around at this poisonous land. This never existed in my timeline. The Overworld never looked as if it was dying, like this." He held his hands out wide, as if encompassing the landscape. "The Minecraft that I knew was never like this."

"So you're saying you come from a different Minecraft?" Hunter asked.

"No . . . I don't know," Gameknight stammered. "Time travel is complicated and timelines are confusing, but what I'm telling you is true. I'm new to this timeline, and all of you are different from the companions I knew in my timeline."

"We understand," Crafter said, nodding his head.

"So you don't think I'm crazy?" the User-that-is-not-a-user asked, relieved.

"We never said that," Hunter replied with a smile. "But, as always, we're with you."

Crafter nodded, as did all the others except Stitcher, who was scanning the terrain, searching for some unfortunate monsters to shoot. Gameknight sighed, then kicked his horse forward, continuing the journey.

The forest was absolutely silent. No birds were chirping, no deer scraping their horns against the tree bark to mark their territory, not even the buzz of bees from the many beehives they saw in the last forest. It was as if all life had been stilled, somehow. Even the wolves and their companions stayed eerily silent. Everyone felt afraid to disturb the deadly silence of this wounded land.

Suddenly they heard the clicking of spiders, and a high-pitched scream from some creature. They urged their horses into a gallop and headed for the sound. When Gameknight crested a small hill, he saw the source of the cry. A strange little creature that looked like a tiny gnome was trapped in a block of spider web and surrounded by spiders. The fuzzy monsters were appearing around him, popping into existence as if being conjured there by magic. In the gnome-like creature's hands, he held what appeared to be a fishing pole. The gray-skinned creature pointed it at the spiders, keeping them away . . . for now. Gameknight knew the sun was still up, but in this biome, the sky was perpetually gray, and even appeared to merge at the horizon with the ashen landscape. The spiders were difficult to see from this distance, only their glowing red eyes easy to pick out.

"He'll never be able to protect himself with that," Stitcher said with a laugh.

The little gray gnome cast out the line. The hook snagged a spider, and then waves of magical energy flowed through the line and into the spider. The monster squealed in pain, but for some reason, so did the trapped gnome. It was as if the gnome was feeling just as much pain as the spider.

"Come on, we need to go help him," Gameknight said.

"He's not our problem," Stitcher said. "I thought we were chasing Weaver and your user friend."

"That user is *not* my friend, and this creature needs our help." Gameknight turned his horse and faced the young girl. "The Stitcher I know would help anyone in need. That creature needs our help. You can see all the spiders appearing; there must be a spawner somewhere."

"That's a spiderwood tree," Woodcarver said.

"What?" asked Gameknight.

"There's a spawner block underneath." Woodcutter pulled out his axe and held it firmly in his right hand, the muscles in his huge arm bulging. "That block under the tree will keep spawning spiders forever. I know how to stop them, but I'll have to take that tree down."

"I don't care," Gameknight replied. "Let's get down there and help that little guy."

He kicked his horse into a gallop as he drew his enchanted diamond sword. Steering with his knees, he drew his iron blade with his other hand and headed straight for the trapped gnome. When he neared, he leapt off the horse and attacked the nearest spider, the one on the end of the fishing line. It disappeared with a pop, ending both the monster's and the gnome's cries of pain.

The little gray-skinned creature stared at Gameknight, as if it were getting ready to attack him, when an arrow whizzed by and hit another of the dark, fuzzy monsters in the back.

"Got him! What a shot!" Stitcher exclaimed gleefully.

"Wolves . . . ATTACK!" Herder shouted. "Let none of them survive!"

Gameknight was shocked to hear Herder utter those words. He was about to glance back at the lanky boy when a clicking sound came from his right. Gameknight turned away from the gnome and faced the spider as it attacked, swiping at him with its wicked curved claws. The User-that-is-not-a-user blocked the attack with his iron sword, then brought the diamond blade down on the monster. It flashed red, taking damage, then tried to scurry away. Gameknight let it run and instead headed for the tree under which the gnome was trapped. The wolves fell on the wounded spider, destroying it in seconds.

Under the tree, the tiny gnome screamed again as it hooked its fishing line into another spider. The bolts of jagged power running down the line looked like multicolored lightning. As the magical energy slashed into the spider, the monster and the gnome both screamed in pain together, their anguish somehow synchronized.

And then Woodcutter was there at the base of the tree, his iron axe already in motion. Next to him stood Fletcher. The fat NPC was drawing arrows and firing with incredible speed. The spiders knew what they were doing and were trying to protect the spawner. Gameknight moved to Woodcutter's other side and stood with both swords ready, their magical enchantments casting a circle of iridescent purple light. Digger moved behind them, watching their backs with his big pickaxe held ready, but not attacking. *Strange*, thought Gameknight. Normally, the Digger he knew would have been on the front lines in an effort to keep the others safe.

A spider jumped at him, the monster's claw scraping against his diamond armor. Before he could counterattack, a pair of flaming arrows embedded themselves into the monster, instantly setting it on fire. Gameknight slashed at the creature, but before he could do any damage, two more arrows hit the monster, making it disappear with a pop.

"Ha, another great shot," Stitcher shouted from somewhere in the gloomy landscape.

Suddenly, the tree trunk finally broke under Woodcutter's blows, revealing a spawner nestled in the ground. Glowing orange embers bounced around within the metallic cage, the body of a spider spinning at the center.

"Digger, break the spawner with your pick," Gameknight shouted.

The stocky NPC glanced at Gameknight, and he saw something in the NPCs eyes he'd never seen before . . . fear.

Putting away his sword, he grabbed Digger's pick-axe and started to hit the spawner. Cracks began to form around the metallic cage. The spider was spinning faster and faster; soon it would spawn. He swung the pickaxe with all his strength, hitting it again and again and . . .

Finally, the spawner shattered. The remaining spiders, realizing their reinforcements would never come, retreated and scattered into the gray landscape.

Flaming arrows flew from the top of a tree, hitting one of the retreating monsters, then another and another until the spiders disappeared with a pop. The wolves shot after them, their white fur standing out against the drab landscape.

"Ha! I got one more!" Stitcher exclaimed.

"Let them go," Gameknight shouted, then glanced at Herder. "Call the wolves back . . . let them go."

He turned away from the boy, but heard the twang of a bowstring again. He glared up at Stitcher. She just smiled and leapt down from the tree.

With a sigh, he approached the tiny gray gnome. Instantly, the lethal fishing pole was pointed right at Gameknight's chest.

"Just relax, I'm not gonna hurt you," the User-that-is-not-a-user said. "I just want to cut away those spider webs."

Crafter was suddenly at his side. The creature gazed at the NPC's armor and could see the hem of his black smock sticking out from beneath the metallic plates, the gray stripe visible at his collar.

"That's right, I'm a crafter," he said. "We're here to help."

The gnome glanced at Gameknight999, then back to Crafter. He struggled to turn and look back at Woodcutter and Digger. The little creature wore a huge backpack that seemed to be made of leather or some kind of brown fabric, the edges of the pack catching in the webs and becoming more entangled. Turning back to face the User-that-is-not-a-user, the gnome nodded, his dark gem-like blue eyes fixed on Gameknight's.

The diamond sword sliced carefully through the spider webs, destroying one block of the ensnaring white strands, then another and another until the tiny creature was freed.

Crafter reached out and offered his hand to the gnome, helping him to break free from the last few strands.

"There you go," Crafter said. "You're free now. We're glad we came along and were able to help."

"Plus we got to destroy some spiders as well," Stitcher said as she bent over and picked up an arrow that had missed its target.

The creature glanced at Stitcher. A sad expression came across his gray face as if he was about to console her.

Crafter spoke again. "I'm Crafter, and this is Gameknight999." He gestured to the User-that-is-not-a-user. "These are our companions. What kind of creature are you, and what is your name?"

"Pech . . . Empech," the creature replied in a high-pitched voice. "Yes, yes . . . Pech, Empech."

"What does that mean?" Hunter asked as she approached. She put away her bow, but still scanned the surroundings for more monsters. "Was that your name? Pech Empech?"

"Yes, yes . . . no, you do not understand. I am a pech. My name is Empech. I am one of the three guardians of Minecraft."

"You're a guardian of Minecraft," Stitcher said with a laugh. "You didn't seem to be doing a very good job trapped in that spider web."

"Stitcher, be nice," Hunter chided.

Stitcher rolled her eyes, then notched an arrow to her bowstring and turned to face the desolate, gray forest.

"You should know, child, it is not wise to judge someone by their size," Empech said in a high-pitched voice. "Yes, yes . . . that is always a mistake."

But Stitcher was no longer listening; she was scanning the dull gray forest, searching for something to shoot.

"The one in green . . . you pursue him, yes, yes?" the pech asked.

"Yes," Gameknight snapped. "He had a villager with him?"

"Yes, yes . . . a prisoner," the little gnome said in his high-pitched, almost squeaky voice. "Something wrong with the one in green, same as with you." Empech stepped up to Gameknight and poked him with a stubby finger, then moved even closer and smelled him. "You are something else, yes yes, not of Minecraft."

"He's from outside of Minecraft, from the physical world," Crafter explained. "But he's helping us, as he has done many times, defending the land against the forces of evil."

"A hero?" the pech asked.

"Well . . ." Gameknight stammered.

"A hero's quest, yes yes, you are on a hero's quest."

"Exactly," Crafter agreed. "We must save Weaver, the NPC prisoner, or bad things are going to happen to Minecraft."

"Hero's quest, yes, yes, Empech will help," the little gray-skinned gnome said.

"We don't have a horse for you," Stitcher grumbled. "Unless you can run fast, you aren't coming."

"Empech does not need a horse, nor do you, child. Horses will be of no use, yes, yes, for your destination," said the gnome, a knowing look on his gray face.

"Empech, what are you talking about?" Crafter asked. "Do you know where Entity303 and Weaver went?"

"Yes, yes, Empech saw them, he did."

"Where?" Gameknight asked, pleaded. "Where did they go?"

The little pech stepped to the User-that-is-not-a-user, standing directly in front of him. He only came up to Gameknight's chest, but his large leather backpack extended up over the little creature's head; it seemed impossibly big for the pech.

Empech stared directly up at Gameknight999. The User-that-is-not-a-user was shocked when he looked down into the gnome's deep blue eyes. Up close, they looked like magnificent rare gems and reflected his own image back at him, but his reflection was somehow distorted. He appeared frail and weak in those dark sapphire eyes, as if his body had withered with fear. Somehow, that reflection mirrored how he felt inside: guilty and weak for not protecting Weaver better.

Gameknight shuddered.

"Where did they go?" Gameknight asked again, this time his voice barely a whisper.

"They went to the forest, yes, yes," the gnome said.

"The forest?" Hunter asked as she moved closer.

"Yes, yes, the forest," Empech said again. "The Twilight Forest."

"The Twilight Forest?" Gameknight moaned, then shuddered again. "How can that be? Are you sure?"

"Empech saw the portal in the ground, yes, yes."

"Portal in the ground?" Crafter asked.

Putting away his sword, the User-that-is-not-a-user began pacing back and forth.

"The Twilight Forest is a modified version of Minecraft; a mod, as it's called. If they went through a portal on the ground, then Entity303 must have added that mod to Minecraft somehow." Gameknight began to pace back and forth. "That explains all these new biomes. Entity303 must have added additional mods to the servers. But why would he want to do that?"

"Who cares what that user did," Stitcher complained. "Let's just go get him."

"I agree," Woodcutter added.

Both Herder and Crafter nodded their agreement.

But Gameknight wasn't so anxious to get into that modded Minecraft world. He'd played the mod once, and knew the monsters that waited for them in that forest. With only this small party of friends, he wasn't sure if they could survive this. His heartbeat raced, cold beads of sweat dripped down his forehead, and, for the first time in Minecraft, Gameknight999 knew what it was like to feel complete terror.

CHAPTER 6

INTO THE PORTAL

"**A**re you sure the portal is this way?" Gameknight asked.

Empech nodded. "Yes, yes, it is this way. Empech can hear it."

They walked quietly through the Ominous Woods, the dark soil, faded trees and poisonous rivers having quelled the morale gained from rescuing the tiny gnome. It was a desolate landscape that was filled with sadness and death.

"You can hear it?" Crafter asked.

"Yes, yes, Empech hears the music from the portal."

"Ahh . . . like the music of Minecraft?" Gameknight asked.

The tiny gnome shook his oversized head. "The music of Minecraft has been gone for long time, yes, yes. Empech can only hear faint echoes. That magic is gone from the land."

"The Oracle?" the User-that-is-not-a-user whispered.

No one replied. The pech looked confused, as if he didn't understand the question. Either they didn't know whom he was talking about, or the answer was too painful to offer.

Gameknight stepped over a small, gray bush. His diamond boot brushed against the leaves, causing them to crumble, leaving behind just the stems as remains. It was a sad sight.

"This way, yes, yes. Empech can hear it louder."

The tiny creature adjusted his large pack and marched up a small hill, moving next to Gameknight999. For a moment, he studied the gnome. He was just about half the height of a full-grown villager, with a head that seemed too big for his body. An oversized lower jaw stuck out from his face, with tiny white teeth sticking up. If they were sharp, they could have appeared terrifying, but with the pech's diminutive size, there was nothing there that could be remotely scary. His eyes were a deep blue that almost appeared faceted, and again reminded Gameknight of rare gems. They were lit from within, causing them to glow ever so slightly and making them stand out against his completely bald, gray head. But when the pech looked you straight in the eyes, the reflection was sometimes unsettling, as Gameknight had learned first-hand.

Empech wore a forest-green shirt and pants, though the pants did not go all the way down to his ankles; they were closer to shorts than trousers. His feet had three stubby gray toes that reminded Gameknight more of an animal's foot than a person's . . . strange. His pack clanked and jingled as he walked, making everyone wonder what was held within.

"There, yes, yes," Empech said.

Gameknight glanced in the direction the tiny gnome pointed with his fishing pole. On the ground, he saw a ring of flowers surrounding a small pool. But as he drew near, the User-that-is-not-a-user saw the pool was not filled with water. Instead, it was filled with the same sparkling sheen he'd seen a hundred times in a Nether portal. The lavender surface undulated and pulsed as if alive. When they drew near, the portal moved faster, somehow sensing their presence.

"This is the portal to the Twilight Forest, yes, yes."

On the ground, Gameknight found a piece of yellow cloth. He instantly recognized it as part of his friend's smock. He bent and picked it up.

"They were here. Look, this is from Weaver's clothing." The User-that-is-not-a-user held the yellow scrap up for the others to see.

"The wolves can smell the scent," Herder added as he patted the thick fur of the alpha male, the pack leader. "They're anxious to find this Entity303 and exact some justice."

"And save Weaver too . . . right?" Gameknight asked.

"Oh . . . well, yeah, of course," the lanky boy replied.

"We're all anxious to save this villager, this friend of yours," Crafter said.

"Weaver's path is through that portal. I must follow. He is the key to getting Minecraft back to the way it was," Gameknight said. "That boy *must* be put back into the past so that the timeline can be repaired, or I fear something bad will happen to all the servers."

"Yes, yes, the land suffers," Empech added. "There is evil at work, and it strains the fabric of Minecraft."

Gameknight stared down at the little gray gnome and nodded, then turned his gaze to his friends.

"You need to know, there are dangers in there that none of you have ever faced," Gameknight said. "I must follow them and free Weaver, but if you want to stay . . . I'd understand. But I don't know if I can do this on my own."

He cast his gaze upon all of the villagers, going from face to face until Gameknight's eyes fell on Digger, the stocky NPC tilting his head to the ground.

Digger slowly looked up and stared at Gameknight.

"Topper would just about be the same age as Weaver," Digger said softly, his gravelly voice cracking with emotion.

Crafter moved to the big NPC's side and put a hand on his strong shoulder.

"It's OK, Digger," the young NPC said. "Maybe you should stay back, and, uh, guard the village."

He shrugged Crafter's hand off his shoulder, then took a step closer to Gameknight999.

"I couldn't take care of Topper . . . I failed," Digger said, his face creased with sorrow as a single square tear seeped from his solemn, green eye and tumbled down his cheek. "I'd rather die than fail like that again."

"But Digger, what about your daughter, Filler," Crafter said. "You have . . ."

The big NPC glared at Crafter, signifying the discussion was over. "I'm going."

He moved away from the rest of the group and turned his back to them. Gameknight could see his shoulders shaking and knew Digger was weeping. He took a step forward to comfort his friend, but Crafter put up a hand and stopped him.

"Just leave him be."

"I don't understand what's happening," Gameknight said. "What's this about Topper? Why is he so sad?"

"Well," Crafter began, "you see . . . Topper . . . well . . ."

"We aren't getting any younger here," Stitcher interrupted. "The longer we mess around here, the farther ahead Weaver and your little friend, Entity303, gets. Let's move."

"Stitcher's right," Fletcher added in a deep voice. "We need to move fast so we can save that boy. Are we all going?"

They all slowly took a step toward the portal.

"All of you ready?" Gameknight said. He glanced to his left and found Digger at his side, his eyes slightly red.

"Then let's do it," Stitcher said.

And together, the companions stepped into the portal and disappeared from the Overworld.

CHAPTER 7

THE TWILIGHT FOREST

They appeared in a strangely lit forest. The blue sky of daytime had darkened, allowing the sparkling presence of the stars to just barely shine through. It was the twilight time, the passing of day into night or night into day, when the sun would normally be halfway behind the horizon. But rather than finding the sun sliced in half by the horizon, there was no sun at all, only the twilight sky and sparkling stars.

Around them fireflies floated about, their glowing yellow bodies moving through the forest like ethereal spirits. Some landed on the unusually tall trees that filled the forest, the light from their radiant bodies spilling out and coating the ground with a warm yellow illumination.

"What is this place?" Hunter asked.

"This is the Twilight Forest," Gameknight explained. "It's a modified version of Minecraft that Entity303 somehow added to the servers. I played it once, long ago, and only saw the smallest portion of the world."

The villagers glanced around in amazement. Extraordinarily tall trees spread their long branches out in a canopy much like the roofed forest in the Overworld, except these trees were at least three to four times taller.

Their cinnamon-brown bark was spotted with tiny silver dots that looked like thorns from a distance, but were really round splotches of metal embedded in the trees' trunks. Lush green grass covered the ground right up to the bases of the trees, the blades waving the constant east-to-west wind.

Stitcher glanced around nervously while the other NPCs just took in the spectacular view.

"We must be careful." Gameknight said. "You never know what's hiding behind the bushes or trees."

"So you're saying there might be monsters around?" Stitcher asked with a smile.

"Well . . ."

Just then, an arrow zipped through the group, narrowly missing the young girl. Stitcher notched an arrow and fired so quickly, Gameknight thought at first she hadn't even aimed. But a *thunk* came from the distance, coupled with a raspy cry of pain, and then she fired two more times, each arrow finding their target.

"One less skeleton," she said, her head held high.

Zombies could be heard moaning in the distance, but they were too far away to be of any concern . . . for now.

"As I was saying . . . we need to be careful," Gameknight continued. "There are more than just zombies, spiders, skeletons and creepers here in the Twilight Forest. There are also monsters that are far worse."

"This is gonna be fun," Stitcher said.

Gameknight just rolled his eyes, though inside he was still worried about Stitcher's new personality.

Just then, a majestic howl cut through the chilly air, shattering the peaceful silence of the forest. Gameknight jumped as the sound startled him.

"The wolves have picked up the scent of Weaver and Entity303 again," Herder said, his voice resonating with pride in his animals.

"Then let's get moving." Stitcher paced back and forth like a caged animal, anxious to catch her prey. "The longer we stand here, the farther ahead they get."

"Right, let's . . ."

Suddenly, a screech came out of the trees. Gameknight drew his sword and turned toward the sound just as a brown creature with a long tail streaked by, its claws scraping his diamond helmet.

"What was that?" Digger exclaimed.

"Flying monkey," Gameknight replied. "We aren't in Kansas anymore."

"What are you talking about?" Hunter asked, then fired an arrow up into the air at a passing blur, missing her target.

Twang . . . Twang!

Stitcher's bow sang as she fired two quick shots. The screeching changed into a howl of pain, and then silence.

"That's how you do it," she said as she glanced at her sister, a satisfied smile on her small, square face. "It's not a flying monkey anymore."

"She takes too much joy in that," Gameknight said to Crafter in a low voice.

"What'd you say?" Stitcher demanded.

"Nothing," Gameknight replied. He glanced at Crafter, a worried look in his eyes.

"Let's get moving," Woodcutter said.

"Wolves . . . follow," Herder said, his voice cutting through the quiet landscape like sharp steel.

The wolves led them through the magical forest. Gameknight had forgotten about the many incredible things in this mod. Many of the strange animals stared at the intrepid adventurers, daring them to come close. There were deer with huge racks of antlers, some of the animals locking horns with their rivals. A group of boars, like large and mean-looking pigs, walked across their trail. The dark brown animals breathed heavily as they stood their ground, their white tusks somehow gleaming in the dim light of the forest. He couldn't remember if these animals would become hostile if provoked, so Gameknight recommended they steer clear. They moved around the group, the wolves keeping a watchful eye on the boars.

As the group followed Herder's animals, the forest became denser, with large ferns blocking many of the paths. This forced the party to take a circuitous path across the terrain, slowing them down.

"We should just go straight through the bushes instead of taking all these curves," Stitcher grumbled. "This is slowing us down."

"It's the path the wolves are following, so Entity303 must have gone this way as well," Herder replied.

"I don't care; this is too slow!"

"The young one is impatient, yes, yes," Empech said, his high-pitched voice filled with squeaks and bird-like chirps. "But impatience leads to rash decisions. Careful thought is always better, yes, yes."

Stitcher grumbled something under her breath as she turned away from the tiny gnome.

They continued through the dense forest for an hour, seeing more animals cross their path, all of them harmless, so far. The clicking of spiders could be heard high overhead, the monsters hiding in the leafy rooftop, but with the trees being so tall, the fuzzy monsters were not a threat for now.

Eventually, when the forest opened into a new biome, the companions had to stop and gaze upon the landscape in amazement. Before them stretched a mushroom biome, but it was nothing like the mushroom islands of the Overworld. Everywhere, broad white stalks extended in clusters of a dozen or more high up into the air. Some were thick and squat, while others were unbelievably tall and skinny. The mushrooms' caps, some of which were easily twenty blocks off the ground, if not more, were red and white and beige, some with bright spots and others all solid colors. The bright red and pristine white domes were like brilliant beacons in the half-light of the Twilight Forest, the colors almost shocking to their eyes.

As they moved through the strange biome, a new cluster of thick white stalks emerged from the haze, the spotted red domes capping the structure high up in the air. Holes that almost looked like windows were carved into the sides of these fungi, some filled with flickering light that could only be from a torch.

"Are those bridges between the giant mushrooms?" Digger asked, his normally booming voice quiet and withdrawn.

"I think you're right," Gameknight said.

"The wolves are heading straight for them," Herder said. "Entity303 must have gone near those things."

They moved toward the giant mushrooms, following the wolves. The furry white animals were like ghosts, their soft padded feet allowing them to move noiselessly. Everyone in the party tried to mimic the majestic animal's quiet nature, but the clanking of their armored plates and the jingling of Empech's pack made it impossible. As they neared, more walkways and bridges could be seen extending from one large mushroom to the next. There were wooden railings on the sides of the raised causeways, clearly indicating these were not naturally occurring things.

"I think it's some kind of mushroom castle," Gameknight said.

"Yes, yes, the Mushroom Kingdom," Empech said, his blue eyes glowing bright. "They are kind creatures, the Mushrites, kind and peaceful, yes, yes."

"Come on, let's keep up with the wolves," Hunter said.

The wolf pack streaked across the forest floor, weaving around the bright and dark stalks. The strange plants gave an almost alien appearance to the terrain, as if this were a different planet; Gameknight imagined it was a mushroom planet in outer space somewhere. The pack leader gave off a loud howl, then stopped at an open door that led into the mushroom structure. Gameknight stood next to the door and drew his enchanted diamond sword.

"These are peaceful creatures," Empech said. "Weapons will not be needed."

"We don't know what Entity303 might have left for us in there," Gameknight said. "It's best if we're prepared." He glanced at Digger and Woodcutter. "I think you two should stay out here and guard the exit with some of the wolves."

He glanced at Herder. The lanky boy pulled some long, tangled strands of dark hair away from his face and nodded. He knelt next to the pack leader and whispered something. The mighty animal barked once, and several of the wolves fanned out to guard the entrance.

Gameknight went in first, followed by Hunter and Stitcher, their enchanted weapons casting an iridescent purple glow on the white walls of the mushroom. Behind them came Herder with the alpha male, and then Crafter, Empech and Fletcher bringing up the rear. Stairs spiralled their way up the massive stalk. At intervals along their ascent, passages extended out of the stairwell and across bridges to the neighboring mushrooms. Moving from one level to the next, the companions explored all the rooms and bridges, searching for any of the mushroom people. In every chamber, they found the same thing . . . nothing.

"There should be Mushrites here, yes, yes." The blue glow in the little gnome's eyes was getting dimmer. "Something is not right."

They went higher up into the mushrooms, exploring the spotted red cap of one. A large red chamber, complete with tables, chairs, and beds was found completely empty, but bowls of beetroot stew sat on the tables, still steaming.

"What happened here?" Hunter asked. "Their food is still warm."

"They either ran away, or . . ." Fletcher began.

"They were destroyed," Stitcher concluded. "Look, some of the chairs are overturned, and a couple of bowls of soup have been spilled. These people didn't just run away, they were destroyed during their meal."

The companions looked around the room and saw the truth in her words. This was a battlefield for a very one-sided battle. Gameknight glanced at all the soup bowls, some of them large and some smaller, likely for children, and felt sad. With no weapons lying on the ground or discarded tools, it was clear these gentle people were unarmed, and didn't have a chance. This had been a massacre.

"Why would Entity303 destroy these people?" Gameknight asked. "He didn't need to do that. It would have been easy enough to just go around the Mushroom castle."

"Perhaps causing the suffering of others masks his own pain, whatever it might be," Crafter said.

"Check the throne room, yes, yes," Empech said. "We must check on the King."

The little gnome turned and headed out of the room, back toward the central stalk. Gameknight followed him with the others searching some of the side rooms and chambers, hoping to find survivors. The pech began moving faster, running up the stairs that spiraled to the top of the gigantic structure. Gameknight sprinted, trying to keep up, but the little creature moved unbelievably fast.

They reached the top of the castle after climbing what seemed like a hundred steps. The stairs ended at a set of large, ornately decorated doors. Empech swallowed nervously, then pushed the doors open. Before them sat a large hall occupying probably half the red and white spotted dome of the giant mushroom. Tall columns of wood stretched up to the ceiling with flickering torches decorating their sides casting a warm yellow glow on the surroundings. At the far end of the chamber sat a large chair made of gold, and on it a creature sat slumped over, its short arms hanging off the sides.

"The king!" Empech screeched with alarm.

They dashed across the hall, the pech moving even faster than before. He stopped next to the golden throne and carefully lifted the King's head. His head was large and round, colored bright red with a smattering of white spots on the side. His body was thin and lean, with short stubby arms and equally thin legs. The mushroom creature wore an elaborately decorated robe with sparkling gems sewn into the garment's delicate stitching.

"Your Majesty," Empech said as he carefully lifted him to a sitting position. "What happened here?"

"User . . . attacked . . ."

The Mushroom King stopped speaking as his red eyes fell upon Gameknight999. He tried to scoot backward in his chair, but there was no place to go.

"This is a friend, yes, yes," Empech said. "He is here to help."

"Your Majesty, who did this?" Gameknight asked. "What did this user look like?"

"The user wore steeleaf armor," the king said. "He had a . . . a sword that glowed yellow and . . ." He struggled to breathe for a moment. "A prisoner, there was a prisoner."

"Weaver," Gameknight hissed. "Where did they go?"

"Nag . . ." the king struggled to say, but he was getting weaker. He struggled to breathe again, his health dangerously low.

Gameknight pulled out a loaf of bread and handed it to the ruler, but he pushed it away, shaking his head.

"I did not protect my people," the king said, an unspeakable sadness resonating in his voice. "This is the end."

"No, your Majesty," Empech said. "Take the food and be healed. Your kingdom can be rebuilt."

"But can the lives . . ." he strained for breath.

The white spots that adorned his red mushroom head seemed to fade, turning slightly gray.

"Can the lives of the lost be rebuilt?"

He took another difficult breath, a labored wheezing sound coming from the ruler.

"Can the horrors that my . . . my subjects endured be . . . erased?"

"Your Highness, you must eat, yes, yes."

The king shook his head, then turned and gazed into Empech's eyes. Gameknight999 could only imagine what reflection he saw in those two dark blue gems. An expression of horror came across the monarch's face, and then finally his HP gave out, and the ruler disappeared with a pop.

"So passes the great Mushrite King," Empech moaned as tears streamed down his gray face. "A great tragedy, yes, yes."

"He will be avenged, Empech," Gameknight growled. "I promise you, Entity303 will be made to pay."

"Careful what you seek," the sad gnome said. "Revenge can punish the predator as well as the prey, yes, yes."

Gameknight looked down at the strange gray-skinned creature. The User-that-is-not-a-user saw his reflection in those dark blue crystalline eyes, but he still had that same frail appearance, his guilt over Weaver's capture deflating his confidence. Now, though, there was a new feature to his visage; his face appeared angry and evil, as if the thirst for revenge was corrupting his very soul. Gameknight quickly glanced away.

"We must leave this place, yes, yes. There is nothing left here but emptiness and pain."

"I agree," Gameknight said. "We continue the hunt."

They ran down the stairs, collected their companions, and followed the wolves onward through the mushroom forest. But the whole time, something the mushroom king had struggled to say was bouncing around in Gameknight's head, warning him of danger.

CHAPTER 8

FOLLOW THE LEADER

Entity303 and Weaver moved through the snowy forest, leaving the large walled enclosure behind. The scraping of hard scales across the frosty ground filled the air as the angry creature behind them continued to search for its assailant. The sound reminded Entity303 of sheets of metal being dragged across a stony path. He smiled.

I hope you enjoy my little surprise, Gameknight999, he thought.

The hissing of the gigantic monster grew quieter as they moved farther from the enclosure, but the pain-filled wails of the zombies were still audible. Suddenly a loud cry of pain pierced the air, followed by another and another, then grew silent.

"Apparently that massive thing doesn't like zombies or the other mobs very much," Entity303 said with a laugh. "Did you see how it went after the skeletons? That thing really wants to destroy everything."

Weaver said nothing; he just glared at his captor. Entity303 could see the fear had faded from the boy's eyes. The villager had been terrified when the huge beast had charged. It made Entity303 laugh at the time, though he'd been a little concerned as well; he certainly wasn't going to tell the villager that.

Their feet crunched on the frozen blades of grass, a light dusting of snow coating everything. Pine trees dotted the landscape, at some places their branches spreading wide and touching. A frosting of white covered the leafy blocks, creating a serene and peaceful landscape. Entity303 smiled. He'd worked on the snow when he'd still been on the Minecraft programming team, but the lead developer didn't like his idea of creating snow serpents that would devour users and villagers . . . cowards!

"What was that about back there?" Weaver asked.

"I just wanted to get that creature nice and angry for when your little friends came by."

"Not that," the NPC snapped. "I meant back at that giant mushroom. You killed all those creatures for no reason."

"I did that for two reasons. First—to show you the depth of my resolve. I will do anything to see my plan through to fruition, and destroying a few programmable mushrooms is nothing to me."

"Those were living creatures like you and me!" Weaver's square face turned red with rage. "You had no right!"

Entity303 drew his sword in a quick motion. Instantly, Weaver stopped walking and stood still. When the blade cleared Entity303's inventory, it began to glow a bright yellow, as if some kind of power source resided within. The user moved it close to Weaver's face. Tiny cubes of sweat formed on his square face as the heat from the blade washed over him.

"My strength and my superior intelligence give me the right, villager," Entity303 growled. "Do you want to question my rights any further?"

Weaver said nothing; he just glared at the user.

"And second—I wanted your little friends to also know that I'm serious. I'm going to lay waste to this land and there is nothing those fools following us can do about it. My actions in the mushroom castle were done just to clarify my intent to my prey."

He put away his sword and continued walking, yanking on the rope to get his prisoner moving. Entity303 glanced to the left. In the distance, he could just make out the edge of the glacier that hid in the haze. They would be going there soon to pay a little visit to the queen, but not yet. There were other places he needed to lead Gameknight999 and his foolish companions first.

"You know you're all alone in this," Weaver said to his captor.

Entity303 could see out of the corner of his eye that the boy was dragging one boot in the snow as he walked. He was likely trying to leave a trail so his friends would be able to follow them . . . good.

"Smithy probably has an army of villagers with him," the NPC continued. "He isn't gonna stop chasing you until you're caught and punished for your crimes."

"You are such a fool, villager."

"My name is Weaver!"

Entity303 laughed. "A program with a name, how delicious. But names are for living things, not computer-controlled toys."

"I'm not a toy," Weaver snapped. "I'm a living creature like you and that tree and that animal over there. We are all alive, and no amount of insults will change that."

They reached a stream that was too wide to jump across, but it was only one block deep and could be waded. Entity303 moved into the slow waters and pushed through the liquid, the stream only coming to his waist. As he forded the stream, he jerked the rope, causing Weaver to fall face first into the waters, getting completely soaked. The user smiled, then pulled on the rope, dragging the fool out of the water and onto the banks.

Weaver coughed as he struggled to his feet. He was now freezing and started to shiver. His yellow smock clung to his arms and legs, and his chest was now covered with a light dusting of snow. Entity303 had made him discard his armor after the mushroom kingdom, making the villager more vulnerable.

He smiled down at the boy. "You're a little wet."

Weaver growled, then shook his brown hair, flinging water in all directions. Some of it landed on Entity303.

"You see, villager, you aren't real, you're just a random collection of electrical impulses zipping through a CPU in a computer somewhere."

Weaver's body stiffened with anger, his rage causing the shivers to stop for a moment.

"My virus, Herobrine, modified your code ever so slightly, giving you the ability to have some memory and make decisions and choose where you want to go, but that doesn't make you alive. You're just a program with some artificial intelligence sprinkled on top. But soon I'll correct this situation and put all of you back to how you were, a bunch of mindless segments of computer code shuffling about through the landscape. And then, just when the developers of Minecraft think my mischief is complete, I'll tear apart the connections between worlds, causing the whole pyramid of servers to come crumbling down, destroying everything. They'll learn not to mess with Entity303."

"Smithy will never allow that!"

Weaver took a step closer to the user and glared up at him with his bright blue eyes, refusing to look away. The boy's defiance amused Entity303.

"Smithy?! You are truly a fool." Entity303 stopped and faced the young NPC. "You think that he's Smithy? Ha . . . what a laugh; this is going to be fun. That user you yelled to in front of the village wasn't your famous leader, Smithy. That blacksmith died during the Great Zombie Invasion. I watched it happen in the narrow pass through the mountains. The person you think is Smithy is really Gameknight999, a user like me. He took Smithy's place, put on his armor and stole his sword.

How do you think your great leader was able to use two swords? Magic? It wasn't one of your pathetic villagers; it was Gameknight999, a user . . . like me!"

"No, I refuse to believe it!"

"Ha ha, you can deny it all you want, but that's the truth. It's unfortunate you'll probably never have a chance to confront the liar, since I doubt he will survive what I have in mind for him, but then again, you might not survive either. Now be quiet, I have a little business with a Yeti."

"No, I don't believe you," Weaver moaned. "He wouldn't lie to me, he's my friend."

"You're so naive, villager. I wish I could be there when you finally confront him; that will be delicious. Now be quiet; we need to move fast."

They ran through the snowy forest, curving around thick towering pine trees and tall spruces. A herd of deer moved out from behind a cluster of ferns, the majestic animals standing tall and proud. Huge horns extended from the creature's heads, splitting again and again until the points were difficult to count. Entity303 ignored the animals and continued on their path. Out of the haze he spotted their destination: a large hill. A dark opening stood at the base of the mound. Icicles hung down from the entrance like icy fangs, making the opening resemble the terrifying maw of some gigantic beast.

Something moved about within the cave behind the opening, squat shapes that appeared to be all torso with very small arms and legs. They were what Entity303 was searching for.

"So what are you doing here in this strange land?" Weaver asked.

"I have need of your little friend, Gameknight999," the user said as he slowed to a walk.

The forest took on an uneasy silence, as if it were waiting for something to happen.

"That's not his name, it's Smithy."

Entity303 smiled.

"You see, I know my limitations and my strengths," he replied. "I'm good at software, but not fighting. I need your little friend and all his cohorts to destroy some monsters for me and unlock a certain fortress. I'm going to lead them around this landscape until they kill everything necessary to unlock the White Castle. That's the first part in my plan." He laughed. "When I get what has been locked in that castle, then I'll be able to really punish those who fired me from the Minecraft programming team."

"What are you talking about?" Weaver asked.

Entity303 ignored the question. Continuing through the frosty terrain, he pulled on the rope, keeping Weaver close. When they were maybe a dozen blocks from the icy entrance, he stopped.

"I'd ask you to just say put, but for some reason I don't think you would," Entity303 said.

He moved his prisoner to a tree, then wrapped the rope around it, tying him firmly to the trunk. A firefly floated about and settled against the tree, just above the boy, casting a yellow glow that looked like a magical halo around Weaver's square head.

"Now if I were you, I'd be quiet," Entity303 said in a low voice.

"Why should I do what you ask?"

"Because there are direwolves walking about, fool. They move in packs of twenty, so if you want to attract their attention, that's fine with me. I'm sure they'll leave your clothes behind when they're done."

Weaver took a nervous swallow as his eyes darted about. A distant howl floated to them on the breeze. The user smiled.

"I'll be back soon; don't go away." Entity303 laughed as he pulled out his glowing sword.

He quickly checked his inventory for healing potions, then moved to the entrance of the frozen cavern. Freezing, cold air streamed out of the chamber, making Entity303's breath turn to clouds of billowing fog. The chill bit at his skin, numbing the tip of his nose. Inside, he could see columns of ice hanging down from the ceiling, though the rest of the cave was bathed in darkness. Reaching into his inventory, he pulled out a torch and placed it on the ground. Instantly, a circle of yellow light spread out around him, pushing back the shadows. More of the short, stocky creatures could be seen moving about inside the cave. They were covered in white fur, with scaly blue skin ringing their face and hands. The largest of the monsters had six blue protrusions sticking out of his head; they resembled horns. The monster stood almost three blocks tall, with muscles rippling along its arms and chest. It was a ferocious beast.

"Hey, Alpha Yeti, I'm here for you," Entity303 said in a loud, booming voice.

The monster turned and stared at the cave entrance. A strange breathy wail floated out of the cavern. It was a cold sort of sound, like the last breath from some kind of gigantic, frozen beast. It made chills run down Entity303's spine and tiny little square goosebumps form on his arms.

The Alpha Yeti approached. It threw a block of ice that shattered on the ground, throwing shards of ice in all directions. Entity303 easily stepped aside. Reaching into his inventory, he drank a potion of speed. Now he was ready.

"I'm really sorry about this, yeti, but I must destroy you," the user said with a smile. "You see, I need one more piece of your fur to complete something special, and I don't think you'll just give it to me willingly . . . so I must take it."

The monster just stared at him, then threw another cube of ice.

"It's nothing personal; it's just business."

The monster growled and stormed toward him.

"This shouldn't take too long," Entity303 said, then dashed forward and began to destroy the Alpha Yeti.

CHAPTER 9

FLETCHER

They left the mushroom biome behind and moved into a snowy forest. The air was cold and biting, freezing Gameknight's nose and cheeks. His breath puffed out before him like smoke that quickly disappeared as it left his mouth. This reminded him of the wintery biomes in the Overworld, but there was something still unusual about it. Far to the left, he could see a structure that looked like a massive translucent wall. It was almost as if it were made of blue glass. . . . *That's strange,* he thought.

The atrocity at the mushroom castle weighed heavily on Gameknight's mind. He was confident it was meant to be a message from Entity303; the evil user was demonstrating his willingness to destroy anything to achieve his goal. Now they understood each other perfectly.

Crafter was furious. He couldn't believe anyone could be so ruthless. Hunter and Stitcher were both anxious to exact some revenge, though Stitcher talked about it as if this were all some kind of game. Woodcutter and Herder formed theories as to why the crazed user would do something so terrible, trying to come up with some justification that would explain this insane behavior. Digger and Empech remained silent, but the shock of what they'd seen was still etched deep into the scowls they wore on their square faces.

Fletcher seemed the angriest, though he was also the quietest. He was boiling with anger, his eyes almost glowing with rage, but he was keeping it all bottled up. The large villager hadn't spoken a word since leaving the mushroom biome, but his body was tense, like a coiled spring ready to explode in some unknown direction. Gameknight felt he needed to get the large villager to talk.

"Fletcher, tell me of your family," Gameknight asked.

The villager seemed shocked by the question. An uneasy silence fell across the group, only the crunch of their boots on the freshly fallen snow making any sound.

"You know what happened to my family." Fletcher adjusted his iron armor, his large shoulders and round belly fitting poorly under the chest plate and leggings. "After all, you were there."

"I'm sorry, but I don't remember," the User-that-is-not-a-user said.

"How can you not remember?" Fletcher growled, a deep, sad look on his face.

"I didn't live through that timeline. In my past, Weaver was an important person and things progressed differently for me than they did for you. Can you tell me what happened?"

"Well, Herobrine was in dragon form," Fletcher explained. "I don't know if you remember that?"

Gameknight nodded. "Yes, he did that in my time-line as well."

"We'd been fighting for days. The monster kings threw everything they had at us. Everyone who could hold a blade or aim a bow was on the walls fighting."

"I remember."

"We lost so many good friends," Fletcher said in a low voice.

"Builder," Hunter said, then raised her hand in the air, fingers spread wide.

"And Farmer," Crafter said, raising his hand.

"And Cutter," Herder said.

"And Tanner," Woodcutter said.

"And Topper," Digger said, his voice quiet and cracking with emotion.

They all spread their fingers wide, giving the salute for the dead, then clenched their hands into fists and slowly lowered them.

"Many lives were destroyed in that battle, but finally, it seemed as if we were going to win," Fletcher said. "That was when Herobrine himself joined the battle. He attacked and turned everything into end stone just after a massive attack by the spiders. Those fuzzy beasts . . ." Fletcher grew silent as the nightmare replayed itself through his memory. He moved away from the rest of the group and walked by himself, hiding his tears from the others.

"Great . . . now look what you've done," Stitcher said with a frown.

"What did I do?" Gameknight asked softly. "What happened?"

Crafter moved closer and spoke softly.

"His family became entangled in the spiders' webs," the young NPC explained. "They were caught by Herobrine's transformation wave. Fletcher had to watch from the safety of an obsidian platform while his family was changed from flesh and blood to pale end stone."

Crafter grew quiet as he too relived the terrible moments. The birds and animals in the forest seemed to feel the solemn nature of the moment and grew quiet. The only thing audible was Fletcher's sobbing. Gameknight didn't know what to say.

When there were no more tears left to be shed, Fletcher returned and finally broke the silence. "If we had been able to destroy more of the monsters before Herobrine arrived, maybe those spiders wouldn't have been there." The big NPC sighed.

"When we fought that battle in my timeline, we used minecarts with TNT in them, and hidden TNT cannons to blast the monsters," Gameknight said.

"What do you mean? Minecarts with TNT? Cannons?" Crafter asked.

"Much of it was actually your idea, Crafter," Gameknight said. "You were the TNT master . . . in my timeline."

"I wish we'd had that in our battle," Fletcher said.

"They were restored when the dragon was killed, weren't they?" Gameknight asked.

Fletcher sighed, then glanced down at the ground with fists clenched. A lone tear trickled down his flat cheek.

"Gameknight, Herobrine destroyed everyone that was transformed," Crafter said. "Even though they were no longer a threat, Herobrine flew around and shredded them with his dragon claws, regardless if they were warriors, women, children, the elderly . . . he destroyed them all."

"You mean, your wife and daughter . . ." Gameknight's voice trailed off as the sorrow of what he had just asked Fletcher to relive hit him hard in the chest. "Fletcher, I'm so sorry. I didn't know."

Fletcher sighed as more tears tumbled down his cheeks.

"We ended up destroying the dragon in the end," Stitcher said in a loud, triumphant voice. The volume of her comment was shocking, shattering the uneasy silence.

"But too late," Fletcher moaned.

The User-that-is-not-a-user placed a hand on the large NPC's shoulder. Fletcher turned and stared straight into his eyes, then moved a little closer. He reached into his inventory and pulled out a shattered piece of end stone wrapped in a soft red cloth.

"This is a piece of my daughter," the large villager said, his blood-shot eyes filled with despair. He then leaned in close and spoke in a quiet voice, his words only meant for Gameknight's ears. "If getting Weaver back into the past will save my family, then I'll do anything, even sacrifice my own life."

"No one is gonna sacrifice their life," Gameknight whispered. "We're all gonna survive whatever Entity303 has in store for us. We'll stop that crazy user and fix all the damage he's done to Minecraft."

"I hope so," Fletcher said as he wiped his cheeks clean.

One of the wolves far ahead howled. It was the forward scout.

"They found something," Herder said with a smile.

"Come on, let's see what it is!" Stitcher exclaimed. She sprinted forward, jumping up and down like a child excited for a surprise.

The rest of the party ran toward the howling wolves, as now more of the proud voices had joined the animal's song. When they sprinted around a cluster of trees, Gameknight saw a huge stone enclosure, the walls decorated with the undulating shape of some kind of serpent. Bright fireflies sat on the side of the wall, their fat bodies glowing bright green, casting some light on the surroundings.

Near the wall sat an oak tree. Gameknight pulled out a shovel and quickly dug up some dirt blocks, then built a set of steps. He climbed to the top of the tree and peered down into the courtyard. The snow, for some reason, did not fall in the enclosure, making things on the ground easy to see. There were numerous creatures moving about; a small herd of deer munched on grass while a group of boars moved about in the courtyard, doing whatever boars do.

"Weaver's scent went into that enclosure," a voice said at his side. Gameknight turned and found Herder standing next to him. "We need to go in there and see where they came out. Or maybe they didn't come out and there's a tunnel or cave in there."

Gameknight scanned his surroundings. The ground in the enclosure was covered with grass, stone slabs sprinkled throughout. Maybe twenty columns of cobblestone stood tall throughout the courtyard, with a wide platform of stone slabs at the top and bottom.

They were probably six blocks high and a good place to put some archers, just in case.

"Why do you think these walls are here?" Crafter asked from the ground.

"I don't know," Gameknight replied.

"I'm not thrilled with the picture of a serpent on the walls," Hunter said as she drew an arrow from her inventory and notched it to the bowstring.

Stitcher paced about next to her, the younger sister clearly anxious to get in there and see what would happen.

"Empech recommends caution, yes, yes," the little pech said from the ground. "It is not clear if this wall was meant to keep intruders *out*, or something else *in*."

"Weaver went in there," Gameknight said. "I think we need to do the same."

"Excellent," Stitcher replied, grinning.

"Something ancient lies within these walls, yes, yes," Empech murmured. "Empech can feel it through the fabric of Minecraft; something angry and dangerous."

"Probably just a spider," Stitcher said. "Let's get started. Weaver's getting farther away as we stand here."

"I hate to say it, but my noisy little sister is right," Hunter added. "We have no choice. If we're gonna catch Weaver, then we need to follow his trail."

"OK, everyone up onto the wall," Gameknight said.

He stepped from the tree to the top of the wall, then moved further from the leafy blocks to make room for the others. When everyone was on the wall, he glanced to his friends, then nodded his head. They all jumped down into the enclosure at the same time. Instantly, a scraping sound filled the air.

"Did you hear that?" Digger asked. "I heard something."

"Me too," Woodcutter said, his axe held at the ready.

"Move forward," Gameknight said.

The companions walked slowly forward, stepping over stone slabs and around pools of black sand.

Suddenly, a hissing sound, like that of a massive balloon slowly leaking air, reached their ears. Then a scraping sound, like heavy plates of steel being dragged across the ground, filled the enclosure . . . and was getting louder.

Gameknight saw something begin to emerge through the haze. It was on the far side of the enclosure, but heading straight toward them. At first it just looked like a large cube bobbing about in the air, but as it neared, the creature materialized through the fog of Minecraft. It was a snake, a gigantic, scaly green snake. It had a massive head that was as tall as Gameknight, with eyes glowing blood red and filled with rage. Its mouth yawned open, a line of pointy white teeth decorating the jaw. It stopped for a moment, staring at the intruders.

"The Naga," Empech said in a high-pitched whisper.

"Maybe it's not hostile?" Digger said in a low, shaking voice.

"It is certainly hostile, yes, yes. Empech can feel its anger. All should stand still and . . ."

The massive green snake suddenly bellowed an ear-splitting roar and charged straight at them, its body smashing through stone pillars like they were made of paper. The monster seemed to come straight at Gameknight999 as if it had been expecting him. Every nerve in the User-that-is-not-a-user's body told him to run, just run away. He didn't want to fail his friends; he just wanted to disappear, but he knew he couldn't do that.

He glanced around to see if anyone noticed his fear . . . no, his panic. Terror filled every aspect of his being, the panic pulsing through his body with every heartbeat. But he knew he had to do something; Weaver was counting on him, and Gameknight didn't want to fail him again. So instead, he focused on what was important: Weaver and his other friends.

The giant green snake seemed to move in slow motion, its thick scales dragging against the ground.

Be strong and have faith, child, a scratchy voice said in his head. It seemed as if it came from some memory, the voice vaguely familiar. And for a moment, it filled him with the faintest flicker of courage.

Gritting his teeth, Gameknight999 drew his iron sword from his inventory with his left hand, his diamond blade with his right, and charged straight at the creature, yelling at the top of his voice.

"FOR WEAVER!"

CHAPTER 10

THE NAGA

Gameknight999 leapt high into the air just as the mighty Naga reached him. He flew over the massive square head, its jaws snapping at him, just barely missing his diamond boot. He landed on the ground, and spun, swinging his sword at the body that slithered past. His sword clanked against the hard, green scales as if they were made of iron. He swung again and again until the point of his blade finally slipped between some of the scales and found soft flesh. The monster flashed red and screamed in pain, then turned and charged at its attacker.

All he could think to do was run. Arrows zipped through the air. The User-that-is-not-a-user could hear them bouncing off the rugged scales, but occasionally one of them would land with a *thunk*, the pointed shaft finding its way between the armor plating that covered the Naga's skin. The monster wailed and turned again. Gameknight could hear the scraping of scales against the ground moving away as the Naga sought another target.

Just then, pain erupted through his arm as a clicking sound filled the air. Gameknight spun, swinging his sword. A small spider was behind him, reaching out with a wicked looking curved claw, its fuzzy black body standing out against the grassy blocks. Gameknight blocked the attack with his iron sword, then brought his diamond blade down upon the creature. It screeched in surprise and pain. The spider tried to back away, but the User-that-is-not-a-user did not relent. He drove the attack harder until the monster disappeared.

Glancing around the enclosure, he saw more monsters emerging from along the wall; a couple of zombies, a few more spiders, and two skeletons in chainmail.

"There are more monsters about!" Gameknight shouted. "Everyone watch each other's backs."

The Naga heard his voice and quickly turned, gliding toward its enemy. A herd of deer tried to get out of the way of the giant green monster, but the massive serpent was too fast. The Naga smashed through the deer without even slowing, and the innocent animals were instantly destroyed.

"NO!" Gameknight shouted. He charged at the monster, anger fueling his courage.

Arrows pinged off the monster's scales, some of them sticking into its flesh. The Naga screamed in pain and rage, but kept its beady red eyes glued to Gameknight999. It loomed over him, about to attack.

Suddenly, dodging to the left, the User-that-is-not-a-user slashed at the monster's head just as its jaws closed with a crash where he had just been standing. Gameknight stabbed at the Naga with his diamond blade, scoring multiple hits, causing the creature to flash red over and over.

"Gameknight, behind you," Crafter shouted.

Spinning, the User-that-is-not-a-user rolled to his right, just as a zombie swiped at him from behind with its razor sharp claws. He slashed at the zombie's decaying legs, then stood, ready for another attack, when suddenly a pair of arrows hit the zombie, causing it to disappear with a pop.

"This isn't working," Woodcutter said.

Gameknight turned toward the NPC and could see cracks in his iron armor; he'd taken some damage. The User-that-is-not-a-user glanced at his other friends and could see similar dents and scrapes in their armor.

"The Naga is slowly hurting all of us while we're only doing a little damage here and there," Hunter yelled. "We need to draw it into a trap and surround it."

"I like the sound of that," Stitcher added.

"OK, all of you spread out in a big arc with bows ready," Gameknight said. "I'll bring the beast to you."

Twang . . . twang . . . twang!

"Stitcher, what are you firing at?" Crafter asked, an annoyed tone to his voice. "We need you to pay attention."

"Ha ha, I got him!" the young girl exclaimed with glee. "That'll teach that zombie to show its ugly face. It needed to be destroyed . . . and now it is."

Gameknight was shocked at how causally Stitcher talked about killing things; it was not at all like the girl he knew in his timeline.

"All of you just stay here," the User-that-is-not-a-user said.

He put away his swords and ran back out to the center of the enclosure.

"Naga, where are you?!" Gameknight shouted.

The monster had moved somewhere closer to the enclosure's walls, but the courtyard was so large, the distant walls were not visible through the haze of Minecraft.

A scraping sound filled the air off to the right. Gameknight could see the herd of boars walking about, munching on the small tufts of grass that grew between the stone slabs.

Squawk!

A high-pitched screech came from behind him. Gameknight glanced over his shoulder. A small penguin was moving quickly across the courtyard, an expression of terror on the little creature's black and white face.

Suddenly, the boars squealed in terror as the Naga burst out of the shadows and crushed them all. A skeleton moved up next to the monster and fired an arrow at Gameknight999. The arrow bounced off his armor, doing no damage, but before Gameknight could pull out his bow and fire back, the Naga turned and devoured the monster, destroying it instantly.

This monster isn't just after us, Gameknight thought. *It's going to destroy everything in this courtyard.*

He glanced at the penguin, then sprinted toward the creature. The sound of hard scales scraping against stone and grass filled the air. The Naga hissed as it pursued him. Gameknight knew the huge monster was faster, but maybe he could still avoid it.

When he reached the penguin, he scooped up the tiny creature and held it under his left arm.

Squawk, squawk!

"Yes, hello," Gameknight replied as he sprinted.

The Naga was getting closer. He could hear the monster's heavy breathing; the smell of its rotten breath was almost overpowering. Knowing he had only moments to spare, Gameknight suddenly bolted to the left. A green, scaly blur shot past him, a frustrated roar filling the air as the monster missed its chance to attack.

"Here he comes!" Gameknight shouted to his friends.

Sprinting with everything he had, Gameknight headed toward his friends. They were hiding behind some of the few stone pillars that still stood, waiting to spring their trap. Behind Gameknight, the scraping sound grew louder and louder; the Naga was closing in. As gently as he could, Gameknight tossed the penguin toward his friends, then stopped and drew his bow. He turned with arrow notched and fired. His enchanted bow lit a magical flame on the projectile as it left the bowstring. The arrow soared gracefully through the air and hit the charging Naga in the forehead. The monster burst immediately into flame, causing it to flash red with damage. More arrows soared through the air and hit the beast. Those that struck its body just bounced harmlessly off, while the ones that hit the creature's head seemed to pierce its protective scales and do damage.

"Aim for its head!" Gameknight shouted. "We can only hurt its head; the rest is too well-armored!"

The Naga turned toward the User-that-is-not-a-user and charged, its angry, bellowing cry making the ground shake beneath Gameknight's feet. Suddenly, a zombie moaned behind him. With a quick glance, he saw that a zombie was emerging from the nearby shadows, moving toward the unsuspecting Digger, who stood nearby, his two pickaxes in his hands.

"Digger . . . look out!"

Suddenly, Fletcher barreled into Gameknight, knocking him aside just as the Naga reached him. He'd nearly been crushed; the big NPC had probably saved his life.

The green serpent moved past them and headed for the penguin, a lust for destruction burning in its glowing red eyes.

"Oh no you don't!" Digger yelled.

The stocky NPC charged forward, his big pickaxes swinging wildly. He smashed into the Naga, tearing into the monster with his shining iron tools. The picks dug deep into the green flesh, making it roar in pain as its HP decreased. Arrows from the other members of the group streaked through the air, hitting the Naga again and again until its head was covered with feathery shafts. And then Digger swung with all his might and hit the beast one last time. The creature shuddered, then flopped onto its side, shaking. Moans of despair came from the Naga as it began to shiver more violently. Suddenly, it exploded, showering the ground with glowing balls of XP and a handful of items

Gameknight stood and surveyed the courtyard. He could still hear the sorrowful cries of a few zombies, but they chose to stay in the shadows rather than attack.

"Digger, you saved us!" Crafter exclaimed. "You destroyed the Naga."

"Thank you, Digger," Gameknight said. "When you stopped the monster with your picks, it let everyone else open fire."

The stocky NPC glanced around, looking surprised and embarrassed. "I just couldn't let that monster destroy this penguin. When I saw that little animal just standing there in the path of that serpent, all I could think about was my Topper."

Gameknight put his arm around Digger's shoulder and hugged him. "I knew I could count on you."

Squawk! the penguin added.

Digger glanced down at the little animal, then cast his eyes to the ground, the fire of courage in the big NPC's eyes already fading.

Gameknight sighed.

Reaching down, the User-that-is-not-a-user lifted the penguin off the ground and checked the animal for injuries.

"This animal belongs on the glacier, yes, yes," Empech said as he leapt down from the nearby oak tree, followed by Herder and his wolves.

The little gnome moved to where the Naga had been killed and quickly picked up the items dropped by the green beast. He held up a gold tile that had an image of the Naga's face painted on it, then stuffed it into his oversized backpack. The tiny gray creature then collected the Naga scales that lay strewn about the ground and stuffed them away as well.

"Glacier?" Gameknight asked.

Empech pointed at the icy blue wall that was just barely visible in the distance. "That is the domain of the Snow Queen, and a very dangerous place, yes, yes. When she is displeased with a penguin, she throws them off the glacier. Few survive very long on the forest floor. Empech is surprised the penguin made it this far. She likely became trapped within this enclosure."

"She?" Crafter asked, confused.

Empech nodded. "The yellow on the animal's chest signifies her as a she, yes, yes."

"We need a name for you, little one," Gameknight mused. He thought about penguins he'd seen in movies or read about in books, but the only one he could think about was the evil, villainous enemy of Batman. *No, that's no good.* He looked at the black-and-white penguin again, hoping for inspiration, and then suddenly he had it. "I'll name you Tux, like tuxedo!"

Squawk, squawk! chirped Tux happily.

In the distance, a group of wolves howled, filling the air with their majestic voices.

"They found Weaver's trail," Herder said as he ran across the courtyard. "They exited the enclosure on the far side."

"Come on, everyone," Stitcher said. "I want to catch me that Entity303."

As they moved across the courtyard, Gameknight moved to Crafter's side.

"Why do you think Entity303 led us here, into this enclosure?" he asked.

"Maybe he wanted the Naga to destroy some of us," Crafter replied. "That would reduce the number of his enemies."

"But that doesn't make sense," Gameknight said. "He could have led us into a trap much worse than the Naga. No, I think he wanted us to fight the Naga for some reason . . . but why?"

"Maybe if you hurry up, we can catch him and ask," Stitcher growled, her voice sounding impatient. "Come on . . . we should run."

They reached the far side of the courtyard and found a set of stone blocks that formed stairs. Stitcher sprang up the steps and leapt off the wall, dashing after the wolves. Gameknight reached the top of the wall with Tux under his arm. Below him spread more of the snowy forest, a large hill off to the left. Footsteps could be seen in the snow, a dragging mark amongst the tracks; that was likely from Weaver, telling them he's still alive.

"Don't worry, Weaver, I'm coming for you," he said in a low voice. "I won't fail you again. I'll protect you, like I was supposed to in the past."

A dark, heavy feeling settled in his chest as pangs of guilt filled his soul.

Prrrr . . . prrrr. Tux nuzzled her soft, fluffy head against Gameknight's arm.

"Thank you, Tux," Gameknight said, and stroked the creature's head, causing the fluttery purring sound to grow even louder. He could sense the worry the penguin had for him, as if there was some kind of empathic link between them. Tux's concern for him seemed to help push back the guilt he felt, but not the fear. He knew there were more monsters out there, some even worse than the Naga, and they were waiting for him and his friends.

CHAPTER 11

THE SWAMP

Weaver's trail led the party out of the chilly, snow-covered forest and into a dank and stinky swamp. Decaying sludge, rotting trees, and decomposing leaves covered much of the water, with strange-looking things moving about in the murky depths. Just to be safe, they stayed close to the land as much as possible, not wanting to find out what was really swimming around down there. Tux seemed nervous about the hidden creatures, so Gameknight carried his new friend. After the Naga, they'd all had enough of snakes.

As they trudged through the damp landscape, Gameknight moved next to Crafter and spoke in a low voice.

"I'm concerned about Stitcher," he murmured to Crafter. "It seems as if she has no regard for other creatures; it's like she wants to kill everything. Even if they are monsters, they don't all deserve to die, but I feel like she wants to exterminate every one of them."

"Hunter tells us she was like this only after being rescued from Malacoda's Nether fortress," Crafter replied quietly. "I never knew her before her capture. She was held prisoner in that fortress for a long time, and was tortured and punished many times by the monsters. Stitcher told me she saw lots of her friends hurt and killed by monsters, some of them for no reason at all. I think that experience scarred her pretty significantly."

Gameknight sighed. "I should have been there to protect her."

I failed Weaver in the past, and it seems I failed both Fletcher and Stitcher in this timeline as well, he thought. *These villagers would be better off relying on someone else.*

"We did what we could," Crafter said. "But it took a while to rescue her."

"Wasn't she freed after Mason, Hunter and I led the army to free you from Malacoda's clutches?"

"Mason," Crafter said. "Who's Mason?"

"You remember, he led the army through the Nether, and I came in with a large group of cavalry. We . . ."

Crafter shook his head. "That's not what happened. We attacked, all of us using bows. You fought for days in the Nether until Malacoda finally finished his portal. You and Hunter snuck in at the last instant and grabbed me before they could take me through the portal."

"So they took Hunter?" Gameknight asked, his voice getting louder with surprise.

"Of course not, what's wrong with you? She jumped down on her horse and we rode away."

"Are you telling me Hunter was never Malacoda's prisoner?"

"Ha . . . me, a prisoner of that overinflated gasbag?" Hunter exclaimed. "That would never happen. I wouldn't allow it."

"This time travel thing is too strange," Gameknight said. *Everything has changed so much. I just hope I can repair this timeline and put things right again. If I don't, then Weaver and my friends will suffer for nothing. I don't know if I can do this.*

Gameknight was about to voice his lack of confidence when suddenly, a squishy sound floated out from behind a copse of thick trees. One of the wolves growled. Gameknight held up his hand to stop the group as he waited to see what would emerge. Slowly, the luminous edge of a blue slime emerged from behind the trees, the gelatinous outer layer protecting the creature's inner core, with its dark eyes and open mouth pointed directly at him.

He quickly glanced around and saw a path around the monster. Slimes were slow and would be easy to outrun. Gameknight was about to point out the path when a flaming arrow streaked through the air and hit the monster. The slime screamed from within its squishy layers, the sound coming to their ears as a muffled cry. Another arrow zipped through the air and struck the beast followed by another. The slime split in two, then charged toward them.

"Stitcher, I didn't tell you to fire," Gameknight complained.

"I know," the young girl said as she stepped forward. "I saw you eyeing an escape path, so I made the right decision for you."

She fired again, loosing three arrows in rapid successions, causing the blue cube to split into four pieces.

"The magma cubes in that fortress destroyed countless villagers, many of them my friends," Stitcher said as she fired again. The tiny slime cubes screamed in pain, their cries getting higher as they became smaller and smaller.

"But this isn't a magma cube," Gameknight protested.

"Who cares," she replied. "A monster's a monster. Now are you gonna fight or just stand there?"

He knew he had no choice now. Drawing his blade the User-that-is-not-a-user charge forward.

"Wolves . . . destroy!" Herder shouted, a vicious expression on his face.

Before Gameknight could reach the slimes, Herder's wolves fell upon the monsters, snapping at them with their powerful jaws and sharp teeth. The tiny jelly-like cubes fell in seconds, leaving behind balls of slime and XP. Once the last of the monsters were destroyed, the wolves continued to follow Weaver's path.

"Now it's a *good* monster," Stitcher said with a vicious smile, then continued forward, following the wolf pack leader.

Gameknight sighed. He glanced at Crafter and gave the young villager a worried look; the NPC returned the look, then shrugged and continued following the wolves. After a dozen blocks, the path suddenly turned to the right, exploring a different section of the swamp. A swarm of mosquitos attacked them from all sides, the wolves yelping at their stings, but fortunately the insects were relatively weak. Their swords swatted the creatures away until they were destroyed.

After another twenty blocks, the trail took yet another sudden turn, now heading to the left.

"Why isn't Entity303 just heading in a straight line?" Crafter asked.

"I don't know," Gameknight replied.

"It's as if he's looking for something," Woodcutter said.

The trail continued to move in a zigzag fashion through the biome, covering more of the stinking, murky area until their path finally led straight out of the swamp and toward the neighboring forest. Gameknight was glad to be out of decaying environment. Seeing the slow rotting of the biome felt like watching the gradual destruction of something that had once been strong and vibrant, but all that was left of that landscape was lifelessness . . . it was oppressive. When they reached the edge of the swamp, they all felt a sense of relief.

Gameknight was glad to leave, but he still couldn't quite put his finger on specifically what he had felt in the swamp. He glanced at Empech and gave him a questioning look.

"Empech felt it as well," the tiny gnome replied as if he heard the unspoken question. "Something tears at the fabric of Minecraft, yes, yes, killing that biome. Empech is sure that swamp will soon strain to point of bursting, perhaps into flames . . . it is unclear."

"I'm just glad we're out of there," Digger said softly. "That place reminded me of terrible things."

And then Gameknight realized that's what he was feeling. The suffering of the swamp was making all of his uncertainty and fear of failure bubble to the surface and slowly erode his courage.

"Me too, Digger," the User-that-is-not-a-user replied. "Me too."

"The firefly forest will be a welcome relief, yes, yes," Empech said in his high-pitched squeaky voice.

"Is that was this biome is called?" Crafter asked.

The pech nodded his oversized head, then smiled at one of the fireflies as it flittered about before the gnome. The golden glow from the tiny insect cast a beautiful halo around the little gnome's gray face.

Gameknight noticed there were glass jars hanging from the trees or sitting on wooden posts all throughout the forest. Each held a glowing insect that shone beautiful rays of light on the forest, adding a splash of yellow color to the already verdant landscape. Everyone in the party breathed in the fresh, woody fragrance of the forest and felt rejuvenated as the oppressive stink of the swamp slowly oozed away from their senses.

"Come on," Stitcher said, "it's time to make up for lost time. Now we run."

Herder said something to the wolf pack leader. The animal gave a growling bark to the other furry creatures, then they all loped ahead, moving like silent white specters.

The rest of the party ran after the wolves, each scanning their surroundings for threats. But as they moved through the forest, Gameknight had the feeling they were hurrying toward some new threat that waited for them ahead—he just wasn't sure what it was. As with all the other monsters in the Twilight Forest, it was likely they wouldn't see the threat until it was already upon them, and that's what worried him. But there was nothing he could do about it now.

CHAPTER 12

POKING THE BEAST

Entity303 yanked on the rope leading to his prisoner, causing the young boy to stumble and fall to the ground.

"Get up, fool," the villager growled. "You're too slow, speed it up."

"I'm going as fast as I can," Weaver replied. "I'm getting hungry and my health is dropping."

He stopped and rolled his eyes at the NPC.

"Fine, eat this."

Entity303 tossed Weaver a couple pieces of meat. The young boy knelt on the ground and allowed the beef to flow into his inventory. Then, he pulled them out with his hands, though his arms above his elbows still tied to the side of his body, making eating difficult.

"How about you untie me so I can eat?" Weaver asked.

"Ha! Not likely."

Weaver sighed. He held the meat in one hand, then leaned over so that it could just make it to his mouth. After the first bite, he gobbled the rest in seconds.

"What is this biome?" the boy asked. "I've never seen anything like it."

Entity303 sneered. "Of course not, you fool. This is a firefly forest biome. It's a common one in the Twilight

Forest mod. But you had no idea how to get into this mod. Only Entity303 has this knowledge; the rest of you villagers are clueless."

Weaver growled at the insult, then sniffed at the meat. "This isn't beef; what is it?"

Entity303 smiled. "It's venison."

"Venison, I don't know what that is," Weaver replied.

"You remember those innocent deer you saw a while back, before I went off to collect my last piece of Yeti fur?" Entity said with a grin. He put his square stubby fingers to his head like antlers and moved about as if he were a deer, then laughed.

"No . . ." Weaver said, a horrified expression on his face. He tossed the remaining pieces of meat onto the ground. "Those creatures were harmless."

"And delicious." Entity303 laughed. "Not eating that meat won't bring those pathetic deer back to life, villager. When you're hungry enough, you'll eat, so pick those up or next time I'll let you starve for a bit."

Weaver scowled at the user, then stepped forward and allowed the meat to disappear back into his inventory again. Once his health recovered, the pair continued through the firefly forest.

Glowing insects buzzed about in glass jars all throughout the forest, the tiny insects seemingly happy in their transparent enclosures. Speckled canopy trees stretched high up into the air, their wide branches reaching wide enough to blot out the twilight sky. Entity303 led them through a small grove of blue, glowing flowers, the petals giving off a magical-looking particle effect. Ignoring their beauty, the user purposely stomped on the flowers as he ran through the field.

"What's that up ahead?" Weaver asked.

Entity303 glanced in the direction the villager gestured. From between the trees, a gray tower stretched upward, far above forest's leafy canopy. It was a cluster of square buildings that rose maybe a dozen blocks into the air until they split apart, forming more towers that loomed high in the air. Walkways stuck out from the main body, with towers rising from those, creating a complex series of buildings that all rose to different heights. But at the core of the stone-brick structure was a central tower that loomed high above the rest, stretching so far up into the air that the top was difficult to see.

"That's our destination," Entity303 said. "This is gonna be fun."

He ran directly to the base of one of the towers, then stopped and pulled out a crafting table.

"What are you doing?" Weaver asked.

"Just be quiet, fool and let me work."

Entity303 reached into his inventory and withdrew multiple pieces of Alpha Yeti fur. He placed them onto the bench in the proper pattern, creating a set of leggings, boots, a chest plate, and a helmet. Removing his iron armor, the user put on the newly formed materials. The yeti armor was white with a single horizontal blue stripe on each piece. They glowed with a magical enchantment, giving off an iridescent purple glow that lit the surroundings with a flickering radiance. His helmet boasted six horns, three on either side, just like the Alpha Yeti.

"Finally, I have this armor," Entity303 bragged. "Do you have any idea how many Alpha Yetis I had to destroy to get all this fur?"

"You're a monster," Weaver accused. "Those creatures were just innocent bystanders."

"So what," the user snapped.

He reached into his inventory and pulled out two bottles, each with a different-colored potion. He held them out to Weaver.

"Drink."

"What are these?" the NPC asked.

"Just do as you are told and drink!"

"They could be anything," Weaver complained. "How do I know you aren't trying to poison me again?"

The user pulled out the green tipped arrow, the honey-thick coating oozing off the tip and falling to the ground, sizzling as it charred the grass. He brought it to Weaver's face, the sharp, venomous tip just an eyelash's length away from his bright blue eyes.

"If I wanted to poison you, I'd just do it. Do you understand me, villager?" Entity303 asked.

"The name's Weaver," the NPC growled, trying to sound brave. The fumes from the poison stung his eyes, making square tears flow down his flat cheeks.

"Ha ha ha, the villager is crying in fear." Entity303 put away the arrow, then leaned close to his prisoner. "Make no mistake about it: if you disobey me or slow me down, I'll give you something to fear . . . my wrath."

The NPC took a nervous swallow.

"Now drink!"

The user put the bottle to his mouth and drank the first potion, then uncorked the second and gulped it down. Entity303 then took two potions for himself and drank. Instantly a set of blue swirls appeared around his body, followed by a set of green swirls from the second potion.

"What were those?" Weaver asked.

"If you must know, they were potions of swiftness and leaping," Entity303 explained. "We're not here to defeat these monsters, just to wake them up a bit. Now follow close if you want to survive."

Before Weaver could reply, Entity303 pulled out a pickaxe and sprinted to the side of the gray tower. He broke two of the blocks with the pickaxe, then pulled out his yellow-glowing sword and entered the tower. Instantly, a pair of zombies fell on him, their sorrowful moans echoing off the barren stone walls. He kicked at the closest monster, driving it back while he went to work on the second. Landing successive hits on the zombie, it disappeared quickly, leaving its comrade all alone. Before it could try to run, the user slashed at it, quickly destroying its HP. The decaying green monster disappeared with a pop.

Entity303 pulled Weaver all the way in, then sealed the opening with fresh blocks of stone.

"We're going to the top of this tower," Entity303 said. "Stay close for your own sake."

The user dropped the rope, allowing the villager to follow on his own. Entity303 smiled; he had no doubt the NPC would follow. If he tried to run away, with his arms still tied to his side, he wouldn't stand any chance of survival. And by the look of fear on the boy's face, the user could tell the villager knew this as well.

Gripping his sword firmly in his hand, the user ran through the next doorway, followed by Weaver. They found a skeleton or two in there, but with the speed potion and their ability to leap up the stairs, the skeletons' arrows never came close. As they moved up into the tower, a darkness deeper than midnight on a cloudy night enveloped the stairs. Quickly, Entity303 pulled out a potion of night vision and drank it. He then held one up to the villager's lips. This time, the boy drank it without objection. Instantly, the shadowy tower changed, the details in the dark recesses becoming visible.

They continued up the stairs, leaping over places where the stairs were missing and knocking monsters off the narrow walkway as they went.

Hopefully, some of Gameknight999's friends will fall through those holes and get hurt . . . or worse, Entity303 thought.

They reached a level where a half dozen skeletons, if not more, were waiting. A spawner was set in the ceiling, the glowing embers within lighting the spinning shape of a new monster about to be created. Entity303 destroyed a few of the monsters, just to reduce the arrows that would be following them. His attacks made the creatures angry. *Good, they'll be ready for my pursuers.*

As they climbed the stairs, more monsters attacked, some incredibly strange and ferocious, but with their enhanced speed and leaping ability, the vicious creatures were not a real threat.

Finally, Entity303 could see the topmost part of the tower. A wooden ceiling, with glass blocks inset, stretched across the tower overhead. Through the glass, he could see a skeleton-like creature clothed in a purple robe moving about. Countless works of art were visible through the glass floor; paintings he'd seen a million times in Minecraft. That skeleton was their objective.

Pulling out some blocks of dirt, the user created a barricade behind them, to keep the monsters below from interfering with what he had to do.

"You need to stay really close to me now," Entity303 said to Weaver. "This is where it gets dangerous. We're about to face a friend of mine, the Lich King. You'll want to be careful and quiet."

"The Lich King? What are you talking about?" the boy exclaimed. "All those monsters back there weren't the dangerous part?"

The user laughed.

"Up there is the king of this castle . . . the Lich King," Entity303 explained. "He is a magical skeleton with many tricks up his sleeves and is a dangerous opponent. Well . . . not for me, but dangerous to your little friends that are chasing us. If you want to survive, you'll need to stay close to me."

Weaver took a nervous swallow and nodded.

They moved up the stairs to the top floor. Inside was the Lich King, a skeleton clothed in a purple robe that had intricate gold stitching along the edges and intricate golden designs on the back. The monster wore a crown of gold, with small green gems adorning the top. Shining golden shields revolved around the creature, making it seem impossible to hit. Blue smoke billowed out of its crown, only to quickly dissipate, creating a gray haze in the room that made the air taste acidic and smell of ash. In the creature's hand was a wand made of bone, the end blackened as if burned by some kind of deadly magic. It flicked the wand at the pair, and what looked like an ender pearl streaked toward them.

"Back up, quick!" Entity303 shouted.

The blue-green ball streaked past them, trailing a line of sparkling particles. It hit the ground and exploded, a wave of heat flowing outward.

"We should get out of here," Weaver said. He moved toward the stairway again, but his captor grabbed the rope and pulled him close.

"Not yet," the user replied.

"You dare enter my tower?" the Lich King asked. "Shadows . . . get them!"

Just then, two more skeletons appeared, each seeming identical to the Lich King, though they didn't wear robes and their bones were completely black. It was as if these were the King's shadows, though they were equally as deadly as the Lich King himself. The Lich shadows flicked their wands at the intruders, launching more explosive attacks. Entity303 and Weaver easily avoided the attacks by speeding to the other side of the room.

The evil user pulled out his bow and fired an arrow at the painting nearest the Lich King. It struck the portrait and shattered it, causing the frame to fall to the floor.

"No!" rasped the king.

Entity303 fired another arrow at a different painting, then chose another target, and destroyed it as well.

"My paintings . . . NO!" the Lich King screamed.

The user put away his bow and stared at the monster.

"Those who are currently pursuing me told me to do that," Entity303 lied. "Tell those who follow that I'll be with the Snow Queen, waiting for them. There's a trophy there that needs collecting."

The Lich King snarled and fired a glowing orb at them. The user quickly stepped aside and let the ball of destruction slip past him, hitting a wall. The explosive blast knocked a few more paintings to the ground.

"OK, now that they're angry, it's time to go," Entity303 said.

He streaked back to the stairs, dragging Weaver along with him, though the NPC needed no encouragement.

More explosions rocked the chamber as they fled down the stairs.

The user directed Weaver into a side passage that led into one of the small towers that stuck out from the side of the main structure. He quickly shattered the blocks he'd placed on the stairway, giving the monsters full access, then sprinted into the small tower.

"Why did we do that?" Weaver asked.

"I want those monsters nice and furious when your friends get here," Entity303 said.

"So we're just gonna wait here for them?" the boy said hopefully.

"Ha! Of course not, you fool. We're leaving."

"How? The monsters block all the stairways. If we go back down there, we'll be destroyed."

"We aren't going down the stairs, villager," Entity303 said. "We're flying out of here."

"What?"

The user laughed again, then broke open the side of the tower, creating a large opening. Then he removed his yeti chest plate and put on a pair of gray wings.

"You better hold on tight if you want to live," Entity303 told Weaver.

"What are you gonna do?" the boy asked, sounding worried.

Instead of replying, Entity303 just yanked on the rope, pulling Weaver close to him, then jumped out of the opening. The pair plummeted toward the ground for a moment, but as they fell, the wings opened. When the Elytra wings caught the wind, they soared upward like a massive bird, skirting the tops of the trees. Behind them, Entity303 could hear the Lich King screaming in rage and the rest of the bloodthirsty monsters growling and snarling, anxious to destroy something soon.

Entity303 smiled, then flew toward the next monster he had in store for Gameknight999, toward the Snow Queen.

CHAPTER 13

THE LICH TOWER

The wolf pack leader returned from the looming structure and moved to Herder's side. The animal's body was rigid, its fur sticking out and its eyes burning red. The creature growled as it glanced back at the tower.

"Weaver's trail leads right up to that gray tower," Herder said. "The wolves can sense monsters . . . a lot of them."

"Great," Gameknight moaned.

"Great!" Stitcher exclaimed.

"But they can't find any trail of them leaving the tower," Herder added. "It's like they went in and never came out."

He gave her a scowl, then glanced at Empech. "Do you know anything about this tower?"

The gnome shook his head. "Empech can sense an ancient creature at the top of the tower, yes, yes. And he is not alone." The pech moved around the cluster of canopy trees and stared up at the top of the tower. "The creature up there is very angry, yes, very, very angry. Empech can feel his rage through the fabric of Minecraft." He turned and focused his sapphire eyes onto Gameknight999. "There is much danger here. Empech recommends caution."

"There's some *really* good advice," Stitcher said sarcastically, rolling her eyes.

"Stitcher, be nice," Hunter chided.

"I'm just saying, it's not the most helpful . . ."

"Gameknight, what's the plan?" Crafter asked.

"Let's follow Weaver's trail and try to enter the tower where Entity303 did." The User-that-is-not-a-user pulled out a shovel. "Make sure everyone has some dirt. We might need to build some defenses."

Gameknight dug up two-dozen blocks of dirt, and the others did the same. When he was done digging, the User-that-is-not-a-user pulled out an apple and ate it quickly, followed by a loaf of bread. Others in the party also ate, making sure their hunger was minimized and their health was at a maximum.

"Ok, let's go," Gameknight999 said.

They followed the wolves to the base of the tower until they reached the building's wall. Gameknight was stunned at how far up into the air the structure reached. There was no visible entrance, but open catwalks and balconies could be seen high up in the side of the structure.

"Look, there are two cobblestone blocks here," Digger noted. "But the rest of the wall is stone brick. It's as if someone broke in and then sealed it up quickly."

One of the wolves moved to the cobblestone and sniffed, then howled.

"That's where they went in," Herder said, patting the furry animal on the side.

"Then that's where we're goin' too," Stitcher said.

She pulled an iron pickaxe out of her inventory and smashed the blocks of stone. Instantly, the air was filled with the sorrowful wails of zombies and the clattering of loosely fitting bones. The clicking of spiders and strange ghostly sounds added to the cacophony.

"Come on, let's go have some fun," the young girl said.

A loud growl came from the dark opening. With a speed Gameknight thought impossible, Stitcher put away her pickaxe, pulled out her bow, and fired a flaming arrow into the darkness. Instantly, a zombie caught fire as the magical arrow made it flash red. She fired two more times, silencing the monster, then moved into the tower.

Gameknight charged after her, shouting out orders.

"Woodcutter, Digger and Empech, watch our backs. Everyone have your bows ready."

With a torch in his left hand and his diamond sword in his right, Gameknight followed Stitcher into the shadowy tower, Hunter and Crafter at his side. He placed the glowing torches in the shadows, splashing a warm yellow light on the walls and floors.

They had entered from one of the smaller towers. The walls of the structure were lined with books and shelves. A narrow hallway pierced one side of the chamber and led to a larger building.

They moved through the corridor and into the main structure. Passages opened on every wall, the walkways bathed in darkness. Gameknight ran to the nearest passage and placed a torch on the ground. Instantly, he was greeted by the sight of glistening claws; zombies . . . lots of them. Behind the monsters, a metallic cage hung from the ceiling, glowing embers within the cube showing it was a spawner.

"There are spawners in the adjoining rooms!" Gameknight shouted as he slashed at one of the decaying green zombies. "Seal the doorways with dirt!"

He placed a block of dirt on the ground just as a set of claws scratched across his chest plate. Gameknight readied an attack, but a pair of arrows appeared out of the darkness and hit the monster, pushing it back a step. Knowing another pair of arrows were about to appear at any moment, he simply ducked and placed another torch on the ground. When he stood, the monster was gone.

An arrow—this one aimed at him—streaked past his head. He rolled to the left, then turned to face the skeleton archer. When he stood, he saw Woodcutter slashing at the creature with his iron axe. Shards of bone flew in all directions as the monster tried to back up and escape the onslaught, but Woodcutter did not relent. In seconds, the monster was destroyed.

Gameknight moved through the rest of the room and placed more torches on the ground. With the chamber fully lit, they saw the rest of the monsters had been destroyed, but there were more zombies and skeletons coming down the two stairways that led to the ground. One of the stairways was made of wood, while the other was formed from slabs of stone.

"Which way?" Crafter asked.

Gameknight could see some fresh gouges in his diamond armor.

"Stone," he said. "Digger, seal up the wooden stairs with something. We don't want monsters sneaking up behind us."

The stocky NPC glanced around, his eyes darting to the wooden stairs, then back to Gameknight999. The tower was filled with the noises of monsters, and it sounded like most of them were heading down the stairways.

"Digger, seal the stairs," Gameknight repeated.

The big NPC glanced at the stairs again but didn't move. Fletcher darted past him and moved up a few steps. When arrows began raining down on him, he quickly placed blocks of dirt and stone on the stairway, then retreated and joined the others.

Squawk!

The penguin was looking up the staircase at the first landing. Gameknight moved up a step, then another, when the sound of paper rustling filled the air. It was as if someone was leafing through a gigantic book, the pages shifting back and forth. Suddenly a glowing ball of energy flew down at him, striking the User-that-is-not-a-user square in the chest. It was like being punched by a giant. He flew back a step or two as his body flashed red.

"What was that?" Gameknight gasped.

Squawk, squawk! Tux cried, her screechy voice filled with fear.

He placed a torch on the wall, then glanced up at the landing. Floating in mid-air at the top of the stairs was some kind of magical book, its pages flipping back and forth as if being read by some invisible librarian. Another ball of white light streaked down at him. Gameknight rolled to the side as the magical attack just missed him, striking the ground.

Squawk, squawk!

Another blazing sphere shot through the room, followed by another, but then the barrage abruptly stopped.

Squawk, squawk, squawk.

"What's that shooting at us?" Crafter asked.

"Some kind of magical, possessed book," Gameknight replied.

"Death tome, yes, yes," Empech said.

"Why did it stop firing?" Fletcher asked.

Squawk!

Gameknight glanced up the stair. Tux was standing directly under the death tome. The book was moving about, trying to get a shot at the penguin, but the tiny creature was staying directly underneath the evil book.

"Hunter, Stitcher, take it out!" the User-that-is-not-a-user shouted.

Instantly, two arrows streaked through the air and hit the floating encyclopedia. Gameknight pulled out his own bow and added his arrows to the attack. Pieces of paper flew in the air as the flying terror took damage. It fired more of the glowing balls down at the villagers, but they'd learned to scatter when they saw the glowing orbs approaching. They each fired one more shot and the book disappeared, leaving loose pieces of paper strewn all over the stairs.

"Come on, let's hurry," Gameknight said. "The longer we stay still, the more time the monsters have to attack."

"Now you're talkin'," Stitcher said.

"Digger, pick up Tux for me. I need you to watch her," Gameknight said.

The stocky NPC grumbled something, but he didn't wait to hear. Instead, the User-that-is-not-a-user charged up the stairs, placing torches on the walls.

"Careful, a step's missing here," Gameknight shouted after almost falling through a hole as he ran upward.

Behind him, Herder placed a block of dirt in the hole and continued up the stairs, the wolves staying close, growling at the darkness above.

A group of skeletons came out of a side hallway, their clattering bones giving away their position. Before anyone could act, the wolves charged forward and tore into the pale monsters, biting and snapping at their legs until the bony monsters were destroyed.

More hostile creatures emerged from other side passages, all looking to surprise the intruders, but Hunter and Stitcher's deadly accurate bows kept the monsters off the stairs until someone could place a block of dirt or stone to block their paths. More of the death tomes appeared from the shadows, firing their sparkling balls of pain. Fletcher was hit in the side and Woodcutter in the back, but their armor absorbed most of the damage.

Slowly, the companions battled their way to the top of the tower. With blocks of dirt placed behind them, sealing off any attack from behind, and with all the side passages blocked, the friends could concentrate on the last level.

Above them stood a wooden floor with glass blocks placed in the corners and through the center. Through the transparent cubes, many paintings were visible, decorating the walls, though it appeared some were missing. Above the center of the room, a finely constructed chandelier hung overhead, casting a warm glow throughout the chamber.

Just then something floated across the floor. The User-that-is-not-a-user couldn't see what it was, but there seemed to be blue smoke trailing behind it . . . *That's strange,* he thought.

"What was that?" Digger asked.

Gameknight shrugged, unsure.

"Who cares, let's go get it," Stitcher said confidently as she notched an arrow to her bow. Crafter put a calming hand on her shoulder.

"Herder, do your wolves still pick up Weaver's scent up here?" Gameknight whispered. He was hoping they were in the wrong place.

The lanky boy nodded, causing tangles of long black hair to fall across his face. He pushed aside the offending locks, then cast Gameknight a smile.

"He was here," Herder said in a low voice as he patted the pack leader on the side.

The User-that-is-not-a-user shuddered. The unknown creature overhead had him terrified. This whole adventure had become more dangerous with every step through the Twilight Forest, and now they were here in front of one of the bosses.

I can't do this. Gameknight's thoughts sounded weak and pathetic . . . exactly how he felt. He sighed and tried to gather what little strength he had.

"OK, we should move in quick and drive whatever is up there into the corner," Gameknight said. *Maybe we don't have to fight.* He turned and glanced at Stitcher. "If it tries to surrender, we let it . . . understood?"

Stitcher nodded, but Gameknight could still see a thirst for revenge in her dark brown eyes. It made him sad.

"Remember, we outnumber that creature, whatever it is. We don't need to fight it; we just need to know where Weaver and Entity303 went. So move fast and be strong." Gameknight glanced at Digger, but the stocky NPC turned away.

The creature above moved across the glass blocks again, though the blue smoke made it hard to see clearly. Every nerve yelled at Gameknight to just run away.

What if I mess this up? He thought. *I could be leading them to disaster.*

His feet felt leaden, as if they were cemented to the stone slab on which he stood. The fear of failing his friends was so overpowering it almost made it impossible to think. But he knew they couldn't stay here. Monster noises were growing louder below their earthen wall, and the monster overhead was growling. They had to act, now, or all would be lost.

He drew his swords, iron in the left, diamond in the right. Beads of sweat trickled down his forehead and seeped into his eyes, stinging. Using his sleeve, Gameknight999 wiped at his eyes. With a nervous swallow, he glanced at all his friends and nodded, then turned and charged up the stairs to the top floor of the tower as fear pulsed through his every nerve like ice-cold lightning.

CHAPTER 14

THE LICH KING

Gameknight stepped into the brightly lit room and faced what looked like a skeleton wearing a long purple robe. The bony monster wore a bright golden crown with green gems ringing the top of the headpiece. Strange bluish-gray smoke billowed out of the crown. The colorful mist rose into the air, then dissipated, creating a gray haze that filled the vaulted ceiling. It smelled of burning pine and ash, the smoke biting at the back of his throat. Small, translucent gold shields revolved around the creature, protecting its chest but little else.

The wolves growled.

"You creatures invaded my tower once," the monster growled. "It will not be tolerated a second time."

"We don't want any trouble." Gameknight slowly put away his swords so as to appear non-threatening. "We just need to know where the other two like us went."

"I am the Lich King, the ruler of this domain," the monster growled. "You make no demands here."

The Lich watched the party as they filed out of the stairway and spread out across the room. He glared at the wolves, causing their fur to bristle outward as the animals' eyes turned bright red. More of them began to growl. Herder reached out and patted the alpha male, calming him and in turn calming the pack.

But when his cold dead eyes fell upon Empech, the monster looked startled. The pack leader growled again.

"You have a third here," the skeleton said. "Perhaps you can be trusted."

"A third?" Gameknight replied. "What are you talking about?"

The Lich King gestured toward the pech with its dangerous-looking wand. It was made of bone, with a midnight black stone on the end that seemed to drink in the light around it.

"Watch out, the monster's attacking!" Stitcher shouted.

"NO!" Gameknight yelled, but it was too late.

The young girl fired her bow at the creature's head. The arrow seemed to soar through the air in slow motion as it flew toward the monster. But before it could hit the bony skull, it was deflected away by some kind of invisible shield.

The Lich King screamed a blood-curdling scream, then flicked his wand toward Stitcher. A green orb shot out of the wand straight toward her. Woodcutter tried to pull her out of the way just as the sphere exploded, throwing the pair across the room, both taking damage.

"Shadows, ATTACK!" the monster yelled.

Instantly, two more creatures appeared, each shaped identically to the Lich King, but instead of pale white bones, gold crown and flowing purple robes, these monsters were pitch black, as if they were the ruler's shadows. Each held a weapon similar to the Lich King's. The three monsters flicked their wands at the intruders, firing exploding balls at them.

Gameknight zigzagged across the floor, dodging the attacks as glowing orbs exploded around him. When he finally reached the Lich King, he swung his diamond sword with all his strength. The blade crashed into the rotating shields and bounced off, making a loud clanking sound. It was like he'd just hit the side of an armored tank. His sword vibrated in his hand, making his arm hurt; those shields seemed impenetrable.

"Look out, Gameknight," Crafter yelled.

He rolled to the right, then zigzagged across the floor as one of the skeletal shadows fired a shot at him. He sprinted toward the monster and swung his blade at the creature, aiming at its unprotected side. It clanked the same way it had against the Lich King, the shock of the blow causing his sword arm to buzz with pain.

"The shields protect the other skeletons," Gameknight said. "Everyone fire at the king, but keep moving."

They pulled out their bows and fired at the Lich King. Half a dozen arrows flew through the air, heading directly for their enemy. Just as they were about to converge on the monster, the Lich disappeared and teleported behind them. It fired another blast that knocked Crafter and Hunter across the room, taking damage. One of the shadows fired at the wolf pack, scattering Herder and the animals. Gameknight rushed to Crafter's side, but was struck by a glowing orb from one of the Shadows. He was knocked backward, skidding across the wooden floor and smashing into the corner farthest from the stairs.

Gameknight watched as the skeletons fired on his friends, the glowing balls exploding amongst them, throwing them all across the room. Screams of pain and fear filled the room, but then the User-that-is-not-a-user realized the screams were his. He was terrified and didn't know what to do. Fear ruled his mind, and it was not just fear of this monster, but fear of failing his friends. He'd always been able to figure out a way to defeat Herobrine and his monster kings, but here in this modded Minecraft, everything was different. Gameknight had nothing to offer. He felt as if he was drowning and was a dead weight around his friends' necks; he was just dragging them down with him. The fear of failure was so overwhelming, it made him afraid to even try. And so, instead of getting up and fighting, Gameknight999, the savior of Minecraft, the King of the Griefers, the Defeater of Herobrine, just slunk back into the corner and shook.

"Everyone get to the stairs!" Crafter yelled. "RETREAT!"

The villagers ran for the stairs as the skeletons attacked, doing more damage as they sprinted for safety. The wolves clustered around Herder as he limped to the stairway. They all dove into the stairwells that descended below the chamber floor—all of them, that is, except for the User-that-is-not-a-user.

"Gameknight, get out of there," Crafter shouted.

The two shadows turned and began closing in on him, the space between the dark monsters slowly shrinking. Gameknight started to sprint, but after taking just a single step, the Lich King appeared between the pair, blocking off his escape route.

"You're like the last one," the skeleton growled. "Not a villager, but something else. He invaded my tower and hurt many of my subjects, just as you have."

"We don't want any trouble," Gameknight said as he backed up into the corner of the room. He felt the walls against his back.

"You attacked me for no reason, and now you will pay the price. Your fate will be an example to all who think to bother the Lich King. Shadows . . . destroy the fool."

The dark skeletons held out their bone-handled wands. Just then a bellowing voice filled the room with sound.

"NOOOOOOO!"

Fletcher moved back up the steps and sprinted toward the monsters.

"No Fletcher, go back," Gameknight yelled, but he could not be heard over the big villager's screams.

The chubby NPC dashed across the room and barreled into the monsters as if he was a bowling ball going for a strike. The Lich King and one of the shadows were knocked to the ground while the third monster was shoved to the side. Fletcher shot past the violent creatures and reached Gameknight's side.

"Fletcher, what are you doing?" Gameknight said.

"Just make sure you save Weaver, so I can have my family back," the big villager said, a tear trickling from one eye.

Fletcher grabbed Gameknight by the back of his armor and lifted him off his feet. With the strength of three men, he threw the User-that-is-not-a-user toward the stairway. Gameknight sailed halfway across the room before hitting the floor, then slid the rest of the way. Crafter and Stitcher grabbed one of Gameknight's hands and dragged him into the stairwell.

Glancing back to the corner, Gameknight saw the Lich King and his Shadows slowly closing in on the doomed villager. Fletcher had his sword out, ready to attack, but the creatures were careful to stay out of reach.

"Destroy him!" the Lich King said in a dry, scratchy voice.

They fired their exploding balls of death at the villager. With no other option available to him, Fletcher swung his sword at the orbs. He knocked one aside, making it veer back at the Lich King, exploding in his face. The other balls descended on the NPC, detonating around him and making him flash red.

"Save my daughter and wife," Fletcher cried out, his voice barely audible over the explosions. "Please Gameknight999, save my dau . . ."

And then the fat NPC disappeared, his items clattering to the ground. Fletcher was gone.

CHAPTER 15

REVENGE

Someone guided Gameknight999 down the stairs, but he wasn't sure whom.

"Fletcher is gone," the User-that-is-not-a-user moaned.

"That monster up there murdered him," Stitcher growled.

Gameknight sat down on one of the stairs and wept. Tux leapt out of Digger's arms and moved to his side. The penguin nuzzled his soft head against Gameknight's side, making a fluttery purring sound that provided a small bit of comfort. Glancing down at the creature, Gameknight gently stroked Tux's soft feathery head.

What have I done? Gameknight thought. *I knew I'd fail, and sure enough . . .*

Waves of sorrow and guilt smashed down upon him. Fletcher had lost so much because of him; his wife and daughter were destroyed because of Weaver's abduction, and now the big, friendly NPC lost his life saving Gameknight999.

"That should have . . . been me out there and not . . . Fletcher," he sobbed.

"We have to do something," Stitcher hissed. "We need to avenge our friend, Fletcher."

"Revenge has a way of taking more than it gives, yes, yes," Empech said.

"I don't care," Stitcher snapped. She turned and glared at Gameknight999. "Entity303 brought us here for a reason, and we aren't gonna find out why until that monster up there is on his knees begging for his life. You let Fletcher be destroyed. Are you gonna just sit there and let that happen to the rest of us, or—" Suddenly an explosion rocked the tower as one of the glowing orbs smashed into the stairway opening. One of the wolves yelped in pain. "Or are you gonna fight?"

Gameknight looked at his friends. Many of them had tearstained cheeks and red, puffy eyes. They all were scared, with the exception of Stitcher, who was furious. Another explosion smashed into the opening above them, shaking the tower. Tux squawked in fear, then moved behind Gameknight for safety. He stared down at the terrified penguin. The creature peered up at him with her dark eyes, an expression of terror on her soft white face. Tux was counting on him to keep her safe. Glancing at his friends, he could see the same thing on their faces.

"Gameknight, we have to do something," Crafter said. "If we just stay here, eventually, the monsters from below will make it up here. We need to move."

"Maybe we should leave the tower and get away from here?" Digger said.

"We don't know where they went after coming here," Gameknight said, his grief turning to anger. The hollow wheezing sound of the Lich King filled the air. "Our only hope to find Weaver is through that skeleton." He glanced to the top of the stairs. "Woodcutter, what's the Lich doing now?"

The tall NPC crawled up the stairs, then stood quickly and surveyed the room, then quickly ducked and moved down the stairs just as another green ball of death exploded just above him.

"The Lich King is on the far side of the room with the two darker skeletons," Woodcutter said. "But something strange has happened."

"What is it?" Crafter asked.

"Well . . . it looks as if the Lich King is missing one of his shields."

"He's missing a shield?" Stitcher asked, her brown eyes filled with violent thoughts. "How is that possible? They deflected every arrow and blocked every sword. How can that be?"

"I'm not sure, but it did happen." Crafter said. "Did one of you break its shield?"

"Maybe Fletcher destroyed it," Hunter said. "You know . . . before they . . ." She couldn't finish her statement.

Gameknight pushed his way to the top of the stairs, and stuck his head into the room, taking a quick glance. The Lich moved across the back of the room. Clearly one of the shields were missing.

And then the puzzle pieces started to tumble around in his head. There was a solution here, but it wasn't clear. *Maybe if we . . .* Suddenly, the image of a ghast filled his mind.

"Ghasts," Gameknight said, nodding, as a plan began to form in his mind.

"Ghasts?" Crafter asked.

As the plan solidified, Gameknight's fear seemed to move back to the shadowy recesses of his mind. He knew what to do to defeat these monsters and keep the rest of his friends safe.

The User-that-is-not-a-user turned to Crafter and nodded his head. "Yep, ghasts. I know what to do, but I need all of you to stay here."

"I want to help!" Stitcher said, her voice filled with anger. "That was my friend who got killed up there."

"I know, but there can only be one target for this to work," Gameknight replied. "All of you stay here. If I'm right, I'll call for you to come up when it's time."

"And what if you're wrong?" Digger asked.

"Then you all should all get out of here."

"Be careful, child," Empech said. "Revenge can turn a heart to stone."

"This isn't for revenge," the User-that-is-not-a-user said. "This is for Weaver."

Gameknight moved to the top of the stairs, careful to stay low. He pulled out a block of dirt from his inventory.

"What are you gonna do with that?" Stitcher asked from below him.

"Why, destroy the Lich King, of course," he replied with a smile, then ran out into the Lich King's chamber.

The Lich King and his Shadows instantly fired at him. Gameknight ducked and bobbed about, avoiding their attacks as he ran for the corner. He could see there were only four shields revolving around the skeletal monarch; clearly, one of them was missing. Darting to the corner of the room, the User-that-is-not-a-user quickly placed a pair of blocks on the ground, leaving one side open.

Squawk, squawk.

Gameknight glanced down and saw Tux at his feet, the penguin's feathers ruffled with anger. A glowing green orb shot toward the pair. The User-that-is-not-a-user quickly placed two more blocks on the ground, sealing himself and Tux into a little dirt-lined hid-ey-hole. The sphere exploded against the dirt, but did no damage.

He breathed a sigh of relief.

"You see, Tux, I realized Fletcher showed us how to defeat the Lich King," he said to his little friend. "His sword deflected one of those glowing balls back at them. When it exploded, it destroyed one of those shields. So Fletcher's sacrifice showed us how to defeat the Lich King."

Squawk.

"That's right, all we need to do is knock some back at him to get those shields down, and then we can attack. Now stay behind me."

Gameknight listened for the monster's raspy breathing; it was coming from the right side of their little enclosure. Gameknight pulled out a shovel and dug up one of the dirt blocks. As soon as the brown cube disappeared, Gameknight found the Lich King staring at the pile of dirt blocks. A wicked smile spread across the monster's bony face, then it fired.

A glowing ball of explosive death streaked toward the pair, the sphere trailing a line of green particles. Gameknight waited for it, thinking about all the times he'd done this with ghasts. The ball came closer and closer until . . . the User-that-is-not-a-user swung his sword, hitting the sphere firmly in the center. The ball bounced off his blade and flew back toward the skeleton. It hit the Lich King's shields, exploding on contact; when the explosion had faded away, Gameknight could see that now there were only three of the shields.

The lich moved away, allowing one of the Shadows to take its place. The dark monster fired explosive balls at him, but Gameknight was already plugging the hole and moving to the left side. With his shovel, he broke the dirt block and held his sword at the ready. The Lich King was there, scowling at him.

"What are you waiting for, skeleton? Why don't you shoot at me?"

"You are not welcome here," the monster snarled. "I will teach you the price for your intrusion."

The skeleton flicked his bone wand, the dark gem on the top growing even darker, then fired a green ball at them. Gameknight swung at the projectile, but timed it incorrectly. The glowing sphere bounced off his sword and flew to the far wall. When it exploded, the blast tore pictures off the walls, scattering them across the floor.

"Get him, Gameknight," Stitcher shouted from the stairway. One of the Shadows turned and fired at the voice, but the young girl had already ducked below the entrance.

"You skeletons were never good at shooting anything," Gameknight taunted. "You're no good with bows, and you're not much better with those wands."

The Lich King snarled at him, then launched an attack at him. Next to the skeleton king, one of the Shadows did the same. Two glowing balls of death streaked at him, and he knew he had only one chance at this. If he missed the terrifying orbs, he'd likely not survive their combined explosion. The blazing spheres of destruction flew toward him in slow motion, his fear drawing out time to an excruciating snail's pace. As time seemed to slow, Gameknight999 gripped his sword firmly, and waited for what would happen next. He could feel beads of sweat forming on his brow and slowly trickling down the sides of his face.

Using every bit of experience he had from batting flaming balls of fire back at ghasts and blazes, Gameknight swung his blade, striking both of the glowing balls at once. They bounced off his sword and flew back at the Lich King, smashing into the revolving shields and making two more disappear.

Pulling out a block of dirt, he sealed the wall of his little shelter; it was almost like being in the Alamo. He reached down and picked up Tux, then jumped into the air and placed a block under his feet. Dropping the penguin, he readied his sword. Now the Lich King and the Shadows could see the upper half of his body above the blocks of dirt. The Shadow on the right side fired a green ball at him. Gameknight glanced at the Lich King, then waited for it to reach him. He leaned back and slapped at the ball, sending it toward the lich. The ball headed straight for the monster, but unfortunately, the Lich King flicked his bone wand and fired his own ball. The two spheres collided in mid air and exploded, but didn't harm the last shield.

Gameknight growled in frustration, then dug up the block under his feet with his shovel, lowering himself and Tux behind the barrier of brown cubes. He could hear the hollow, almost mechanical breathing of the Lich King. He was moving back and forth, teleporting from the left to the right.

"I don't think he's gonna make this easy on us," Gameknight said. "I have to go out there to end this. You stay here."

He pointed to the ground, hoping the little penguin understood. Using his shovel, he removed the bottom block. When he started on the top block, Tux moved out of the enclosure, squeaking and squawking.

"No!" Gameknight shouted.

He broke the top block, then darted into the room just as the Lich King waved his wand at the tiny animal. The User-that-is-not-a-user watched in horror as one of the green balls of destruction flew straight at Tux.

Gameknight sprinted with every bit of strength he had. It was a race, his legs versus the glowing ball of death; one of the two would claim Tux.

Leaping into the air, Gameknight dove, but not for his penguin friend. Instead, he dove for the space between the deadly sphere and Tux. Like a tennis player, he swung at the projectile with a backhand stroke, knocking the sphere back toward the skeleton. It smashed into the Lich King, destroying the last of his shields.

Gameknight landed with a thud on the wooden floor, expecting the Shadows to open fire while he was vulnerable. But when he glanced up, he found the Shadows had disappeared; their lives were somehow linked to the shields. The magical wand in the Lich King's hand then changed with a flash, turning from the bone-handled weapon capped with a black gem to one that was colored a sickly green.

"His shields are down!" Gameknight shouted to his friends.

"This isn't over, fool," the Lich snarled.

The skeleton flicked his bone-handled wand. The tip glowed a bright green, and then suddenly three zombies appeared before him, their claws glistening in the flickering light from the overhead chandelier.

One of the monsters swung at Gameknight, its claws whistling through the air as they just barely missed his head. Before he could swing his sword, an arrow hit the monster in the side, making it flash red with damage. The User-that-is-not-a-user swung his blade at the creature, striking it in the shoulder just as another arrow hit the beast. It disappeared with a pop.

"Yeah!" Stitcher exclaimed proudly.

"All of you, take care of the zombies," Gameknight shouted.

Sprinting across the floor, the User-that-is-not-a-user dodged the green monsters and headed straight for the Lich King. The bony creature flicked his glowing green wand again. Three more monsters appeared, but Gameknight ignored them; he knew his friends would watch his back. Leaping high into the air, he landed next to the Lich King, his diamond sword already moving in a blur. He struck the monster twice before it even knew what was happening.

A zombie moaned right behind him. Gameknight rolled to the left, then stood with his iron sword now in his left hand. The Lich King put away his wand and pulled out an enchanted golden battle-axe. Iridescent waves of purple magic flowed up and down the handle of the enchanted tool, the razor-sharp edge rippling with fiery heat.

The monster swung the axe at Gameknight's head. With his iron blade, he blocked the attack, then struck the skeleton with his diamond sword. The Lich King groaned as he flashed red, taking damage. The creature screamed in rage and swung at Gameknight again, then teleported behind him, but the User-that-is-not-a-user was expecting it. He'd fought Herobrine and Erebus numerous times, and it was a common ploy.

Gameknight held his diamond blade behind him, protecting his back as he spun around. Sure enough, the monster's battle-axe clashed with Gameknight's weapon, causing a shower of sparks to fly up into the air. The User-that-is-not-a-user brought his iron sword down onto the creature when he finished the turn, striking the Lich King twice. The skeleton staggered backward, surprised by the iron weapon, only to feel the bite of the diamond sword following quickly after.

With his HP almost exhausted, the monster fell to the floor, dropping his sparkling weapon, the golden crown falling from his bony head. The monster had collapsed near the dropped items from Fletcher's inventory, the villager's favorite bow and sword lying by the creature's feet.

Gameknight extended his diamond blade and held it next to the creature's neck.

"Now you're gonna tell me where the others went," he growled.

And for the first time, an expression of fear covered the Lich King's face.

CHAPTER 16

A NEW DIRECTION

Gameknight moved a step closer to the fallen Lich King, the tip of his diamond sword scratching the edge of its bony throat. Glancing over his shoulder, he could see the last of the zombies had been destroyed and his companions were moving toward him. The skeleton glanced at his crown, then his dark eyes shifted to the axe that lay only inches from his skeletal hand.

"Don't even think about it," Gameknight growled.

The monster glared up at his captor and sighed.

"Now talk . . . what happened with Entity303 and our friend Weaver?"

"You mean the one like you and his prisoner?" the Lich King asked with a wry grin. "Yes, he gave me a message for you, but I'm not sure if I remember it or not."

"Tell us what we need to know, or I'll shoot you right now!" Stitcher said. She strung an arrow and readied it to fire, causing her bow to creak under the strain.

The wolves moved forward, growling.

"You'll just destroy me anyway," the monster said. "Why should I help you?"

"Because Gameknight999 keeps his word," the User-that-is-not-a-user said. He sheathed his sword and stepped back away from the skeleton. "Give us the message and we'll be gone from here with you still alive."

The Lich King glanced up at Gameknight999, then nodded his head.

"Very well. Your enemy said something about the Snow Queen. I don't remember the exact words, as I was trying to destroy him at the time."

Gameknight glanced at Empech. "Do you know of this Snow Queen?"

"Empech knows of her, yes, yes. Very dangerous, yes, yes, very dangerous indeed."

Gameknight nodded, considering the information. He turned back to the Lich King, who was staring up at him. The creature moved its hand toward the sparkling crown that lay just out of reach.

"Watch out, he's reaching for the axe!" Stitcher exclaimed.

"No, wait!" Gameknight shouted, but it was too late.

Stitcher fired two shots with lightning speed. The arrows hit the skeleton, taking the last of his HP, causing the monster to disappear with a pop, a confused and frightened expression on his pale face.

The Lich King's items scattered across the floor; his green-tipped wand, the enchanted gold axe, some armor, a fat yellow bug, assorted other items, and a gold tile with the monster's face painted on the surface. Empech stooped and quickly picked up the tile, then placed it into his large backpack.

"Stitcher, why did you do that?!" Gameknight yelled, his face creased with anger.

"He was reaching for a weapon," she replied. "I was protecting you. Besides, why should we have spared him? That monster killed Fletcher."

"I think he was reaching for his crown, Stitcher," her sister replied. "You didn't have to shoot him."

"Whatever," the younger sister replied, sounding unconcerned.

"The elder sister speaks the truth, yes, yes," Empech said, shaking his large head. "Too much violence . . . too many of Minecraft's creatures being destroyed, yes, yes. All is getting out of control."

Gameknight didn't reply. He heard the accusation in Empech's voice. This was getting out of control and too many were dying. They weren't rescuing Weaver, they were just dancing to the tune Entity303 was playing for them. First the Naga, now the Lich, and next would be the Snow Queen. How many of his friends had to die before he ever caught up with them?

The room was quiet save for the sounds of monsters far below in the tower. The occasional scratching of zombie claws against their blocks of dirt filled the air; those creatures could still sense them up here and wanted to attack.

Great . . . more violence.

Gameknight sighed, then glanced at his friends. They all seemed to look back as if they felt sorry for him, like they all knew this was his fault. Gameknight thought they didn't want to blame him directly, for they pitied him. Some of them glared at the items dropped by the skeleton, their unibrows creased with anger, but Gameknight assumed it was really directed at him.

The Lich King isn't responsible for this tragedy; I am, he thought. *Fletcher was my responsibility, just like all these people are. I couldn't protect Weaver, and I couldn't protect Fletcher's wife and daughter, and now I've failed Fletcher as well.*

He sighed then moved to Fletcher's items. He sat on the floor, allowing some of his now-discarded tools to flow into Gameknight's inventory. Tux waddled forward and stood next to him, her soft feathers rubbing against the back of his hand. One of the wolves limped across the floor and stood at his other side. The animal leaned over and licked Gameknight's cheek. He reached out and stroked the creature's white fur but was shocked at what he felt. The wolf's fur was burned slightly all the way to the skin, and matted with sweat. The creature was clearly in pain.

"I should have just gone by myself," Gameknight said in a low voice. "I shouldn't have involved all of you. You're all wounded and Fletcher is dead, because of me."

"That's not true," Crafter objected. "We all know you did your best."

"My best . . . what a joke."

"The young crafter speaks the truth," the little gnome said. "Empech sees Gameknight999 doing great deeds and defeating monsters just to save his friend."

"You don't get it; none of you do," The User-that-is-not-a-user stood and walked toward the Lich King's items. There was a large yellow bug with a brightly glowing body lying on the floor. The creature looked up at him with two dark eyes, then crawled closer on its six stubby legs until it was sucked into his inventory.

"I froze in that corner," Gameknight continued, pointing to where Fletcher had perished. "I was so afraid of those skeletons that I just moved away from them and tried to curl up in a ball and hide."

"We all get afraid in battle," Crafter said. "That's nothing to be ashamed of."

"Yeah, even I get afraid sometimes," Hunter added.

"Not me," Stitcher said.

The older sister glanced at the younger, then just shook her head disapprovingly.

"What?" the young girl asked defiantly.

"You don't understand. I was terrified, not of the skeletons, but of failing. I don't know if it was being afraid of losing a battle for the first time, or maybe . . . losing your faith in me, or maybe losing faith in myself. But don't you see, I gave up and Fletcher had to come and save me. He sacrificed his life for me, but I wasn't worth it! His death is my fault." He stopped to take a breath and wipe the tears from his eyes. "How many more of you must die because of me being afraid to fail . . . being afraid to even try?"

No one said a word; they all just looked down at Gameknight999, the expressions on their square faces, even Stitcher's, were all sympathetic.

"Empech hears Gameknight999 and knows he speaks the truth," the little gnome said in his high squeaky voice.

"What are you saying?" Crafter chided.

The NPC reached down to stop the pech from saying more, but the little creature stepped forward before he could be stopped.

"Responsibility is a difficult burden to bear, yes, yes. Sometimes, it is a load that is freely accepted, and sometimes it is thrust upon someone, whether they like it or not, yes. Gameknight, you have freely accepted your role in Minecraft, for good or ill. At times, like today, you may regret this decision, but let me tell you, child, *you* are the one who must see this through; there is no other."

"Why?" Gameknight asked, pleaded. "Why must it be me?"

"You know the answer to that, child, as surely as you know your own name, yes, yes."

Empech stared down at him. Gameknight thought the strange little creature was expecting some kind of revelation.

"What? I don't know the answer, all I know is a friend lost his life trying to save me."

"After your friend was killed, did you run away?" Empech asked.

"Well, no, I had to finish the battle."

"Empech saw you run out here and face the three monsters all alone, yes, yes. That was not the deed of a coward, it was the deed of a hero."

"But Fletcher . . . he . . ."

"We do not get to choose when we will be successful or not; the random events around us make that choice." The gnome looked down at the weapons on the ground, a disgusted expression on his gray face. He kicked the bone-handled wand of the Lich King, the green gem at the end now dark. The weapons slid across the wooden floor toward Gameknight999. It collided with the great battle-axe and both items flowed into the User-that-is-not-a-user's inventory. "But Empech is certain, failure comes to visit us all eventually. You must learn from it and accept it with the same grace you use to accept success. If you let your fear of failure dominate who you are, then all your decisions will be clouded with doubt."

"But how do I find the courage I need when I'm terrified?" Gameknight asked, his eyes now red and swollen from weeping.

"You look to your friends, yes, yes," Empech said. "Fletcher gave you courage to finish this battle victoriously."

"But it cost him his life!"

"Yes, but he chose to sacrifice himself for you, and for his wife and his daughter," the pech replied. "Fletcher knew his responsibility was to protect his family, and the best way he could do that was to save you, so you could save Weaver, yes, yes. Repair the timeline and all will be mended." Empech moved closer so he was staring straight up into Gameknight's eyes. "You must choose whom you want to be, then follow that path." He lowered his voice to just a whisper. "Whom is it you want to be, child?"

The words echoed in his head like thunder.

Whom do I want to be? Gameknight thought.

He considered everything that had happened to them: the monsters . . . the battles . . . Fletcher. Minecraft was a much more dangerous place now because of the mods Entity303 had somehow loaded into the pyramid of servers. That user had poisoned Minecraft, and Gameknight999 had to somehow put it back the way it was supposed to be.

But why me? Why must I be the one to fix it?

You know why it must be you, a high-pitched voice said in his head. *Just have faith.*

Surprised, Gameknight glanced down at Empech and found the little gnome nodding his head.

You can hear my thoughts?

Empech just smiled.

Why must it be you? Empech's voice echoed in his head.

Because I'm better with a sword? Gameknight wondered.

The little gnome shook his head.

Because I have more experience?

Empech stayed motionless, not responding.

Because of my bow . . . because of my knowledge . . . because of my speed or strength or . . . The possible reasons flowed from him, each sounding empty in his head. He thought of every possible answer, but none of them felt right, and yet he refused to give up. Reaching deep into his soul, Gameknight thought about what it was that really made him special. He could feel something down there in the depths of his inner being, but he couldn't quite see it.

And then something started to bubble up from within the deep recesses of his soul. With his eyes closed, Gameknight reached for the fuzzy, insubstantial thing that was more of an idea than anything else. Slowly, square faces began to materialize from within his mind. They were the faces of his friends, the faces of villagers and creatures and everything about Minecraft. There was one wrinkled and gray-haired face that he instantly recognized as the Oracle from his timeline, and she was smiling at him. In fact, they were all smiling at him with hope and confidence showing on their face.

And then it came to him. The one idea that had helped him defeat Herobrine and all his monster kings and keep Minecraft safe: he wasn't alone. *I can't fail, because I'm not alone,* he thought. *Only WE can fail.*

Because he had all these people around him, whenever he was ready to give up, there were always people around to lean on and ask for help. He'd been chasing

Weaver and feeling guilt about his abduction because he'd thought this was all his fault, but that was impossible, because they were all in this together.

He realized now that he couldn't fail these people, for the only failure was in not trying . . . Fletcher had taught him that. The image of the Oracle in his mind nodded her head, then gave him one of her warm, grandmotherly smiles. She then winked at him, broke apart into three pieces, and dissolved back into his memories.

Slowly, Gameknight999 opened his eyes and found Empech staring up at him, smiling a huge toothy smile.

"I get it, Empech," Gameknight said, nodding his boxy head. He stood a little straighter. "I was afraid to fail because I was trying to do this all on my own."

"But we're here with you, too," Digger said. The big NPC stepped forward and picked up Tux, then placed a reassuring hand on Gameknight's shoulder. "You're never alone in Minecraft . . . never."

"I know. I guess Weaver's abduction made me sorta forget that."

"Well, don't let that happen again," Hunter said, and punched him in the arm.

Gameknight smiled as he rubbed his shoulder.

"I forgot we're stronger together than I am on my own," the User-that-is-not-a-user added. "And maybe I should share some of this responsibility with all of you when I'm afraid I can't see the solution."

"You think?" Hunter added sarcastically.

"Gameknight, we're in this together," Crafter said. "And none of us are going home until Minecraft is repaired."

Digger then stepped forward. He walked past Gameknight and picked up Fletcher's bow. The big NPC looked down at the weapon, then held it out to the User-that-is-not-a-user.

"I want my Topper back," Digger said in a weak voice that cracked with emotion. "I'll do whatever it takes to fix Minecraft—even if it means doing what Fletcher did—to get my son back."

"Digger, you don't have to . . ."

The big NPC put a finger on Gameknight's mouth, stopping his words.

"This is not the timeline I want." He glanced around the room at the other villagers. "It's not the timeline any of us want. Minecraft is wounded and is dying. None of us talk about it, but we've all felt it. Entity303 has poisoned the pyramid of servers and is destroying our universe. We need to stop it, somehow. I will do anything . . . no, *we* will do anything to fix it. Gameknight999, we have faith in you, even if you fail. We just need you to try."

Gameknight reached out and took the bow from Digger's hands, a tear now trickling from his eye.

"I will try, starting right now." The User-that-is-not-a-user glanced at Empech. "Take out that square tile that the Lich King dropped."

The gray gnome took off his huge backpack and rummaged around for a moment, then pulled out two gold tiles. One had the face of the Lich King painted on it, and the other showed the Naga.

"These are trophies, and are part of the progression in the Twilight Forest mod," Gameknight explained. "I remember these. Each boss drops one when they're defeated."

"What are they used for?" Woodcutter asked.

"That's the thing, they aren't used for anything except for . . ." Gameknight became still as the puzzle pieces began to tumble around in his head. Three gold tiles appeared to his mind's eye, and a huge castle, and a forest of thorns, and . . . their path formed within his mind, and the User-that-is-not-a-user smiled.

"What are you grinning at?" Stitcher asked.

"He figured it out," Crafter said, his bright blue eyes filled with hope.

"I know where he's going," Gameknight said.

"So do we," Stitcher said. "He's heading to the Snow Queen; the skeleton told us."

"No, that's not his destination." Gameknight pointed to the gold tiles in the pech's three-fingered hands. "These tiles are keys that open something in the Twilight Forest, I just can't remember what right now, but I'm sure it will come to me. All I know for sure is that we're gonna need a third key. That's what we're gonna do . . . get a third key."

"But don't we need to follow him to the Snow Queen?" Herder asked.

"No, we aren't gonna do what he wants us to do anymore," Gameknight said. "It's time we followed our own path. We only need one more trophy and then we have all the keys. By then, I'm sure I'll remember what the keys unlock. We're gonna get there before Entity303 does. But to do that, we'll need to move fast."

"And we'll also need to face another boss?" Digger asked.

Gameknight nodded his head. "I fear we've destroyed the easy ones already. The Snow Queen, as I recall, is nearly impossible to defeat if you can't fly. So we're gonna do something unexpected."

"Then where are we going?" Crafter asked.

"Someplace none of you are going to like, especially you, Tux," Gameknight said as he reached out and petted the little creature on the head. "We're going to the fire swamp."

CHAPTER 17

EYES IN THE TREES

"**W**hat are those fools doing? They aren't following my trail," Entity303 said from atop a gigantic tree.

He watched as the tall skinny villager moved to the north, surrounded by a pack of wolves, the stocky NPC at his side. The last of his pursuers emerged from the stone tower, the two redheads firing arrows through the opening in the wall until it was sealed up. Entity303 did a quick count and found one of them missing.

"Ha ha ha," the user chuckled. "It seems the Lich King took care of one of your friends for me."

"What do you mean?" Weaver asked from the forest floor. He was tied to the trunk of a rainbow oak tree, a bottle of poison balanced precariously on the shaft of an arrow embedded in the bark. If he struggled, the bottle would surely fall on him.

"You are certainly dense, villager." Entity303 shifted his position in the top of the gigantic tree to get a better view. "There seems to be one less person in their company. Either someone really liked it in the Lich Tower and decided to stay, or the skeletons and other monsters destroyed one of them for me . . . perfect."

He gazed down at his pursuers. Gameknight999 stood out amongst the other villagers, his dual swords and shining diamond armor marking him as their leader. With a word from the skinny NPC, the wolves moved outward, their white fur standing out against the lush green grass that covered the ground of the firefly forest. They formed a perimeter around the villagers, likely acting as an outer guard. Once the wolves were in position, Entity303 heard one of the animals howl. The entire group then started to move northward; the opposite direction from the Snow Queen's fortress.

Entity303 glanced over his shoulder. The edge of the glacier was easily visible through the haze and he knew Gameknight999 and the others could see it as well. But why weren't they heading toward it?

"Maybe the Lich King double crossed me," the user said to himself.

"What did you say?"

"Be quiet and let me think!" he snapped.

Why are they heading north? There's nothing there but swamp and more swamp, Entity303 thought. *What is Gameknight999 up to?*

"I wanted to see the Snow Queen destroy some of your friends, but it seems that's not going to happen," the user said, clenching his fists in frustration.

Moving to the edge of the tree limb, he glanced down at the ladder he'd placed on the side of the tree, then smirked and jumped off the impossibly high tree branch. Leaning forward, he opened his Elytra wings and glided gracefully through the air, banking in huge curving arcs as he reveled in the wonderful feeling of flight. Carefully, he glided around a tall canopy tree, its limbs reaching out over the neighboring trees as if trying to shelter them from the absent sun. A few rainbow oaks with their color-shifting leaves looked like miniature multihued kaleidoscopes between the soaring plants and seemed even smaller compared to the gigantic tree he'd been in. Eventually, as with all things, his flight slowly came to an end as the ground approached.

After a graceful landing, Entity303 removed his Elytra wings and replaced the Yeti chest plate. He rubbed the furry white armor and thought of all the Alpha Yetis he'd had to destroy to attain this armor; it made him smile.

Moving to Weaver, the user carefully grabbed the splash bottle of poison and put it back into his inventory.

"So, it seems your friends have lost our trail, or they've given up on saving you," Entity303 said with a smile.

"Smithy will never give up," Weaver said defiantly. "When he catches you, he's gonna make you sorry."

"You still don't get it, do you?" the user said. "Your pathetic friend, Smithy, is not whom you think he is. He's really . . ."

"I refuse to believe you!" Weaver growled. "Smithy is my friend. He's the leader of our village and would never try to deceive us. So stop your lies and let me go before it's too late for you."

"Let you go?" He laughed. "You're my insurance policy. I'm not going to let you go until everything in Minecraft is destroyed. When my plans are impossible to stop, then maybe I'll strand you and your friends on some unstable world and let you watch the end of Minecraft together. Ha ha ha." The user laughed as if it was the funniest thing he'd ever said. Weaver scowled at him.

Moving to the trunk of the rainbow oak tree, he loosened the rope that held Weaver to the trunk, though his arms were still securely bound by more lengths of rope.

"Come along, villager, we're going to follow your pathetic little friends for a while."

Entity303 yanked on the rope, drawing Weaver closer. He quickly pulled out a cloth and stuffed it in the boy's mouth, then tied the loose ends behind his square head.

"There, maybe that will keep you quiet. I don't want you yelling to those villagers and letting them know where we are, at least not yet."

Pulling on the rope, the user led Weaver to the north, following the trail made by his enemies.

"What are you up to, Gameknight999?" Entity303 growled. "What have you figured out?"

Weaver tried to mumble something but the cloth kept him quiet. The user glanced at the boy and saw an expression of defiance on his square face. Carefully reaching into his inventory, he pulled out the poison arrow again and gave the villager a little poke. Instantly, sickly green spirals formed around the boy's head, his face turning as pale as a skeleton.

Entity303 laughed cruelly, then yanked on the rope again and continued north after Gameknight999 and his friends, the pursued now the pursuer.

CHAPTER 18

INTO THE FIRE SWAMP

They ran through the firefly forest in complete silence, the muffled thump of their boots on the thick green grass the only sound coming from the party. Herds of deer watched them pass, some of the younger ones getting startled and running away while the adults, with their great horned racks, stood guard and cast a watchful eye.

"I don't think I like the sound of this place you're taking us to," Crafter said.

"Nor do I," Gameknight replied. "But in order to beat Entity303, we must take control. The fire swamp will give us the last trophy and enable us to get to his final destination before he does."

"But how can you be certain that user was leading us from monster to monster just to collect these trophies?" Woodcutter asked.

"Because he could have taken us to some more dangerous places than the Naga and the Lich King that don't have any trophies," the User-that-is-not-a-user explained.

"Yes, yes, Gameknight999 is correct," Empech said, the little gnome somehow easily keeping up with their sprint, his tiny legs moving in a blur. "The Goblin King in the dark forest, very dangerous. And the Minoshroom in his labyrinth, yes, yes, few emerge, few survive."

"Empech is right," Gameknight added. "If Entity303 wanted to reduce our numbers, he could have taken us there, and surely many of us would have perished."

Squawk, squawk, Tux screeched, her voice sounding tired.

"Yeah, maybe it's a good time for a rest," Gameknight said.

They stopped in a large clearing devoid of trees, a lazy river carving a sinuous path through the landscape. Bright flowers dotted the grassy floor with blue, fluorescent green, and yellow flowers, each giving off magical particles that floated up into the air, then evaporated, leaving behind the faintest sparkle of light. It was captivating to watch. At the far end of the clearing there was a large mound that looked unnatural for some reason. Grass covered its slopes, merging it with its surroundings, but there was something about the hill that seemed dangerous. The wolves moved next to each other and glared at the mound. Their fur bristled as their tails stuck straight out, a deep throated growl coming from each.

"What's wrong with the wolves?" Digger asked as he set Tux on the ground.

"There are monsters in the distant hill," Herder said, pointing to the mound as he ran his fingers through his tangled hair.

"Monsters?!" Stitcher asked excitedly, already drawing an arrow and notching it to her bowstring.

"It is safe, yes, yes. Monsters will stay in their hill." Empech moved forward and put a calming hand on Stitcher's arm. "Weapons are not needed here, all is safe."

The young girl lowered her bow, but kept a watchful eye on the grassy knoll.

"Speaking of weapons," Gameknight said, "I picked this up after the Lich King disappeared." He pulled out the bone-handled wand with the large green gem embedded in the end. "Empech, any idea what it is?"

"The Lich King's wand, yes, yes," the gnome said.

"Well, I know it's the Lich King's wand," the User-that-is-not-a-user replied. "But do you know what it does?"

"It is rumored the Lich King has three wands, yes. Empech heard of the Scepter of Life Draining, the Twilight Scepter, and the Zombie Specter, but it is not clear which this is."

"That's the one the skeleton king was using to conjure up all those zombies," Hunter said.

"Maybe we can use it and the zombies will be on our side," Woodcutter suggested.

"Dangerous experiment, yes, yes. It is wise to be cautious with this and only use it if the situation is dire."

"Perhaps you're right," Gameknight replied, putting the scepter back into his inventory.

As he did so, his hand brushed against something warm in his inventory. Reaching in, he pulled out the Lich King's battle-axe. The weapon pulsed with magical power as if it were alive. But there was something else about the axe; it didn't fit in Gameknight's hands, as if the axe was rejecting him. He felt the heavy weight of the sparkling weapon and knew this thing needed strong arms and firm hands to wield it properly. He thought about Carver from long ago in Minecraft's past; he would have loved this tool. But then his eyes fell on Digger, and he wondered. . . . He put away the weapon, then moved his gaze across the others.

"Let's get moving," Stitcher said. "We need to stay ahead of Entity303. I want to get to this fire swamp of yours and battle whatever is there." She continued running to the north.

"The younger sister is quick to find violence," Empech said with a sigh.

"It wasn't always that way with her," Gameknight said. "In my timeline, she was the last to pick up a weapon and the first to make peace."

"Not anymore," Hunter said as she got up and started following her sister.

The wolf pack leader barked once, then loped after the young girl, the rest of the pack spreading out to form a protective ring. The companions headed north, following Stitcher, each with a bow in their hands, eyes scanning the strange forest through which they passed.

Gameknight slowed a bit, allowing Digger to catch up with him, Tux held under one arm. The stocky NPC had taken to watching over the young penguin, as if it somehow eased the pain he still felt over the loss of his son, Topper.

"Digger, I have something for you," Gameknight said.

The NPC's blue-green eyes shifted to the User-that-is-not-a-user. "What is it?"

"It's the Lich King's battle axe. I have the feeling, for some reason, that you'll be needing this." Gameknight reached into his inventory and held the Lich King's battle axe in the air. The glistening head was heavy and drooped toward the ground.

"I don't understand it, but I feel like you need to have this," Gameknight explained. "Something about it makes me think this is critical, and I need you to use this weapon when the time is right."

"Why not give it to Woodcutter? He uses axes all the time."

"I don't know how to explain it, Digger, but I feel you're the one who needs this, not Woodcutter." Gameknight took a step closer and placed the axe in his friend's timid hands.

"Huh . . . it's much lighter than I would have thought," Digger said. He swung it through the air. The keen edge made a whistling sound, leaving a glowing trail as if the magically heated blade was burning through the air.

Gameknight moved a little closer and lowered his voice so that only the two of them could hear. "I know you're afraid; so am I. But something deep down in my soul tells me that I need you at my side with this axe in your hands. It doesn't make any sense, and I don't understand it, but I fear if you're not right next to me with this axe, then someone will fall in battle, and I couldn't bear to know it might be you." The User-that-is-not-a-user looked directly into the stocky NPC's eyes. "I need you with me on this adventure. Filler and Topper need you."

Digger sighed, then nodded his head.

"All right?" Gameknight asked, trying to sound enthusiastic, but he could tell from the expression on Digger's square face that he was still afraid.

TWANG . . . twang, twang.

"Yeah!" Stitcher exclaimed, as if she'd just won some kind of prize.

"What is it?" Gameknight said as he sprinted toward the front of the formation. He reached Crafter's side and saw Stitcher just a few strides ahead.

"One less zombie for us to worry about," the young girl said. She glanced over her shoulder, a radiant smile on her face, though her eyes were still filled with anger.

"Stitcher seems so angry," Gameknight said. "I worry about her."

"She seems normal enough to me."

"That's the problem," the User-that-is-not-a-user replied. "She has a constant tone of violence about her that all of you have accepted as normal."

"Well, she was held in that nether fortress as a prisoner for a long time," Crafter said. "If we'd been able to slow down Erebus and Malacoda back then, they would have captured fewer prisoners, and maybe she would be different now. But those two monsters moved across the Overworld pretty much unchecked . . . you remember."

"No, I don't. That wasn't my timeline. I remember destroying Erebus and slowing Malacoda's forces by using lots of TNT and fireworks. Most of those things were your ideas, because of what Weaver taught you when you were younger. But with him being taken away from the timeline, you never learned those things."

"This is very confusing," Crafter said.

"Weaver's abduction has affected all of you," Gameknight continued in a low voice. "Look at Digger; he was a pillar of strength and courage in my timeline. Herder was the most calm and trusting person in all of Minecraft, and Stitcher had more empathy for others than anyone in existence."

"And what about me?" Crafter asked.

"I think you most of all were changed, Crafter. You would never have accepted these attitudes from another villager, much less your friends. But you have accepted them as they are, instead of how they could be." Gameknight weaved around a tall tree with fireflies clinging to its spotted bark. "You were the heart and soul of Minecraft in my timeline, and you pushed everyone to be the best person they could be, even if it was difficult. I remember you once told me a story about a boy in your village named Fisher . . . do you remember it?"

"There was one boy by that name, but he drowned in the lake when he was young; never learned how to swim . . . so sad."

"That didn't happen in my timeline," Gameknight snapped. "But anyway, Fisher in *my* timeline taught you that deeds do not make the hero. Rather it is the fears they overcome that define them and make them heroic. You forced me to confront my own fears, as you did with everyone around you. But here in this timeline, you seem to be content with things as they are, instead of pushing against those barriers and trying to make things better." Gameknight sighed. "This whole timeline is all wrong. We need to put it back the way it was."

"How do we do that?"

"We must save Weaver and send him back to the past."

Stitcher slowed to a walk as she came to the end of the forest biome, the fireflies flitting about in the foliage of the soaring trees. The landscape changed quickly from the flowered, life-affirming forest, to something burned and charred. The young NPC pulled out a new arrow and notched it to her bowstring. She scanned her surroundings as Gameknight and the others approached.

"What is it?" Gameknight asked.

Stitcher remained silent as her angry, predatory gaze shifted across the biome before them.

"What kind of land is this?" Herder asked. He reached out and patted one of the growling wolves.

"I remember going through this part of the mod long ago," Gameknight said. "I knew we'd eventually find this place. This is the fire swamp."

"That doesn't sound very nice," Hunter said.

"I agree," Woodcutter added, his iron axe in his hands.

Digger moved up next to him and glanced down at Woodcutter's axe, then pulled out the gold battle-axe from the Lich King and gripped the handle firmly. The stocky NPC shook ever so slightly, unseen to all of their eyes except Gameknight's.

Pools of lava dotted the landscape, with thin tendrils of smoke slowly rising from the ground like dark, ethereal snakes. The constant east-to-west wind dragged the winding lines of smoke, spreading them into an ashen haze that filled the air, making it difficult to see very far. The ground was a burnt brown, with little embers glowing here and there. The occasional tree could be seen with leaves still covering its top, but most of them were bare of their leafy canopy. The empty trees stood as limbless trunks, stark reminders of the death and destruction that was spreading through Minecraft.

A column of fire suddenly shot up into the air, making a sound that Gameknight could only equate to that of a jet engine.

"I think this is probably the worst place I've ever seen, aside from the Nether and the End," Stitcher said.

"The good thing is it can't get any worse," Hunter added.

Just then, a great roar sliced through the air. It was a terrible, primeval sound that made tiny square goose bumps form on Gameknight's skin. The bellowing roar bespoke of a creature filled with strength and anger and violence.

"Great, now it's worse," Hunter said. "If we . . ."

Before she could finish her statement, another roar, slightly higher, was added to the first, and then a low growl from a third creature echoed across the landscape, making a musical chord of malice and hatred.

"There's three of them?" Digger moaned.

"Maybe we can go around them," Woodcutter suggested.

"If we move along that ridge," Crafter said, pointing to a line of trees, some of them charred and burnt, "we could get around those monsters, and . . ."

"No, we can't go around them," Gameknight said. "Those monsters are why we're here. It's their trophy we're here for. There is no other path."

"But it sounds as if there are three of them out there," Digger said. "How do we fight three monsters that sound that huge?"

"There aren't three," Empech said. "Only one creature rules in the fire swamp, yes, yes."

"But we heard three distinct roars," Crafter said.

"Three roars, three heads, one body," the tiny gnome said. "Welcome to the land of the Hydra."

"Hydra . . . I don't like the sound of that," Hunter said.

Another roar boomed through the air, making all of them flinch.

"I don't know about this," Crafter said.

"I do," Gameknight growled. "Weaver needs all of us, and we need him. Come on."

Drawing his dual swords, Gameknight stepped into the fire swamp, heading in the direction of the most frightening roars he'd ever heard.

CHAPTER 19
BROOMS

Entity303 pulled Weaver behind the trunk of the massive oak tree. It stretched up at least thirty blocks if not more. Its base was six blocks wide, and was without a doubt one of the largest trees he'd ever seen.

"I added this mod, just to see how much it could strain the server planes," Entity303 said with a smile as he patted the rough bark.

Weaver just grunted.

"What? You want to say something?" the user said.

He reached behind Weaver and untied the gag.

"You have something you want to add?"

"Yeah. I can't wait until they catch you," Weaver growled. "I'm gonna enjoy watching when you have to face Smithy of the Two-Swords in combat. You won't stand a chance."

"Ha, what a joke," Entity303 scoffed. "I think I'm gonna keep Gameknight999 alive just long enough for you to finally understand the lie he's been perpetrating on you and all the other villagers. You think your famous leader is an NPC like you when he's really a user like me . . . I love it!"

Weaver gritted his teeth and scowled at the user.

"Now it's time to move fast," Entity303 said. "Your little friends have led us to the Fire Swamp, and that can mean only one thing."

He pulled a broom out of his inventory and dropped it to the ground. It sparkled and glowed with magical enchantments. Weaver looked down at it, a confused expression on his face.

"That broom is from a witchcraft mod I put on the servers after Herobrine unlocked them for me," Entity303 explained. "We're gonna use these brooms so we can beat Gameknight999 and his foolish comrades to their destination. Now get on the broom."

Weaver stood his ground, refusing to mount the magical device. Entity sighed, then yanked on the rope, but this time Weaver was ready for it and pulled back at the same time. The tug of war made Entity303 stumble just a bit.

Weaver laughed and gave the user a satisfied grin.

With an unbelievable swiftness, Entity303 drew a sword from his inventory. It glowed a bright yellow but had a blood-red color at the sharp edge. The user attacked, bringing the shimmering blade down onto the villager's shoulder. Weaver grunted and fell to one knee, flashing red as he took damage. Now Entity303 was the one laughing.

"I bet that hurt. You know why?" He moved forward to stand directly over the wounded NPC, glaring down at him. "That's called an infused longsword, and it has magical powers you don't even understand, like being able to go through armor. So if you think I'm afraid of your little friends, you better recalibrate that square head of yours. They still live, but only because I allow it."

The user yanked on the rope and pulled Weaver to his feet. He then pulled out a piece of beef from his inventory and stuffed it in the boy's mouth.

"It won't be helpful if your HP drops to zero, at least not yet. So do as you're told, unless you want to taste my sword again. Get on the broom."

Weaver sighed, then mounted the broom as if it were a horse, his legs dangling on either side.

"Why are you doing this?" the young boy asked. "Why are you leading them all over this strange land?"

"Well, you see, my young villager, I want your little friends to unlock the White Castle for me, and slay the beast that hides within the bowels of that fortress. When they accomplish that, and I'm sure they will, though most will not survive, your foolish friends will be unlocking for me tools of great power, which I can then use to destroy all of Minecraft. By dragging you along as bait, I'm forcing them to do all the dangerous work while I just watch. Ha ha . . . you're all morons."

"We'll see," Weaver whispered, a scowl on his face.

Entity303 just smiled.

"So we're going to this White Castle soon?" the boy asked.

"No, no, I'm not done torturing your friends yet," the user explained. "I want to see them battle the Snow Queen, and maybe do a couple of rounds with the Minotaurs and the Minoshroom in the labyrinth, and then perhaps get lost in the Goblin King's Stronghold for a while. I think a battle down there with the goblin knights, the block-and-chain goblins and the knight phantoms would be fun to watch. There won't be many of your friends left after all that, but oh well."

He mounted his broom, then pulled the rope tight.

"You stay close now, villager. If you fall off your broom, then I'm just gonna let you dangle down and smash into the trees. You hear me?"

Weaver just grunted, an angry frown on his square face.

"Ha ha, you heard me all right," Entity303 said with a laugh. "It's time to fly fast. We have an appointment with a three-headed monster."

And with that, they kicked off the ground on their sparkling brooms and shot through the forest and into the fire swamp, the roars of a distant monster filling the air.

CHAPTER 20

THE HYDRA

An ashen haze hung over the dark landscape, as blocks here and there continually belched smoke into the air. Pools of lava cast an orange glow on the surroundings as glowing embers leapt into the air like kernels of popped corn from an overheated frying pan. Dark ash floated up from the molten stone, adding to the charcoal-gray mist that lurked just off the ground.

The aroma of the place assaulted Gameknight's senses. It smelled of smoke and ash and sulfur and dust . . . but that was the good part. With every breath, it seemed as if he could taste the air. His tongue felt as if he'd just licked the remains of an old campfire and everything seemed to be covered with a thin layer of grime. The fire swamp was almost worse than the Nether.

A gray block with a dark center sputtered a small puff of ash. Empech shot forward, grabbed Gameknight's arm and yanked him back just before a column of fire blasted into the air. The two companions fell to the dark, charred ground. Another sputtering sound off to the left was followed by more flames shooting into the air. One of Herder's wolves yelped in pain when a fiery column licked its side, leaving behind charred fur and a wounded leg.

"Gameknight, what did you take us into?" Herder growled.

"We're here for the Hydra. And if I remember the Twilight Forest mod correctly, that monster is in the center of the fire swamp," Gameknight said as he stood, then helped Empech up. Another sputtering puff of smoke in the distance. A bright yellow-orange tongue of flame shot into the air, the roar sounding like the blast of a tiny hurricane. "I've never seen the monster before, but I have heard rumors that it's difficult to defeat."

"Great!" Stitcher exclaimed, an inhuman hunger in her eyes.

"What's with the fire shooting up out of the ground?" Hunter asked.

"Those are called firejets," Gameknight explained. "We need to listen and watch out for each other."

"I like the firejets," Stitcher said with a strange sort of grin. "They probably cooked everything in this biome for us."

Squawk!

Digger reached down and picked up Tux.

"Don't worry girl, you'll be OK, I promise," the stocky NPC said to the penguin.

Squawk, squawk, she replied.

They moved through the dark, ashen terrain, weaving their way around lava pools and smoking blocks. Many trees were barren of leaves, but a few still had their foliage. The leaves were dark, rusty reds instead of bright greens, and the grass was also similarly colored. Everything in this biome was either gray or some flavor of brown and dark red, and it was all covered with a thin layer of ash.

The wolves moved out in a large circle around the party, each scanning the area for monsters. Gameknight would have liked to have them closer, but Herder would not relent; he sent the animals out on patrol regardless of what was said.

A tremendous growl filled the air, followed by another guttural roar and the gnashing of teeth.

"That your friend?" Stitcher asked excitedly.

Gameknight nodded his boxy head.

She smiled, a look of excitement sparkling in her eyes.

"There's its lair up ahead," the User-that-is-not-a-user said. "The Hydra will be near, so everyone be ready. Herder, you should bring the wolves in. It would be bad if one of them stumbled into the monster."

"My wolves will lead the attack," Herder said, his voice ringing with pride.

"No, just bring them back," Gameknight said. "We'll figure out a strategy when we get closer."

The lanky boy gave him a scowl, then whistled, the piercing sound echoing across the landscape. Instantly, ghostly white forms emerged from the haze that hung over the land and came to his side.

"OK, let's move up quietly," Gameknight said.

The party moved forward, weaving around the burnt remains of an oak tree, then jumping across a small stream of lava. Ahead was a large mound made of reddish-brown dirt, charred grass, and stone. Along the edge, Gameknight noticed the mound was not a solid hill. Instead, the inside was carved out; the mound only forming a hollowed-out half of a dome. And standing at the center of the dome was their prey, the Hydra.

The monster emerged from within the earthen dome, its heads moving out of the shadows first, followed by the hulking remainder of the giant's body.

Hot needles of fear pierced every inch of Gameknight's body as he stared in disbelief at the creature.

"That is the Hydra, yes, yes," Empech said. "An ancient monster that was erased from Minecraft long ago, but brought back to life by your adversary."

Gameknight said nothing; he just stared. It was the largest monster he'd ever seen in Minecraft. It stood on two large feet, a long, scaly tail stretching behind it like a massive, ridged snake. Its body was covered with thick scales, the sides and back colored a dark blue, while bright green scales spread across its chest and legs. Three gigantic heads sat atop long necks similar to the Ender Dragon, the green scales protecting the front of the necks. The monstrous faces had blazing red eyes, terrifying mouths, and sharp white teeth that seemed to shine brightly even though there was no sun in the constant twilight of the biome. Green, bony ridges ran down the back of each neck, coming together into a single line of scaly protrusions that extended down the long, dangerous tail.

"We're supposed to fight that?" Digger asked, his shaking voice barely audible over the roars of the Hydra.

Squawk, Tux said with a shaking voice.

"Maybe we can climb up over the hill behind the creature," Crafter said. "If we're careful, it might not see us."

Suddenly a laugh filled with vile contempt came from behind the monster. Gameknight moved closer until he could see through the smoke and ash. Behind the hydra stood Entity303 in enchanted white armor. Six blue horns stuck out from the back of his shining white helmet, giving him the appearance of some kind of snowy creature. An expression of pure hatred was carved into the user's face as he stared at Gameknight999. The user glanced up at the Hydra and smirked, then stared back at his nemesis. A rope extended from one of his blocky hands, the other end wrapped around a small boy: Weaver!

"What are you waiting for?" Entity303 shouted, pointing at him with a glowing yellow sword. "Why don't you come and take my prize from me, if you dare."

He yanked on the rope, pulling Weaver closer to him. One of the heads of the Hydra turned to see the source of the sound. The user pulled out a splash potion and threw it on himself, then Weaver. Instantly, the pair disappeared, the invisibility potion hiding them completely.

The Hydra, seeing nothing, turned back and stared at Gameknight999 and his friends.

"You know why I brought you here," Entity303 yelled. "If you want to see this villager remain alive, then you better get to work. I expected you at the Snow Queen's palace, but the fire swamp will do as well . . . for now. If you get too hot from this confrontation, then maybe the Snow Queen's Aurora palace will cool you down next. Ha ha ha . . ."

"Smithy, he's heading for the White . . ." Weaver yelled, but then grunted and went silent.

"Now, that's a shame; I had to hit your little friend over the head," Entity303 said. "I'm sure he'll be OK . . . well, maybe." The evil user laughed again. "You better get to work, Gameknight999. Your unconscious friend here needs your help. It wouldn't be good for you to let my trail get too cold. Ha . . . too cold . . . Snow Queen . . . I'm hilarious!"

Entity303 grunted with effort, then grew silent, his footsteps causing small puffs of ash to rise off the ground as he moved deeper into the hollow earthen dome, then disappeared through an opening in the back of the hill.

"He's taking Weaver away," Gameknight exclaimed. "We need to stop him!"

"Um, I think the Hydra there might be in the way," Hunter said.

"It's too big," Digger moaned.

Crafter nodded his head, his long blond hair falling across his face. "I don't know if we can do this."

"We need to deal with that beast somehow," Stitcher growled. "Any ideas?"

"Yeah, I have one," Gameknight said.

He drew his diamond sword with his right hand, the iron blade with his left, then turned and smiled at his friends.

"FOR WEAVER!" he screamed, and charged straight at the Hydra.

CHAPTER 21

PIECES OF THE PUZZLE

Gameknight charged straight at the monster, his enchanted diamond sword held high. The Hydra's three heads swiveled and glared at him as he approached, their red eyes like burning coals. The center head opened its mouth, the many razor-sharp teeth glistening from the internal fire. Tiny, glowing embers danced on its tongue as it pulled in a huge breath, then spat balls of fire at him.

Rolling to the left, the User-that-is-not-a-user felt the heat of the projectiles as they streaked by his head, the smell of smoke and sulfur filling his senses. More fireballs fell around him. Gameknight danced around them carefully, ducking and weaving as they plummeted toward him. The burning spheres sat on the ground, shouldering for a moment, then exploded, tearing holes in the dark red landscape.

The right head moved near the ground, then opened wide. A stream of flames flowed out of the monster like the fiery exhaust from a rocket. Patches of the ground began to glow where the flames hit, the last few tufts of grass burning away, leaving only ash. Gameknight turned, zigzagging, hoping the monster could not move as quickly as he could. Fortunately, he was right. The

User-that-is-not-a-user was able to stay ahead of the flaming torrent, but just barely.

The left head spat a fireball at him. It landed in front of him, the sphere glowing on the ground. Gameknight sprinted toward it, then jumped over the explosive, allowing it to explode far behind. Moving up to the monster, Gameknight999 swung his diamond sword with all his might. The weapon hit the green and blue scales and bounced off as if they were made of steel, the blade vibrating in his hand, making his whole arm ache. The creature did not flash red, nor did it cry out in pain. In fact, it seemed the Hydra didn't even notice his blows.

The three heads turned their attention to Hunter and Stitcher, who were firing their arrows at the monster. Their pointed shafts made a pinging sound when they bounced harmlessly off the monster's scales, doing no damage; they were like fleas annoying a massive dinosaur. Gameknight took advantage of the distraction to run away from the monster and reconsider his plans. As he sprinted across the warm sand, a firebomb struck him in the back, then exploded, throwing him forward. Pain erupted throughout his body as his diamond armor cracked under the assault. Digger ran forward and tossed Gameknight over his shoulder, then retreated just as another fireball streaked down at them. It tore another crater into the ground as they escaped, the heat from the fiery blast singing Gameknight's hair a little. When they were out of range, Digger carefully set his friend on the ground.

"Are you OK?" Digger asked.

Squawk squawk!

"Yeah," the User-that-is-not-a-user replied as he reached out and patted Tux on the head. "I'm OK, thanks to you."

Digger smiled, then looked away, his moment of bravery almost embarrassing to him.

Gameknight sheathed his weapons, then turned and faced his companions.

"I don't think your plan of charging right at the creature worked very well," Hunter said as she returned to the others, Stitcher at her side.

"Those scales are impenetrable. My sword just bounced off them."

"My arrows too," Stitcher growled.

"The scales cannot be destroyed," Empech said.

"It would have been nice if you'd told us that earlier," Stitcher growled.

The tiny pech ignored her. "The Hydra is only vulnerable in one place," Empech said as he took his huge pack off and set it on the ground.

"You gonna share with us where that place is at?" Stitcher asked impatiently.

"The Hydra is completely covered with scales, from head to foot, yes, yes. But when it opens its mouth, the ancient beast can be injured."

"You mean we can only hurt it inside its mouth?" Crafter asked.

The pech nodded his head.

"Are you saying the place with the massive, razor sharp fangs and streams of fire coming out, that's where it's vulnerable?" Stitcher rolled her eyes, then shouted. "That's a lot of help!"

She stormed away, standing next to a charred tree and staring at the monster.

"So we need to attack it in the mouth?" Gameknight asked.

Empech nodded his head, then pulled a crafting bench out of his pack.

"Empech, what are you doing?" the User-that-is-not-a-user asked.

"Your armor, it will not be sufficient." the little creature said. "There is a reason why the Naga is the Naga, yes, yes."

He pulled out the Naga scales and began crafting them into something, his hands a blur. In seconds, he tossed Gameknight999 a green chest plate, then crafted a set of leggings.

"Put these on. The Naga armor will give you some protection against the fire, but be warned; nothing will protect you from the monster's teeth. The Hydra can crush anything with its jaws, yes, yes. You must not get within reach of those teeth. Fight it from a distance, yes."

Finally, the pech pulled out some leaves that seemed thick and stout, a steely blue tint to each.

"Steeleaf," Empech said, "very strong, yes, yes." He quickly crafted a shield and tossed it to Gameknight999.

"You mean use bows on the Hydra?" Crafter asked.

"Bow and arrow will cause only the smallest harm," Empech replied.

Gameknight looked back at the monster. Craters dotted the landscape where the fireballs had exploded and torn terrible wounds into the landscape.

What am I going to do? he thought. *Weaver was right there. I could have saved him if I'd been fast enough. I failed him again.*

Gameknight stared at the place where his friend had been standing and sighed.

How many of my friends must get hurt, or worse, in this battle that I've already messed up?

He glanced at the monster again. One of the mouths opened wide, releasing a gout of flame that sprayed across the landscape, turning an oak tree into a massive candle.

How am I going to do this? he thought, his words echoing in his head like pathetic pleas.

Like the ghasts, a high-pitched, weak voice said in his mind.

The words sounded as if they were coming from far away, very far away. They were barely audible over his own self-criticisms.

Like the ghasts, yes, yes, the squeaky voice said again, this time a little louder. *Like the Lich King.*

Gameknight turned and stared at Empech.

You can only do what you believe you can do, yes, yes, the gnome's voice said in his head.

"What I believe I can do?" the User-that-is-not-a-user asked.

"Are you talking to yourself?" Hunter asked, but Crafter placed a hand on her arm, silencing her questions.

Gameknight glanced at the Hydra. The monster spat a burning fireball at them. The glowing sphere fell to the ground before reaching them, then exploded.

Ghasts . . . of course. I can do that!

And then, suddenly, the puzzle pieces started to tumble around in his head, his newly remembered belief in himself driving away the haze of uncertainty. There was a solution here, and the User-that-is-not-a-user was going to find it.

"Ghasts . . . it's just like the ghasts," Gameknight said as the solution solidified in his mind.

Empech nodded, a smile creasing his gray face.

"I know what to do, but I need all of you to stay here." The User-that-is-not-a-user stared at all his friends, making sure the message was clear. "It's important that the Hydra is focused just on me, so all of you stay here and watch my back. Do you understand?"

"You want us to stay here while you go out there and face an undefeatable monster with your fancy green Naga armor?" Stitcher asked. "Is that it?"

The User-that-is-not-a-user nodded his boxy head.

Drawing his diamond sword, Gameknight999 charged toward the Hydra, the monster's six eyes glaring straight at him.

CHAPTER 22

FLAMES AND FANGS

The Hydra's burning red eyes tracked Gameknight as he approached. The central head let out a thunderous, growling roar, causing the other two heads to join in. The sound echoed across the desolate fire swamp and rippled out into the surrounding forest, but Gameknight ignored it. He had a plan, and he was going to see it through.

The monster launched a barrage of attacks when he was in range. It opened one of its mouths and belched fireball after fireball at its attacker. Gameknight stopped running and waited for the flaming spheres to descend upon him. With his sword held like a bat, he swung at the balls, knocking them back at the beast.

The first couple shots went wide, but the next one bounced off his sword and went straight back at the monster. It exploded near the open mouth.

The Hydra flashed red.

Yes!

It bellowed in pain and stomped its tail on the ground, then fired another volley. Gameknight didn't move a single step. He wanted the timing to be perfect. With beads of sweat dripping down his forehead, he waited for the balls of fire to reach him, then swung again, knocking the explosive orbs right back at the monster. Again, it roared in pain as more of the firebombs detonated near its head. The Hydra attacked one more time, this time launching the balls even faster. But Gameknight was ready; he'd done this countless times in the Nether with ghasts. He knocked the spheres back as if he were in an easy tennis match, sending the flaming balls right into the monster's mouth. It screamed in pain as the head flashed bright red, then disappeared.

"One down!" Hunter yelled from behind.

Gameknight smiled, but then was shocked as another head emerged from the monster's body, followed by a second head; the head that had been defeated was now replaced by two. The hydra now had four heads!

Sparkling embers danced around one of the mouths. Before he could move, a torrent of fire flowed from the monster, bathing the landscape in flame. Gameknight jumped backward, then turned and ran as a wave of fire crashed toward him. The heat from the attack was so intense it singed some of the hairs on the back of his neck. But as quickly as it started, the stream of fire stopped.

Suddenly, Hunter was at his side.

"I told you I need the Hydra focused on me," Gameknight said. "Go back."

"Nope," she replied with a smile. "I'll make sure the Hydra is focused on you, but it will also be focused on me . . . WATCH OUT!"

A fireball streaked down at the pair. Hunter knocked the projectile aside with her sword. Gameknight turned and swung at the next one, sending it back at the beast. But now, two of the heads were attacking from opposite sides of the monster's body. If he'd been alone, likely Gameknight would have been overwhelmed.

Standing shoulder to shoulder, they batted back the burning spheres, aiming for the open, tooth-lined mouths. Another of the heads turned toward the duo and opened fire. Suddenly, Woodcutter was on Hunter's shoulder, his iron axe smashing into the burning sphere. And then Crafter came forward, followed by Digger. The stocky NPC held both pickaxes ready in his hands, but out of the corner of his eye, Gameknight could see them shaking.

Slowly moving forward, the group pressed closer to the monster, batting more and more of the burning spheres back at the Hydra. Another head flashed red one final time and disappeared, only to be replaced by two more. Now there were five of the hideous heads either launching fireballs at the companions or spraying the landscape with sheets of flames. Smoke billowed into the air, making it difficult to see. The air was warm and tasted of ash. Deep breaths hurt Gameknight's chest a little.

One of the center heads tilted upward to the sky and let out a thunderous roar that echoed across the scorched landscape. It was joined by the others . . . a chorus of deadly animalistic screams all singing together. The heads then tilted toward its attackers and opened fire. The burning spheres were coming at them from all sides now, some landing on the ground at their feet and sitting there for an instant before exploding.

Suddenly, Herder sprinted in front of the group, his iron shovel in his hand. As he ran past, he swung at a burning sphere that sat on the ground in front of his friends. The firebombs leapt off his shovel and shot into the air, some of them exploding before they reached the monster, but others hitting home. Another head flashed red and disappeared, but this one was not replaced.

"One down!" Gameknight shouted. "Everyone forward."

They moved closer to the Hydra, making it easier to hit the monster with the deflected fireballs, but they also had less time to react. A fireball slipped past Crafter's sword and smashed into his armor. Gameknight could see cracks forming across the chest plate.

"Hunter, Stitcher, get behind us and use your bows," Gameknight said.

"Empech said they would do no good," Hunter replied.

"Aim for their mouths," Gameknight replied. "If the fireballs hurt them, then maybe a flaming arrow in their mouth will do the same."

The two girls stepped back and pulled out their enchanted bows.

Herder shot across the front of their formation again, and struck at a burning sphere that sat on the ground. It flew into the air, but exploded right after leaving his shovel. The blast knocked him to the ground. Digger sprinted forward, picked the boy up and carried him away, the edges of his iron armor glowing slightly with heat.

Another fireball made it past their weapons, this one smashing into Woodcutter. The tall NPC screamed in pain and fell to one knee as another fireball streaked toward him. Gameknight dove to the side and hit the flaming sphere just as it was about to strike the NPC. It bounced off his sword and flew into the mouth of the Hydra, destroying another head. Only four remained.

Glancing at his friends, Gameknight could see all of them were getting wounded. If they didn't end this battle fast, someone was going to perish.

Pulling out the blue-green steeleaf shield, Gameknight charged forward.

"All of you stay there. I'm ending this."

With the stout shield held out in front of him, the User-that-is-not-a-user charged, closing the distance to the beast. The monster's heads all tracked him, their bright red eyes burning with hatred. It fired more fire-bombs at him, but with Gameknight so close, all of the deflected shots went straight back at the monster. Glowing embers sparkled in the mouth of the left head. Gameknight held up the shield as a spray of flames spewed from the monster's mouth. Gameknight quickly ran around the monster's feet, moving to the right side. The left head continued spraying its fiery breath, but now it was hitting the other heads. The center head flashed red as it took damage from the flaming spray, causing it to disappear with a pop.

The right head opened its mouth to spit more fire at Gameknight. Suddenly, two flaming arrows streaked into its exposed throat, causing it to flash red, then disappear; only two more heads remained.

The steeleaf shield was getting hot and beginning to glow. Cracks were forming across the back; it wouldn't last long. When the shield disappeared, Gameknight would have no defense against the spray of fire.

The monster turned to get a better angle on him. It swung its massive tail across the ground, likely intent on knocking him to the ground. Gameknight jumped into the air just as the tail hit his feet. He stumbled for a moment and had to drop his diamond sword to reach out to the ground and cushion his fall. Bouncing quickly back to his feet, he drew his enchanted iron sword.

Another fireball streaked down at him. Swinging the blade with all his strength, he hit the burning sphere right into the mouth of the left head. It flashed red just as two flaming arrows streaked into its open mouth. The head disappeared with a pop, leaving behind only one terrible set of burning eyes and razor sharp teeth.

Intelligence seemed to flicker within the bright red eyes. Gameknight could tell the monster was studying him, deciding which attack would be best.

And then it struck.

Instead of shooting out fireballs, the creature lowered its head and snapped at Gameknight with its massive teeth. It tore the leafy rectangle out of his grip and tossed it aside.

The Hydra growled victoriously.

Gameknight rolled away from the head, then gripped his sword with both hands. Over the monster's ridged tail, he could see his friends watching. Digger held his pickaxe in his hands. He then gripped the handle with both hands and held it over his head as if he were going to throw it.

"Of course!" Gameknight said to himself.

The Hydra turned toward him and opened its massive jaws, getting ready to bite down on its next victim. But as the Hydra opened its mouth wide, Gameknight threw his enchanted iron sword with all his strength. It tumbled end over end, narrowly missing a large tooth, then stuck into the monster's throat. The creature closed its mouth in shock, causing the blade to dig into the vulnerable flesh.

The monster flashed red.

It bellowed an ear-splitting roar, then snapped at Gameknight, who was already moving. The sharp teeth narrowly missed him, but the sword, still stuck in the Hydra's mouth, dug in again, causing it to flash red one last time. The beast gave off a sorrowful moan of pain and sadness, then fell to the side, writhing in agony. With one final, sorrowful roar, the Hydra shuddered, then exploded. The blast threw Gameknight backward a dozen blocks, and when he hit the ground, everything went black.

CHAPTER 23

KEYS TO THE CASTLE

A silvery mist swirled around his legs. It was cold and clammy, like the tentacles of a squid . . . or a ghast. Strange trees began to emerge from the mist, stretching high into the air. Their branches spread out, forming a canopy that covered the twilight sky in places, blotting out the sparkling stars.

A firefly buzzed past, then settled on the dark skin of the canopy tree, the glow from the bug creating a yellow circle of light that spread through the forest, driving away the darkness.

I'm in the Land of Dreams, *Gameknight thought*. I'm not awake.

But if he wasn't awake, then where was he?

Suddenly, he saw someone dressed in sparkling white armor, the blue stripes across the chest plate and leggings standing out in stark contrast to the pale surface. Six blue extrusions stood out from the iridescent helmet, giving the impression of being some kind of monster . . . like the Alpha Yeti.

Entity303! Gameknight suddenly realized it was his enemy.

He saw the user running through the forest with Weaver in tow, a rope wrapped around the boy's body, pinning his arms to his side. Their bodies were partially transparent, as they were awake and not in the Land of Dreams. Suddenly, Gameknight's favorite bow, with the Infinity, Flame and Punch enchantments, appeared in his hand. Gameknight drew back the string, the Infinity enchantment making an arrow instantly appear. He aimed it at Entity303, but slowly lowered the weapon; his arrow would have no effect on someone that was awake.

"If that three-headed monster hurt any of my friends, I'm gonna make you sorry," Weaver said.

"Ha ha ha . . . you're funny, villager," the user replied.

The boy growled, his eyes burning with anger.

Gameknight floated through the forest, following the pair. They ran toward a massive chunk of ice that was maybe thirty blocks tall. He figured it was the Snow Queen's glacier; that was where Entity303 wanted them to go next.

"Well, if I can't hurt you, at least I can follow you and see where you're going," Gameknight mused to himself.

The pair reached the foot of the glacier, then Entity303 removed his chest plate, and put on what looked like a jetpack.

Industrial-craft, that must be one of the mods he added, Gameknight thought.

Entity303 yanked on the rope and pulled Weaver close, then slowly lifted off the ground. Gameknight drifted after them, rising in the air.

Suddenly, a massive wave of chilly water crashed down upon him, forcing him to the ground. Gameknight tried to stand, but another wave fell on him, knocking away the trees and the glacier and everything around him until . . .

Gameknight999 woke with a start. He was on his back, staring up into a twilight sky where stars were just beginning to peek through the darkening heavens.

"Is he awake?" a voice asked.

He sat up and glanced at her. Hunter cast him a smile, then put the empty bucket back into her inventory, square droplets of water still lining the rim.

"About time," she said.

"What happened?" Gameknight asked.

"When the Hydra exploded, you were blasted through the air until you finally landed here," Crafter explained. "I guess you passed out for a bit."

"Well, I'm awake now." He shook his head as a dull ache filled his skull, the pain blossoming with every beat of his heart. Gameknight stood and glanced back to where the Hydra had been standing. "Where's Weaver? He was going up to the top of the glacier and . . ."

Finally, clarity came to his mind, and he remembered he'd been in the Land of Dreams. Weaver and Entity303 were far away from here.

"He's gone," Stitcher said. "What'd you expect? Entity303 would just be standing there, waiting for us?"

"Stitcher, be nice," Hunter chided.

"Well . . . if we didn't have to stand around and wait for him to wake up," the younger sister added, sounding frustrated, "we'd be following their trail now."

"I know where they are now, but we aren't gonna follow their trail," Gameknight said.

"What do you mean?" Crafter asked.

"He said they were heading to the Snow Queen next," Stitcher said. "They left a clear trail through the forest. It'll be easy to follow."

"I don't care," Gameknight said. "We aren't playing his game anymore. We're gonna play *our* game now."

"How hard did you get hit in the head?" Stitcher asked.

Gameknight looked down at the young girl, expecting to see a playful smile, but instead he found an angry scowl growing across her square face.

"Entity303 is gonna lead us past all the bosses until he manages to get more of us destroyed. I'm not letting that happen. You see, I played this mod a long time ago."

"You mean you knew about all this stuff?" Stitcher asked, a tone of accusation to her voice.

"No, I only explored the smallest amount, but I did see one thing."

"What was that?" Crafter asked.

"The White Castle."

"The White Castle?" Hunter asked. "What's that?"

Gameknight spotted his sword on the ground and moved to it. He bent down and picked it up, then put it back into his inventory. A sputtering sound filled the air for just an instant, then a geyser of flame shot into the air far to their left.

"The White Castle was supposed to be the end of the Twilight Forest mod," he explained.

"So what about the White Castle?" Woodcutter asked. "Why go there?"

"Weaver yelled that to us right before Entity303 hit him over the head and knocked him out. It made me remember what the trophies are for, to unlock that castle. Instead of letting Entity303 lead us around, we're gonna go to the White Castle before he gets there."

"But there are three challenges to the white castle. First, a deadly thorn forest surrounds it. If you fall into it, you have no chance of survival."

"That sounds lovely," Hunter said with a smile.

"Second, to get in, you must have three trophies to open the doors, which we already have."

Empech pulled off his huge pack and set it on the ground. He opened the top and pulled out three square golden tiles, each with a different symbol on them. The first had the face of the Naga, complete with leafy skin and bright red eyes. The second shining square had the face of a skeleton on it, a golden crown adorning its head: the Lich King. And the last one had the blue and green face of the Hydra staring out of the tile: the drop from the gigantic monster after it was destroyed.

"Perfect," Gameknight said. "These are the keys to getting into the castle. If we get there before Entity303, then we'll have the advantage of surprise."

"But where do we go when we get into the castle?" Crafter asked.

"The dungeons under the castle were set up to hold lots of creatures," Gameknight explained. "Some say there are multiple levels that go deeper underground, but I've never seen them. I've heard there is a huge hidden chamber under the castle, built for some kind of monster."

"And what waits for us there?" Digger asked, his voice shaking just a bit.

"That's the strange thing. This mod was never completed, but I bet Entity303 has something there waiting for us. Probably he needed us to get the keys for him so he can get in, for some reason."

"But we're gonna get there first!" Stitcher exclaimed. "And this time, we'll be waiting for him."

"Right!" Woodcutter added, his shining axe reflecting some of the still-burning flames, making it appear as if it were ablaze.

"That user must be stopped, and Weaver must be saved," Gameknight said in a confident voice, more to himself than to the others. "The timeline must be repaired so all these mods to Minecraft can be eliminated, and Weaver is the key. He *must* be sent back to his own time, or I fear something terrible is going to happen to Minecraft."

"Like what?" Crafter asked, his bright blue eyes filled with trepidation.

"The thing with mods is that they aren't very stable when there are a lot of them running at the same time." Gameknight held the gold tile with the Hydra's face on it. The bright red eyes made him shudder. Moving to the tiny gnome, he placed it back in his pack. "You see, Entity303 somehow added lots of mods to Minecraft, but I'm sure he didn't spend the time to figure out which would function properly and which would conflict with each other. There are mod packs out there, like the DireWolf20 modpack, that are very stable. Direwolf20 spent a lot of time testing all the mods, to figure out which would work and keep the world stable, but I bet Entity303 didn't do that."

"So you're saying the world might become unstable?" Crafter asked worriedly.

Gameknight nodded his head.

"What does that mean? Put it in simpler terms," Stitcher growled impatiently.

"OK, you want simple . . . the pyramid of server planes might collapse, and everything could be destroyed. That's probably Entity303's plan anyway. So, if we don't save Weaver and restore history, then everything will be at risk."

Everyone remained silent, the thought of that level of destruction unthinkable, yet they all knew it was possible.

"So then, maybe we should get going," a hollow, scared voice said. It came from Digger.

The stocky NPC moved to the opening at the back of the hill through which Weaver and Entity303 had escaped. Gameknight could see the big NPC was afraid, his normally bright green eyes dimmed with fear. He shook almost imperceptibly. "Are . . . any of you coming with me?"

"Absolutely!" Stitcher shouted, the sudden volume causing many of them to jump.

"Don't scare us like that," Hunter said and punched her sister in the shoulder.

"What?" the younger said with an innocent smile.

"Digger's right, let's get out of here," Gameknight said. "Empech, do you know where the castle is located?"

"Empech saw the edge of the thorn forest off in that direction, yes, yes." He pointed to the north with a three-fingered hand.

"All right, let's go," the User-that-is-not-a-user said. "We move fast. Leave anything behind you don't need:

furnaces, beds, minecarts . . . leave anything you won't need in battle."

"What about TNT?" Crafter asked.

"We absolutely want that!"

Reaching out, he patted the young NPC on the back, then sprinted through the opening and headed to the north, the deadly thorn forest and White Castle not yet visible in the distance.

A chill covered his body as he thought about the unknown monster that likely lurked somewhere within the white structure, waiting to ensnare them in its deadly embrace . . . or worse.

CHAPTER 24

PREDATOR FOLLOWING THE PREY

Entity303 paced back and forth, pulling Weaver along with him. He glared down over the edge of the glacier at the forest below. His enemies should have had time to reach the edge of this frozen biome by now. But where were they?

Stopping his impatient march, he pulled off the jetpack and put it back into his inventory.

"Where did you get that flying machine?" Weaver asked. "It doesn't seem . . . natural."

"I've added more things to Minecraft than you can even comprehend," the user said. "This jet pack is nothing compared to some of the other mods here. You and your pathetic friends have only seen the tip of the iceberg."

"Iceberg? What's that?"

Entity303 just laughed, then turned and faced the home of the Snow Queen, the Aurora Palace. It was a massive, multi-colored thing with sheer vertical walls that stretched high into the air. The surface shined, as if it was made of smooth glass. Brilliant blues and reds and oranges and greens and yellows all flowed from one to the other in a spectacular show that reminded him of the Aurora Borealis in the physical world. On one side, at the base, a broad set of stairs led to a single door in the wall. The user knew monsters, like the Aurora guardian with their chilling ice swords and the Ice Cores with their crystalline shards, lay waiting for Gameknight999 and his friends; and that was just in the first room. Even deadlier creatures waited for the User-that-is-not-a-user and his friends deeper within the icy fortress. The thought of those fools battling the monsters of the glacier made him giggle with delight.

Squawk, squawk.

A foolish penguin stepped up to Entity303, the flightless bird curious about the stranger. Drawing his blade in a smooth, fluid motion, the user struck the innocent bird with his infused longsword, destroying the creature's HP with a single blow.

"What are you doing?!" Weaver cried.

Entity303 moved toward another of the black and white creatures, ready to strike. Suddenly, Weaver yanked on the rope, trying to pull the user off his feet, but the villager slipped on the slick ice instead and fell to the ground.

"Ha ha ha, what a fool!" he shouted.

The penguins, surprised by his loud voice, all waddled away, moving far from the newcomers.

Glancing back, Entity303 stared at the forest behind him again.

"Where are your little friends?" the user asked.

"Maybe they're tired of playing your games," Weaver said defiantly as he stood. "You're not so smart after all, are you?"

Entity303 glared at the NPC, saying nothing, his eyes filled with anger. The smallest of smirks grew on Weaver's lips. And that was the last straw. The user slapped him hard across the face. It knocked the NPC to the ground, where he landed with a thud and a groan.

"You aren't so funny now, are you, villager?"

"My name is Weaver!" he snapped.

"A program with a name, that still makes me laugh," Entity303 said. "No matter. All of you programs will be gone soon enough."

He glanced back down at the forest as Weaver slowly stood. Pacing back and forth, Entity 303 scanned the surroundings, looking impatiently for his pursuers.

"It seems Smithy and his friends are somewhere else," Weaver said, a tone of pride in his voice.

Entity303 raised a hand to strike him again, but the NPC didn't move. He stood his ground and waited for the blow that never came. Instead, the user yanked on the rope that was still wrapped around the NPC's body.

"Stand there and shut up," Entity303 barked.

Weaver smiled.

The user growled, then turned and scanned the forest before them. He expected Gameknight999 and his friends to be following.

I made the trail easy to follow, he thought. *I even told them I was heading to the glacier and killed some animals and zombies along the way, just to make sure they would see the path.*

"Where are they?"

Weaver giggled. Entity303 turned quickly, ready to strike the villager again, but his prisoner spoke, halting the blow.

"Maybe they're on their way to your White Castle."

"Of course," the user said. "He must have figured it out." He turned and glared at Weaver. "Perhaps what you blurted out from behind the Hydra gave them the clues they needed."

The NPC smiled and stood a little taller.

"You think this is some kind of victory? Ha!" Now, Entity303 was smiling. A worried expression came across the villager's face. "That's exactly where I want them, you fool. Of course, I wanted to be there first, to watch my newest creation destroy them, but no matter. My little pet will feast on their HP."

"What kind of monster is there?" Weaver asked.

"Imagine three of the most terrifying monsters your puny little brain could think of," Entity303 said in a low, dangerous voice.

Weaver moved closer.

"But then imagine them merged together into one ferocious beast."

The NPC's face turned white as his eyes grew wide with fright.

"All you've done is slightly delay your friends' destruction." He laughed an evil, maniacal laugh. "We must hurry. I don't want to miss the show." Entity303 glanced back at the Aurora Palace, the multi-colored structure looming high above the translucent blue glacier. "The snow queen will have to wait for another time . . . pity. I was looking forward to seeing how many of your friends she could destroy."

He sighed.

"Oh well." Entity303 yanked on the rope, pulling Weaver close. "You better hang on if you want to live. We're gonna be flying pretty fast toward the White Castle."

And with that, he pulled out his jet pack, tightened the straps, and then activated it, soaring off the glacier and out over the Twilight Forest, Weaver holding on tight. The wind roared past his ears as they picked up speed. Angling upward, Entity303 sacrificed his speed for height, going higher and higher. The ground below became hazy as the glacier slowly disappeared, making the Aurora Palace seem as if it were floating in the mist.

Just then, the jet pack sputtered once, then twice, then ran out of fuel. Weaver grabbed hold of Entity303, his fear clearly visible on his square face.

The User laughed, then took off the jetpack and let it fall. As they began to plummet to the ground, he put on his Elytra wings, then leaned forward. The gray wings popped open wide and caught the gentle currents of the air, allowing them to soar noiselessly across the star-speckled twilight sky.

With a smile, Entity303 banked to the right and headed northward, toward the White Castle, knowing that his prey was out there somewhere, waiting to be destroyed by his wrath.

CHAPTER 25

THE THORN FOREST

The party moved quickly out of the fire swamp and into an acacia forest. Everyone gave a sigh of relief when they could breathe again without having to taste the air of the fire swamp biome. In this arid landscape of bent and twisted trees, open spaces, and gray-green grass, Gameknight felt much more at ease. They had a direction now, and it was not dictated by Entity303; instead, it was a choice *they* had made in hopes of surprising their enemy.

The landscape quickly changed into rocky highlands. Low hills covered with tall pines and spruces blocked their path, requiring them to climb laboriously. As they moved across the hills, their eyes darted nervously about. Caves and shadowy crevasses dotted the rough surroundings. Unseen monsters moaned and clattered and growled from within every shadowy pocket in the rolling terrain, their voices echoing off their rocky enclosures. With all the openings and fissures, it was difficult to move without constantly having to turn around and watch behind and in front at the same time. Herder brought the wolves in close, forming a tight circle of fangs and fur to protect the party from any unwelcome surprises.

"If all remain quiet and do not antagonize the monsters," Empech said in a quiet, screechy voice, "then perhaps the creatures in the shadows will allow us to pass through this land unchallenged, yes, yes," Empech said.

Twang . . . twang, twang.

A quiet squeal of delight came from Stitcher.

"Did any of you see that shot?" the young girl said. "I nailed that white blaze thing from all the way over here."

"That creature was called a basalz," the gnome growled. "It would have left everyone alone if you had kept your bow silent."

Two more of the floating creatures slowly rose from the shadows, the sound of their wheezing mechanical breaths filling the air. One of them fired a sparkling, magical projectile at Stitcher. She quickly moved out of the way, then shot at the left creature while Hunter took down the right, a sad look on the older sister's face.

"Stitcher, we didn't need to kill those creatures," Hunter chided.

"What do you mean? They attacked us!" Stitcher replied, annoyed.

"Only because you killed one first!" Hunter said, sounding frustrated.

"Maybe you should put your bow away," Gameknight suggested, trying to keep the peace. "I'll tell you when to take it out."

"Yeah . . . right," Stitcher replied, rolling her eyes.

"Shhhh," Crafter said. "Everyone be still."

A deep-throated rumble came up through the ground. It was the roar of some kind of beast, its cry making the very surface of Minecraft shake.

"I don't think I want to know what makes a sound like that," Digger said.

Squawk, added Tux.

"Come on," Gameknight whispered urgently. "Let's keep moving. We need to get to the White Castle before Entity303."

The User-that-is-not-a-user ran through the uneven terrain, careful to avoid the many holes in the ground. They approached a dark patch on the ground, as if a circle of shadows had been painted on the landscape. High overhead, a billowing cloud sat high in the air, some kind of cobblestone building in the center.

"The giant's cloud, yes, yes," Empech said as they looked up at it. "Good to avoid that place. Battling with one's self is always difficult."

"What?" Woodcutter asked.

"It doesn't matter right now; we aren't going up there," Gameknight said. "Besides, there it is."

Ahead, the ground rose as if it had been pushed upward by some kind of enormous tectonic force. Atop the rise, the White Castle could be seen, its massive towers and raised walkways standing out against the twilight sky. Around the plateau was a thicket of thorns protecting the slopes that led to the structure.

Gameknight moved up to the edge of the pointy bramble and gasped. Before him stood the deadly Thorn Forest. It rose high up into the air, with thick thorn-covered vines twisting this way and that like spiky, intertwined snakes.

At first glance, Gameknight thought it might be a maze, with spaces just wide enough for someone to pass through, but now, as he stood right next to the barbed plants, he could see it would be impossible to walk through.

Woodcutter pulled out his iron axe and stepped up to a thick branch.

"As I recall, you can't cut through this," Gameknight said doubtfully.

"I can cut through anything," Woodcutter said with a wry grin.

Swinging the axe high over his head, he brought it down on the brown, spiked vine. His big arms strained as he swung the axe down on the plant again and again, but the metallic head seemed to bounce right off each time, taking only the smallest chips out of the obstacle. Slowly, a spiderweb of cracks formed on the face of the barbed surface. The cracks spread farther and farther as Woodcutter threw all his strength into the task.

Finally, the brown, thorny branch shattered, but as soon as it did, new green branches shot out, each bristling with razor-sharp thorns. The newly grown vines sliced across Woodcutter, making him flash red as he took damage, the barbs carving into his armor.

Gameknight leapt forward and pulled the tall NPC away from the spiny branch as the thorns groped outward for anyone else foolish enough to stand near. The two companions fell backward in a heap.

"Thanks," Woodcutter said. "It was almost as if that spiky monster was protecting itself. I felt like it was actively attacking me."

Gameknight stood, then helped the tall villager to his feet. Deep gouges were carved across the front of Woodcutter's iron chest plate. The User-that-is-not-a-user reached out and touched the deep scratches, then glanced back at the thorn forest, a look of trepidation on his square face.

"So, I think it's safe to say we aren't cutting through all that," Hunter said.

"Maybe we could tunnel under it?" Digger asked.

Empech shook his oversized head.

"No, the rock beneath is very hard, yes yes," the tiny pech said. "It can be broken, but many diamond pickaxes would be needed to get through it and reach the White Castle."

The NPCs glanced up to the top of the plateau that was surrounded by the thorn forest. Only the smallest part of the castle was visible over the edge of the prickly forest, the top of a blocky wall shining a pristine white in the twilight lighting.

"If we can't go under, and we can't go through, then we go *over*," Gameknight pulled out an iron shovel. "Start collecting some dirt. We'll likely need a lot."

The villagers instantly went to work, gathering dirt and clay from the surrounding landscape. Suddenly, the *twang* of a bowstring made all of them stop. Gameknight turned toward the sound and found Stitcher with her enchanted bow in her hand. She fired a second arrow, then a third. A sorrowful moan filled the air, followed by a faint pop.

"Were we under attack?" Hunter asked.

Stitcher shook her head.

"Was it Entity303 and a group of monsters?" Crafter asked.

She shook her head again, her crimson hair flinging from one shoulder to the other.

"Then what were you shooting at?" Gameknight asked, confused.

"I saw a zombie, so I put it down," the young girl replied, as if it was obvious.

"Was it heading toward us?" Gameknight asked.

Stitcher shook her head again. "No, I don't even think it knew we were here." She beamed with pride.

"Then why did you shoot it?" Gameknight asked.

"Didn't you hear me say it was a zombie?" Stitcher said. No one answered, they just stared at her. "It was a *zombie*! That's reason enough to destroy it."

"Oh, Stitcher, I don't know what happened to you in your past, but I'm sorry I couldn't protect you better," Gameknight said sadly, shaking his head. He moved to her side and put a brotherly arm around her shoulder as if he were consoling her.

"Get off me," she snapped, shoving him back. "You talk as if there's something wrong with me. THERE'S NOTHING WRONG WITH ME!" She put away her bow and paced back and forth like a predatory animal, danger and strength in every step. "You don't know what it was like be a slave in that Nether fortress. I was there for months, and where were all of you? Nowhere!" She glared at Gameknight999. "I know you rescued me eventually, and I'm grateful, but I suffered as Malacoda's slave for months. I watched my friends perish. I experienced terrible suffering at the hands of those monsters, not because it was necessary for them to hurt us, but because they could!"

Hunter started to say something, but Stitcher silenced her with a glare.

"None of you know what I went through, so don't even think about judging me. This is who I am, so get over it!"

She stormed off, pulling out her shovel and digging up some grass blocks. Gameknight sighed.

"I can't imagine what must have happened to her to make Stitcher so angry and violent," Crafter said.

"It's not the anger that concerns me, it's the lack of empathy for the monsters, the lack of caring about what she's doing," Gameknight said. "I understand anger, because I'm angry much of the time. I'm angry at Entity303, I'm angry at myself for letting Weaver get captured . . . I'm angry at a lot of things. But I also think about how my actions affect others, even the monsters. I saw the terror in the Hydra's eyes when it knew it was going to die. I knew the creature was confused and scared and sad and lonely. I could tell what it was feeling, but I don't think Stitcher can anymore. She's lost her sense of empathy."

"It's not your fault," Crafter said. "I know that's what you're thinking."

"But I should have been able to protect her," Gameknight protested.

"You did in your timeline," Hunter said. "But in this timeline, without Weaver teaching us about TNT, things progressed differently."

"But it's not right," Gameknight snapped, frustrated. "I can't stand seeing any of you suffer. I must fix this, for all of us."

"Well, how about we start by getting over that forest of spikes," Woodcutter said, rubbing the scratches on his chest gingerly.

"You're right; let's get this done," Gameknight said.

He glared up at the thorn forest and growled determinedly, then began to place blocks of dirt.

CHAPTER 26

THE WHITE TOWERS

Building a structure that rose high enough to extend over the thorn forest and reach the top of the plateau on which the White Castle sat was a slow process. A few times, Gameknight999 almost fell as he was placing the blocks, accidently leaning out too far to place the next cube of dirt along an overhanging path. Fortunately, Digger was there to pull him back from the brink and safely onto the dirt path. If he had fallen, it was likely he would have perished.

After careful construction of the raised path, they made it over the deadly thorn forest and finally set foot on the gray plateau. In front of them loomed the White Castle. It was massive, with perhaps twenty towers dotting the area, each with sheer walls that stretched up sixty blocks into the air. Narrow, raised walkways connected each soaring structure to the next one, making a confusing series of causeways that all led somewhere, though it was not clear where. Some of the towers boasted dark roofs with tall spires stretching up high into the air, their tips hidden from sight. At the center of it all was a gigantic central building slightly higher than the other towers and nearly as wide as it was tall. Blocky crenellations ran along the top of the structure, giving it a classic castle-like appearance.

Gameknight carefully examined the structures and walkways. It was clear that they slowly spiraled inward to the main castle, but at some points two or three walkways intersected at one tower. He instantly recognized it as a maze . . . a tower maze. From within the towers, it would be difficult to tell which walkway to take; they would have to be careful.

"So how do we get up there?" Stitcher asked. "You bring some wings with you from the physical world?"

Gameknight cast her an annoyed glance; he was not in the mood for games. Stitcher worried him.

"Look how the walkways are set up," the User-that-is-not-a-user said. "They lead inward to the main building, some at higher levels than others. It's actually a maze. We need to make sure we get on the correct walkway so we can reach the main building at the right level."

"Great, a maze . . . I love mazes," Hunter said sarcastically. "Will there be monsters in there with us?"

Gameknight nodded his square head.

"That's not a problem," Stitcher said, a vicious smile on her face, as if she looked forward to it. "We can take care of anything in there."

Gameknight's chest grew heavy, as if the guilt he felt for her was somehow crushing him.

"Stitcher's comment makes me wonder, what *is* in there?" Crafter asked.

"I don't know," he replied. "In the original Twilight Forest mod, the White Castle was never completed. There were places within it where many monsters could be housed, but they were always empty. The developer of the mod, Benimatic, never said what was planned for the White Castle. All I know is that we'll probably find your typical Minecraft creatures in there, but Entity303 also led us here for a reason. I suspect he's added something that we really don't want to find."

"But it's likely that's where Weaver will be," Herder said. He reached over and patted the wolf pack leader on the side. The animal stared up at the White Castle and growled.

Gameknight nodded. "I'm sure we'll find both Weaver and Entity303 wherever the most dangerous monsters are hiding."

"Well, we aren't gonna find out anything if we stay out here," Woodcutter said. "Let's get going."

"Yeah!" Stitcher said excitedly.

"I think the tower maze starts at that one to the left," Digger said, pointing with his pickaxe.

They moved toward the tall structure. Dark ravens swooped down on them, squawking as they flew by, their black bodies standing out against the pristine white of the castle and towers. Tux squawked back at them, trying to make them go away, but the birds ignored their distant cousin. Stitcher aimed an arrow at one of the dark birds.

"The birds are not a threat," Empech said, his dark eyes focused warily on the young girl.

The gnome reached for something in his inventory, his eyes narrowing as Stitcher pulled back the arrow a little farther. But when Stitcher lowered her bow, Empech shifted his reach and pulled out a loaf of bread, an expression of relief on his gray face.

"Look, there's some kind of door at the base of that tower," Woodcutter said.

Gameknight turned to where the tall villager was pointing, then ran across the plateau toward the wooden door. Suddenly, a wave of fur sped past him as the wolves dashed for the entrance. Herder's animals reached the tower in seconds, then set up a protective ring around the structure, their red eyes checking the area for threats.

As he ran, the User-that-is-not-a-user also scanned their surroundings for monsters; there were none. So far, this had been too easy, and that made Gameknight worry.

When they reached the tower, the User-that-is-not-a-user approached slowly with his diamond sword in his hand. He scanned the surroundings, convinced there should be some threat nearby. Still he saw none; now he was getting really nervous.

The door on the side of the shining white tower was not a normal door, but was made up of small wooden squares, a small red ring at the center of each tile and a larger red ring near the edge. Three of the tiles lacked the red rings, and instead had recessions carved into them. Crafter moved close to the door and studied it with a critical gaze.

"You ever see a door like this?" Gameknight asked him.

Crafter shook his head. He moved his hand along one of the squares, then pressed it firmly. The door didn't budge.

"The trophies, yes, yes," Empech said. "You must use the trophies."

The tiny Pech pointed to the three recessed tiles that ran down the middle of the door, their empty centers yearning to be filled. Empech set his pack on the ground, then pulled out the golden trophies, each adorned with a monster's face. Gameknight took them from the gnome and carefully put one in each recession. They fit perfectly, as if this were their only purpose.

"Press one of the tiles," Empech said.

Crafter reached out and touched the tile with the Naga's face on it. Instantly, it disappeared, then the neighboring tiles vanished one after another, each making a sound like a soap bubble popping, until all of the wooden tiles making up the door were gone.

Suddenly, a skeleton stepped out of the opening. It was draped in a tattered, forest-green shirt and equally torn pants. A golden necklace with a blood red gem at the center hung from the monster's bony neck, the ruby pulsing with magical power. In its hand, the monster held a golden hoe.

"Skeleton druid!" Empech shrieked.

The creature glanced at the gnome, then flicked its hoe toward Crafter. A sparkling green ball of magic streaked right at the young NPC, striking him in the chest. Instantly, green spirals formed around Crafter as he fell to his knees, the enchantment poisoning him.

"Wolves, attack," Herder growled.

The wolves charged at the skeleton, snapping at legs and arms. The monster moved back into the tower as it tried to escape the animals, but it didn't stand a chance. In seconds, it was destroyed.

Gameknight ran to Crafter's side. He offered his friend a piece of steak, hoping food would slow the effect of the poison. The NPC took the meat and ate it quickly, but the spirals around him only grew brighter. He moaned, then fell backward into Gameknight's arms.

Empech reached into his pack and pulled out a glass bottle. He pulled out the stopper and handed it to the villager.

"Drink, yes, yes," the gray creature said.

Crafter took the bottle and drank quickly. The potion of healing stopped the poison from spreading and slowly erased the green spirals that hovered around his head.

"Thanks, Empech," the young NPC said. "That poison was powerful."

"Skeleton druids should be treated with cautious respect, yes, yes," replied the diminutive gnome.

Gameknight helped Crafter to his feet, then moved into the tower. Hunter and Stitcher were already inside, the enchantments on their bows casting splashes of iridescent purple light on the walls. But even with the magical illumination, the tower was incredibly dark.

"The Moonworm Queen, yes yes," Empech said. "The Lich King dropped her and Gameknight999 picked her up. Use the Queen."

"What are you talking about?" Gameknight asked.

"The glowing insect from the tower," the little gnome insisted. "Use the Queen."

And then he remembered . . . the large glowing insect. Reaching into his inventory, the User-that-is-not-a-user drew out the large bug and held it in his left hand. Instantly, its eight legs wrapped around his wrist, not like an attack, but more like a gentle embrace. The glowing creature felt comfortable against his skin, warm and kind.

"Squeeze," Empech said.

Gameknight gave the Moonworm Queen the smallest of squeezes. Instantly, a glowing yellow worm shot out of the creature and stuck to the wall, casting a wide circle of fluorescent yellow light. It lit the interior of the tower, showing a set of stairs that climbed high into the tower.

"Moonworm Queen will give us many more worms than Gameknight has torches, yes, yes," Empech said.

Gameknight nodded his head, then cast the little gnome a smile.

"OK, we have light; now let's go find Weaver," the User-that-is-not-a-user said.

With the Moonworm Queen in his left hand, and his enchanted diamond sword in his right, Gameknight999 climbed up the stairs toward the trap that he knew lay waiting for them.

CHAPTER 27

MAZE OF TOWERS

They ran up the stairs of the first tower as Gameknight placed moonworms on the walls to provide light to see where they were stepping.

"Empech, how many worms does the Queen have in her?" Gameknight asked.

"It is unclear, yes, yes. But the Moonworm Queen can be recharged with torch berries."

"Oh, that's *really* helpful," Stitcher said in a mocking tone. "Anyone have any torch berries?"

"Stitcher, be nice," Hunter said in a low voice.

"Perhaps we'll come across some," Crafter added. "Just keep placing those worms. It helps a lot."

After multiple turns and many flights, the stairway finally came to the next floor. It was dark . . . pitch black. Gameknight approached cautiously, sticking his head up through the opening, then ducking back again in case there were more skeleton druids. Nothing happened.

"We've reached the next floor, but I don't hear any monsters," Gameknight said. "I think it's safe."

"Wolves, forward," Herder commanded, his voice as crisp and sharp as the edge of a sword.

The animals streaked up the steps and moved into the room. The pack leader barked once, signaling it was safe.

Gameknight moved into the room and placed moon-worms on the walls. "There's another door here," he said.

"We can see that, genius," Stitcher replied sarcastically.

He looked at the young girl and just sighed, the guilt of what had made her so cold filling his soul.

"Apparently, we go through the door now," Hunter said.

The door was similar to the one that had let them into the tower: many square wooden tiles, each with a small ring of red surrounded by a larger one. But this time, there was no place for monster trophies.

"Hunter, Stitcher, you two get in the center," Gameknight commanded. "Crafter, get on the left with your bow; I'll be on the right. The rest of you, watch our backs. All of you ready?"

They moved into position, then nodded. Reaching out, the User-that-is-not-a-user touched one of the door tiles. Instantly, they began to disappear, each making a popping sound until every square evaporated. Before them stood a raised walkway that stretched from one tower to the next; it was completely empty.

"No monsters?" Crafter said, confused.

"Why complain?" Stitcher said. "Come on."

She ran across the causeway, the rest of the party following her. They lined up at the next door and Gameknight touched the wooden tile. As with the last, the door disappeared with a cascade of popping sounds, revealing another empty tower bathed in darkness and another stairway leading up into shadows.

This happened in three more towers as the explorers moved higher and higher into the White Castle towers. Finally, they reached a room with a stairway piercing the ceiling, the sparkling stars shining through the opening. Gameknight ran up and moved out onto the roof of the building. Snow fell silently from the perpetually half-day/half-night sky that covered the Twilight

Forest, the white dusting giving a fantastic, almost fairytale quality to the castle.

From atop the tower he could see the entire structure. Sixteen towers stood around a massive central square structure, everything made of pristine white quartz. Between the towers stretched raised walkways, some near the top while others punctured the structures' midpoints like sharp skewers, holding the massive columns apart. Some of the towers near the gigantic central structure gave off a soft blue glow as long vertical stripes of color leaked the cerulean light, bathing the neighboring towers in a wash of color.

The central tower itself seemed deserted. There were no guards along the edges, no archers manning turrets . . . nothing. The lighting was dim enough across the massive structure's roof that zombies and spiders could spawn, but there were too few to be of any concern. They all knew the real danger resided somewhere deep within the castle.

"I can see the path we need to take," Hunter said. She jumped off the quartz blocks that lined the edge of the walkway. "Let's get moving. I'm getting hungry and I wanna finish saving the world before dinner."

They all laughed except for Stitcher.

"Ok," Gameknight replied. "I wouldn't wanna get in the way of your eating schedule. Lead on."

Hunter ran forward and opened the next door. An arrow shot out of the opening as a skeleton fired at her. Before the bony creature could shoot another, Hunter and Stitcher silenced the monster, leaving a pile of skeleton bones that Herder's wolves happily devoured.

They moved quickly through the towers. It worried Gameknight that it was so easy.

"Why do you think there are so few monsters guarding these towers?" Gameknight asked the group.

"You want *more* monsters?" Stitcher replied, sounding shocked.

"No, I didn't say I wanted more monsters. I asked *why* this was so easy."

He reached the next doorway and pressed his hand against the square wooden tiles. Instantly, the concentric red rings turned green and the tiles disappeared with a popping sound. Inside, the shadowy tower was empty except for a set of stairs, one flight going up, the other heading down.

"I just worry that there's something terrible waiting for us." He glanced back at Herder. "Which way?"

"The next bridge is below us," the lanky boy said as he stood precariously on the edge of the walkway, peering down.

As Gameknight headed for the stairs, he fired a moonworm onto the ground at the top of the steps to mark that they'd been here before, then moved down the stairway. It was easy to get lost in all these passages, and leaving a trail to follow was important.

The central castle was growing near; they were almost there.

"Come on," Hunter said. "We're getting close, let's hurry up."

"Caution is advised," Empech warned.

"Caution for empty towers?" Stitcher asked mockingly. "Ha!"

She moved down the steps with her bow ready in her hands, the others struggling to keep up. Pressing on the door tiles, Stitcher opened the door to the next walkway and sprinted toward the tower that loomed ahead.

"Wait for us!" Gameknight yelled.

The young girl ignored him. She opened the next tower and stepped into the darkness with a few of Herder's wolves on her heels, the rest of their party struggling to keep up. Then, pausing for just a moment, the NPC allowed the others to reach her side. As soon as Gameknight stepped into the tower, she sprinted forward again, climbing the next set of stairs. The User-that-is-not-a-user cast a worried glance at Hunter, then followed the young girl, placing more of the glowing worms on the walls to give them a little light. When they reached the top, Stitcher opened the door and peered across the walkway that stretched from the last tower to the huge White Castle. Then she bolted across the bridge and stood at the door that would allow them to enter the White Castle.

For some reason, this last door seemed more dangerous than the rest, as if it held back a flood that was about to crash down upon them.

"Maybe they didn't put a lot of guards in these towers because whatever is waiting for us within the castle can take care of itself," Digger said as he caught up to them and slowly approached the door, Tux held tightly under his left arm. "Maybe only someone insane would want to go in there."

"Someone insane? That sounds like Gameknight999," Hunter said with a chuckle.

"Something lies within the White Castle, waiting, yes, yes." Empech said. "Something unnatural."

"What is it you sense?" Crafter asked the strange little gnome.

"Yeah, what's waiting for us?" Woodcutter asked.

Empech closed his eyes for a moment, concentrating. But when he opened them, those dark blue gem-like eyes looked terrified, as if he could somehow sense his own destruction. He glanced at Gameknght999 and placed his three-fingered hand on his wrist.

"An ancient creature waits, yes, yes," the gnome warned, his high-pitched voice barely a whisper. "It is very dangerous, and angry, yes, yes . . . very angry."

Empech reached into his inventory and pulled out the magical fishing pole, its long shaft reflecting the glow from the moonworms, the golden fishhook pulsing with light as if it had a luminous heartbeat.

"What are you gonna do with that?" Stitcher asked.

"Ahh . . . what?" the gnome replied, seeming dazed, as if coming out of some kind of trance. He stared down at the magical weapon in his hands, a surprised expression on his gray face. "Empech does not know."

Glancing up at Gameknight999, Empech stuffed the weapon back into his inventory and pointed to where a sickly green glow flashed from within the User-that-is-not-a-user's inventory.

Reaching into his own inventory, Gameknight drew out the Lich King's magical wand. The pale bone handle glowed in the fluorescent yellow light, the emerald tip pulsing as Empech's fishing pole had, alive with power.

"The zombie scepter senses danger for the wielder. Empech can feel its power growing."

The User-that-is-not-a-user stared at the wand in his hands, then tucked it away into his inventory.

"It is not clear if the zombies conjured by that wand will be friend or foe," Empech said. "Use of it should only be done in the most dire of circumstances, yes, yes."

Gameknight nodded.

"So, you didn't say what you thought was in the White Castle, Empech," Stitcher said, the tone of her voice almost accusatory. "No more riddles. Tell us something useful, or get out of the way."

The gnome glanced up at Stitcher with a sad look in his crystalline blue eyes.

"The vengeful one wants to know more, yes, yes?"

"Yeah . . . I want to know more." A scowl covered Stitcher's face.

"Very well. What is waiting for all of you is a choice." Empech said, his high-pitched voice soft as a whisper but as hard as steel. "Someone must make a choice. Life . . . or death." He turned and pointed one of his fat gray fingers at Stitcher, then moved it across the others in the party. "One of you will make the choice, and all will suffer the same fate. That is what Empech senses . . . yes, yes, that is what Empech knows."

Gameknight glanced at Crafter and shuddered as cold fingers of dread began to crush his soul.

"Then let's do it," Stitcher snapped.

Casting a worried glace to all of his companions, Gameknight reached out and placed a hand on the door, causing the wooden tiles to slowly disappear.

CHAPTER 28

SECRET ENTRANCE

Entity303 moved to the stone house that stood on the gray plateau, far from any of the white towers that stretched high into the air. His heart still raced a bit after flying over the thorn forest. Gliding to the castle had worked perfectly, but the destination had been a little farther than he'd expected. With his altitude decreasing, Entity303 had just barely made it to the stone plateau, landing on the very edge and almost falling into the deadly brambles. The foolish villager had found it funny, but after Entity303 had poked him with his sword, his laughter quickly evaporated.

A clattering of bones came from the rocky structure. The user knew it was a skeleton druid's house, but he hadn't seen any of the monsters yet. Likely there would be some nearby, brewing their poisons or looking for innocent creature to infect. They were pathetic creatures and he wasn't concerned.

Just then, one of the bony creatures stuck its head out the window; it had probably heard their footsteps. Entity303 fired his yellow-glowing infused bow at the monster, then fired a second arrow quickly. The two projectiles ended the creature's life almost instantly.

Pulling on the rope that was still wrapped around Weaver, he moved quickly into the house. What looked like a small metallic cage hung from the ceiling. Within the enclosure, a smaller version of the skeleton druid spun around as sparkling embers flashed about the edges.

It was a spawner.

Entity303 pulled out a pickaxe and quickly shattered the device, then turned his pick on the fireplace. A piece of netherrack sat burning within the structure, surrounded by red bricks. He put out the flames, then broke the rusty netherrack, revealing a tunnel below the fireplace that plunged downward into darkness. Digging up more blocks, the user exposed a set of stairs that extended into the depths of the plateau, heading in the direction of the White Castle.

"I put this here where I reprogrammed this mod," Entity303 said. "Not only did I capture a little surprise for your friends, but I also made this little secret entrance, just in case I needed it."

"It won't do you any good," Weaver said. "Smithy and his friends are gonna catch you eventually. You're gonna lose, and I'm gonna love watching it."

Entity303 yanked on the rope, causing Weaver to fall to the ground.

"We'll see, villager. Now go down the steps or I'll give you a little taste of poison."

The NPC glanced up at the massive White Castle through the open window and sighed.

"You won't find your friends out there. They're likely finding their way through the towers. That is, if they even made it through the thorn forest." Entity303 moved up to Weaver and pulled him to his feet. "Maybe they're already dead. . . . that would be disappointing. I really wanted to watch their destruction. Hopefully one of them will survive. My little pet down there in the castle is very excited about meeting them."

"You're a monster," Weaver growled angrily.

"Ha, you don't know what a monster really is. But you'll soon see a real monster in action when it destroys whatever is left of your friends. This is going to be fun."

Weaver sighed again, then moved down into the dark stairway. Entity303 followed close behind, placing torches on the walls as they descended.

"I'm looking forward to this battle," Entity303 said to the darkness. "Not even the great Gameknight999 will be able to overcome what I have in store for him." He laughed cruelly, anticipating his enemy's defeat.

They followed the gloomy stairway downward until it ended in a large square chamber that was brightly lit with torches. Three of the walls were made of cobblestone, but the fourth was something different: pure white, just like the castle overhead, the torches in the room making it appear as if it were glowing. The white wall had a door set in it, but this door was made of small wooden tiles, each adorned with red lines forming concentric squares.

"What's that?" Weaver asked.

"That's our way in," Entity303 explained. "I couldn't program it so my secret stairway would go into the castle, but I could bring it to this hidden door." He moved closer to the entrance. "You see those red lines? I'm gonna make them turn green."

"So what?" Weaver sounded confused.

"So if they turn green, then that means your foolish friends have unlocked the castle." Entity303 laughed. "Then we can just walk in without needing the three trophies."

He reached into his inventory and pulled out two splash potions. He threw one onto Weaver, then dropped the other on himself. Instantly, they vanished.

"That's better," the evil user said. "Now, let's get inside and watch my monstrous creation devour your friends. Ha ha ha ha . . ."

Reaching out with an invisible hand, Entity303 pressed on one of the door tiles, causing the red lines to turn green and then disappear one after the other, a popping sound accompanying each.

"Come on, villager." He yanked on the rope. "We don't want to miss the show!"

Entity303 and Weaver moved into the dark passage, the sound of angry monsters filling the air.

"Be careful, Smithy!" Weaver yelled. "It's a trap."

His voice echoed off the dark stone walls, causing the moans and growls to stop for just an instant, then continue, now sounding even more vicious.

"Ha ha ha . . ." Entity303 laughed as they walked through the glowing dungeons of the White Castle, toward the trap that had been laid for Gameknight999 and his friends.

CHAPTER 29

CAVE TROLL

The castle had an old, musty smell, as if no one had been in the building for centuries. Dust covered the ground and rose in tiny puffs as they walked, making Gameknight want to sneeze, the stale dusty air biting at the back of his throat.

By the delayed echo of their footsteps, Gameknight could tell the room, though cloaked in darkness, was massive. He placed moonworms on the ground as they moved along the perimeter of the huge chamber.

"Look at these columns," Crafter said.

The young NPC had a torch in his hand and was standing away from the wall, the golden circle of light illuminating the space around him. A gigantic square column stood before him stretching high up into the air, its size making the villager seem even smaller. It was pure white, like everything else in the castle, its top disappearing into the dark shadows high overhead.

"There's a stairway over here," Hunter called out, her voice echoing off the walls and sounding as if it were coming at them from all sides.

Gameknight scanned the chamber. Hunter was standing at what seemed like the center, the illumination from the torch in her hand making the crimson curls that fell around her shoulders glow red with a magical luster. Before her stood a huge stairway that was maybe a dozen blocks wide, an ornate bannister along each edge.

"There are stairs going up and another flight going down," she added.

"I think we go down," Gameknight said. "Entity303 can't control the roof very well, but he can control the dungeons. I'm sure he has something bad down there waiting for us. I just hope we can get there before he does."

The companions gathered around Hunter, then went down the stairs together. Gameknight led the way with a group of wolves at his side, Herder right behind, constantly directing the animals. The moonworms stuck easily to the stairs as they descended, casting fluorescent green circles of light on the steps, making it easy for the others to see where they were going.

At the bottom of the stairway, they reached another set of the doors with red circles. Stitcher moved forward and raised a hand to touch the square wooden tiles.

"Not yet, Stitcher," Gameknight warned. "Let everyone get into position."

She gave him an angry scowl, then backed away from the door and stood on the group's left side. Hunter took the right side, with Crafter and Gameknight in the middle. Behind them stood the wolves and Herder, who was ready to send them into battle. Woodcutter and Empech stood at the back with Digger in the center, Tux still cradled in his arms.

"Everyone ready?" Gameknight asked.

They nodded.

He reached out and touched the door, then pulled back and drew his diamond sword. As with the others, the wooden tiles slowly evaporated one after another, each *popping* when they disappeared.

Sprinting through the chamber, the User-that-is-not-a-user used the Moonworm Queen to place squirming, glowing worms on the walls and floors. The room was gigantic, and, like the last one, was just too large to fully illuminate with the glowing insects, so Gameknight only lit up the area around the door. Fluorescent green light pushed back the shadows nearby, but left the rest of the room bathed in darkness.

Then, a grumbling sound, like the rumble of an earthquake, filled the room. Huge footsteps pounded the floor as something heavy charged at them from the darkness. The thundering steps grew louder and louder, the ground shaking until Gameknight thought the quartz floor might shatter beneath them. And then a massive creature entered the circle of green light. It was a monster Gameknight had never seen, with pale green skin and thick arms that rippled with muscles. The monster had short, stout legs that seemed too small for its huge body, its feet moving in a blur. A large and bulbous nose, almost like a villager's, dominated the creature's face, with dark, deep-set, angry eyes on either side.

Stitcher turned and fired her flaming arrows at the giant. The magical flames instantly went out when the shafts hit the creature, the feathered ends sticking out of the monster's muscular chest. Not slowing a bit, the behemoth reached up and broke the arrows off, then roared as it charged straight at them, balled fists flying. Gameknight swung his diamond blade at the creature, but it bounced off its green hide as if it were made of stone. With a swipe of its left hand, the creature sent the User-that-is-not-a-user flying, landing with a thud.

"Cave troll!" Empech screamed, his high-pitched voice cutting through the air like a knife.

The troll smashed into Stitcher, throwing her aside as if she weighed nothing. Crafter shot out of the darkness with his enchanted iron sword in his hand. The blade sliced across the monster's stomach, making a sound like steel scraping against steel.

It had no effect at all. The cave troll was stronger and faster than anything the they'd ever battled. Their weapons seemed to be useless.

The monster brushed Crafter aside easily, and then turned to face Gameknight999, who now stood with both blades drawn. The troll advanced slowly, forcing the User-that-is-not-a-user to back up until he was trapped in the corner. With an expression of crazed hatred on its green face, muscles tensed like coiled springs ready to explode, the troll moved forward.

"Someone . . . HELP!" Gameknight shouted as he readied himself for destruction.

CHAPTER 30

THE PRICE OF POWER

Suddenly, a high-pitched scream echoed through the massive hall. Almost a blur, Empech streaked out of the shadows to stand in front of Gameknight999, his backpack jostling about on his back. He held his fishing pole out before him, the golden hook now glowing bright green.

"Stop . . . please," Empech begged.

But the cave troll, now only four blocks away, continued its slow advance.

"Stop!" the little gnome pleaded.

The troll was now two blocks away.

"Empech, run!" Gameknight shouted, but the tiny creature stood his ground.

Then, suddenly, the gnome swung the fishing pole through the air, casting the line forward. The golden hook shot through the air like a bullet and caught in the monster's thick hide. Colorful bolts of lightning streamed down the fishing line, enveloping the troll with sheets of sparkling, deadly energy.

The monster skidded to a stop, flashing red as it took damage. It bellowed a great, sorrowful howl that was filled with such pain and despair it almost hurt to hear. But then, the monster's cries of agony were joined by screams from the gnome. Empech cried out, his voice filled with terrible suffering, as he flicked the rod again, causing more bolts of magical, crackling power to run down the fishing line and envelop the beast.

"Hunter, Stitcher . . . attack!" Gameknight shouted.

He pulled out his enchanted bow and fired at the massive beast. The arrows struck the monster, making it roar in pain. More arrows from the other members of the group streaked out of the shadows and struck the giant, but with each shaft that hit the troll, Empech screamed in anguish as well. The tiny gnome fell to his knees, but kept the pole leveled at the monster, which now stood only a block away.

The cave troll flashed red again and again as more arrows struck the creature. Empech's magical fishing pole continued to pump more of its magical bolts of destruction into the monster. The huge beast and Empech both screamed in pain repeatedly, their agonizing wails exactly synchronized. It was as if they were feeling the same thing.

Tilting its head upward, the cave troll stared at the ceiling, a look of confusion and despair on its green face. A terrible, sorrowful wail escaped its gaping mouth as its HP finally fell to zero. The monster disappeared with a pop, its cries of anguish still echoing in the room.

Empech collapsed to the ground, the sparkling magical weapon falling from his small gray hands.

"Empech, that was fantastic!" Stitcher exclaimed. "I don't know what that fishing pole does, but it's awesome."

The little gnome struggled to his feet. When Gameknight reached his side, he saw tiny square tears streaming from his gem-like, blue eyes and down his gray, wrinkled face.

"Empech cannot do it again, no, no. Empech refuses," he moaned as he wept.

"What is it, Empech?" Gameknight moved to the gnome's side and put an arm around his narrow shoulders, supporting him as he wept. "What's wrong?"

"Empech cannot . . . Empech will not," the little gnome mumbled between sobs.

"You don't have to do anything, Empech," Crafter said as he approached. "It's OK, we're all here to help."

"No, no, Crafter does not understand," Empech moaned.

"All I understand is that this fishing pole of yours is incredible," Stitcher said. "I've never seen anything so powerful. It not only brought that green monster to a stop, it squashed it like a bug!"

She picked up the fishing pole and stared down at it for a second in wonder, then handed it back to the gnome. Empech shook his head.

"No, no, Empech will not touch that again; the price is too high."

"Well, if you don't want it, then I'll take it," Stitcher said.

"I don't know if that's such a good idea," Crafter said. "We really don't know what that thing does."

"I know what it does: it stops monsters," she replied.

"Stitcher, I think you should listen to Crafter," Hunter advised.

"I'm not gonna pass up a weapon that can stop a monster like one of those cave trolls," the younger sister said. "It might give me the power to crush a monster like Empech just did." She stared at her older sister. "I want that kind of power."

"Be careful, young one," the gnome said, wiping the tears from his crystalline blue eyes. "That power comes with a terrible price."

"What price?" she replied. "I'll pay it; just name your price. I can handle anything."

Empech held up his three-fingered hands and stepped back, giving up his claim on the magical fishing pole.

"Arrogance is a dangerous lens through which to view the world, child," the gnome said. "Humility and caution are always sage companions."

"Pffff," she harrumphed, then put the fishing pole into her inventory with a grin. "Less talking and more moving. Gameknight, which way?"

The User-that-is-not-a-user lifted his arm from the pech's shoulders, then pointed to the ground. "We must keep going down, to the dungeons."

"Then let's stop all the gabbing and get moving." Stitcher said, then turned and headed into the darkness, the iridescent light of her enchanted bow casting a faint purple sphere of illumination around her lithe form. Suddenly, the young girl shouted from the shadows, her voice echoing off the cold stone walls. "There's another door over here; come on!"

Gameknight glanced at Crafter. He saw the same look of concern on the young NPC's face that he felt in his own heart.

Stitcher is without any sensitivity or concern for other people's feelings, Gameknight thought. *How did I let this happen to my friend?*

He chest felt heavy as feelings of guilt settled onto his soul like a leaden shroud.

"Hurry up. I'm not gonna wait forever," Stitcher yelled from the darkness.

Gameknight sighed, as did Crafter and Hunter. The party headed in the direction of her voice, their eyes sad at the realization of what had been stolen from her so long ago in the Nether fortress: her empathy.

The group of comrades moved toward Stitcher's voice. The splash of purple light from her bow quickly became visible as they strode through the darkness. Gameknight held the Moonworm Queen in his left hand, placing glowing worms on the ground as they walked. Finally, they reached the young girl's side.

"This must lead somewhere," Stitcher said as she tapped on the door with her bow. "Everyone ready?"

Gameknight sighed with the others. He was tired of fighting, tired of violence and tired of fear, but he knew they had to continue. As they all held their weapons at the ready, Gameknight999 reached out and placed his hand on a tile. As with the others, the squares disappeared one after another, revealing another stairway that extended downward into the bowels of the White Castle, to what lay waiting for them: an ancient beast . . . an angry beast . . . a lethal beast.

CHAPTER 31

THE RUNE DUNGEONS

Like the last wide stairway, this passage was maybe a dozen blocks from one wall to the other. Stitcher moved forward into the darkness and looked down the steps, the shadowy gloom hugging the walls with its terrifying embrace. She went down a couple of steps, then glanced back at the others, an impatient expression on her square face.

"Well?" she asked expectantly.

Crafter moved into the passage followed by Herder and his wolves, a torch in his hand. The furry animals almost disappeared in the ominous hallway, their white fur blending in with the pristine white steps, the darkness making the two merge together.

Gameknight placed a moonworm on the wall. Suddenly, a splash of yellow light lit the stairs and walls.

"Why would they need this to be this wide?" Digger asked nervously. "What were they moving that needed this stairway to be this large?" His voice shook a little.

"Maybe an entire army," Stitcher suggested in a cold voice.

That made Digger shake even more.

"Stitcher," Hunter chided.

"What?" the younger sister replied, sounding exasperated, but no one spoke.

Digger sighed as he stepped into the passage and stared down the steps. Everyone could feel his fear; it was almost tangible in the air, a thread stretched nearly to its limits and about to break. Gameknight put a hand on his friend's shoulder, letting him know he wasn't alone, then moved down the steps with him.

They descended in utter silence except for the echo of their boots slapping against the cold stone stairs. There were no monster sounds to be heard; Gameknight was thankful of that, but the silence forced him to confront his inner demons: his own feelings of failure and guilt. Uncertainty and doubt circled him like vultures around a wounded animal, pecking away at his courage, but Empech's words drove the monsters back: *You can only do what you believe you can do.*

I can do this, he thought, the words driving back the ghostly specter of fear that filled his mind.

They continued down the steps, Gameknight shooting the moonworms onto the walls as they descended.

"It's too quiet," Gameknight said worriedly.

"I like quiet," Digger replied.

"Come on," Stitcher said, "Let's go faster and get this little adventure over with."

The young girl charged down the steps and into the darkness, her enchanted bow in her hands, an arrow already notched. Gameknight tried to keep up with her, placing glowing moonworms farther apart on the walls as he ran to keep up, but Stitcher didn't wait for anyone. The rest of the party hurried to catch her, but were barely able to keep within sight of her bouncing red curls as they descended down the cold, lifeless staircase.

"Stitcher, slow down," Gameknight called, but the young girl ignored them and extended her lead. Finally, she stopped and waited for the others.

"Thank you for waiting," he said.

"I wasn't waiting for you," she replied. "It was just getting too dark. I need your little insect friends there to shed some light on the stairs."

"Well, I don't want to use the Moonworm Queen anymore unless it's necessary. Who knows how many worms are left within her? Does anyone have any torches?"

"I do," Woodcutter said.

The tall NPC moved down a couple of steps, then pulled a handful of torches out of his inventory. He walked down the stairs, placing torches on the wall as he went. The warm circles of flickering, yellow torchlight buoyed their spirits, driving back the shadows and quelling the thoughts of imaginary beasts hiding in the shadowy recesses of their minds.

Soon, they reached another wooden door. As they all stood with their weapons ready, Woodcutter placed a hand on a wooden tile. With popping sounds, the door's tiles disappeared, letting pink light fill the stairwell.

Instantly, the smell of ash and dust filled their senses. Added to it was an aroma the Gameknight could only describe as the smell of a lightning storm, as if something electrical had been fried. A faint buzzing filled the air, like a distant bee flying just beyond eyesight, its relentless wings continuing to beat out its droning hum.

They stood inside a massive cube built in the center of an unbelievably large room. The cube was fifteen blocks on a side and fifteen blocks tall, with translucent walls that gave off the bright pink light. Like panes of colored glass, the transparent sheets of color that formed the walls allowed them to see similar cubes in the distance, each glowing a different color. Within the other colored rooms were creatures moving about, some very big and some small. They writhed and struggled to stand, as if in terrible pain within the radiant enclosures.

Single-block pillars ran along the edges of the cube-shaped cells, dividing the glowing surfaces into smaller sections. The stone columns were built from special blocks with ornate figures and runes carved into their surfaces, the figures shining the same color as the glowing walls.

"What is that?" Stitcher asked, an uncertain scowl on her face.

She reached out and touched the glowing surface with her hand, then pounded on it with a pickaxe.

"It's a force field. I remember seeing these last time I played this game," Gameknight said.

"Game?" Stitcher growled. "Is this a game to you?"

"I mean back in the physical world," the User-that-is-not-a-user stammered. "You know, before I met all of you."

Stitcher gave him a scowl and turned away.

"It's OK, Gameknight," Crafter said. "Tell us what you know."

"Well, the last time I pla . . . explored this world, I found nothing that could break these force fields. We'll probably be seeing more of these as we descend." Gameknight pointed to a door in the side of the glowing cube. "We go that way."

"We're going out there?" Digger asked, gesturing to the additional glowing rooms.

Gameknight nodded, then moved to the door and waited for the others. Hunter and Stitcher moved to his side with arrows drawn, a pack of wolves pacing angrily at their feet. Gameknight reached out and pressed one of the wooden squares. The door evaporated.

Instantly, the wolves started to growl as they sniffed the air.

"Monsters," Herder whispered.

"Come on," the User-that-is-not-a-user said. "This is like a maze down here. We need to find another pink cube with more stairs going down."

They move out into the dark corridor, the group staying close together. The sounds of monsters filled the cold, dusty passage, but thankfully, they sounded far away . . . or was it just an echo of something nearby?

They moved cautiously past a blue cell that contained a strange-looking creature. It was short and stocky, with blood-red wings sticking out from its back that resembled those of a bat. Two sharp horns jutted up from the creature's square head, giving it a devilish look. The monster moaned as if it was in pain, but just glared at the party with venomous hatred as they passed.

"I have a bad feeling about this," Gameknight whispered. "Let's move fast."

With Woodcutter at his side, he started to run. The big NPC was placing torches down every dozen blocks or so, placing each just at the edge of the last circle of light. It was providing them enough light to see, but the stone walls and floors were dark and could easily hide dangerous holes. They passed more blue cells, then green and yellow ones, each holding some kind of terrible creature none of them had ever seen before.

"Why is the stone so dark?" Hunter asked. "It looks like regular stone, but it's as dark as bedrock."

"It's deadrock," Empech said from behind.

"What?" Gameknight asked.

"The walls and floor," the little creature said. "They are made of deadrock. It is like bedrock, but it is no longer connected to Minecraft. Likely, this is an effect of Entity303's tampering with Minecraft. Empech is sure this will eventually spread throughout the land until everything is deadrock,'"

"I don't like the sound of that," Woodcutter said with concern.

The pech just grunted.

"This is probably part of Entity303's plan," Gameknight said. "His mods are doing this, I know it."

"How do we stop this?" Crafter asked.

"There is an ancient prophecy Empech heard," the gnome said. "It may shed some light on this predicament."

"What was it?" Crafter asked.

The pech took on a solemn expression, then his voice became scratchy as if something were caught in his throat, or maybe someone else was speaking through him. *"When the Three are merged into One, the Music of Minecraft will return to hold the land together, before the end."* His deep blue, gem-like eyes glittered with hope.

"More riddles . . . thanks a lot," Stitcher said.

They turned a corner and headed toward a glowing blue cube, the letters etched in the blocks shining the same color. The monster sounds were growing louder.

"What does that mean?" Gameknight asked.

The pech just shrugged as he ran. He was about to say something when a strange, raspy mechanical breathing sound filled the air. A glowing ball of sparkling magic shot out of the darkness and struck the wall just in front of the User-that-is-not-a-user, barely missing him.

"Monsters!" Gameknight yelled.

The party now sprinted through the dark tunnels, Woodcutter placing the torches as fast as he could. They ran from the monstrous wheezing as more sparkling balls of energy streaked over their heads. Now, the sounds of zombie moans could also be heard from behind.

"Great, more monsters," Crafter moaned.

"And I'm out of torches," Woodcutter said between panting breaths.

Gameknight pulled out the Moonworm Queen and shot the glowing worms onto the ground. The yellow glow of the creatures instantly spread outward. But the worms seemed to flicker for some reason.

"Just keep running," Gameknight said. "We need to find the . . ."

"There's the pink force field off to the left," Hunter shouted just then.

Gameknight turned and headed in that direction. When he reached the glowing cube, he pressed his hand to the wooden tiles as the sound of bowstrings filled the air. Stitcher and Hunter were firing back along their trail. Monsters were slowly emerging from the darkness behind them, following the glowing worms on the ground. Many of the creatures screamed in pain as the sisters' arrows found their targets.

"The door's open, come on!" Digger shouted as he shoved his way past his friends, Tux squawking fearfully under his arm.

They moved into the cube, where they stood before another stairway that went deeper into the castle.

"The monsters are coming!" Stitcher yelled behind them as she fired her bow as fast as she could draw arrows.

Zombies and spiders and skeletons came at them from the darkness, but a myriad of unfamiliar monsters, all vicious-looking, moved toward them as well. Gameknight turned as he saw things that resembled blazes but were the color of stone, as well as another dwarfish-looking creature with red bat-wings and bright glowing eyes, along with tiny green hobgoblins with razor-sharp teeth and long black claws, and red creatures that could only be described as demons.

"How do you close the door?" Hunter asked, her fearful voice echoing off the pink force fields.

"I don't know," Gameknight said. "Everyone down the stairs. We'll seal them off with stone and dirt."

The party moved down the dark stairway just as the first of the red, flying dwarfish monsters entered the pink cell. They built a barricade behind them as the creatures reached the first steps. Growls and moans and snarls echoed through the passage as they tore at the barrier of blocks with nails and teeth.

Once the wall of stone and dirt was complete, Gameknight relaxed and turned to his companions. They were clearly terrified by the mob they just escaped, but their barrier had diminished their growls to mere background noise.

"What now?" Crafter asked.

Gameknight glanced at the dark, descending stairway. "Down. I'm sure we'll find Weaver at the end of this stairway."

He pulled out the Moonworm Queen and placed a glowing, wriggling worm on the wall, the light from the tiny creature buoying their spirits a bit. But just then, a ferocious, thundering growl from below filled the air, followed by a great crash that made the ground shake.

Gameknight shook as lightning bolts of fear stabbed at his every nerve. The great, angry howl echoed through the stairway over and over again until it finally dissipated, leaving a terrifying silence. He took in a dry, sour breath of air, then glanced at his friends. They all looked frightened beyond words, with the exception of Empech. The tiny gnome gazed at the User-that-is-not-a-user and nodded his head, a look of faith in his crystalline blue eyes.

Gameknight sighed. "I guess we have to go down there."

The others stared at him and nodded, though none of them, not even Stitcher, looked pleased.

"Here we go," he added, then turned and descended the dark steps, toward the most terrifying sound he'd ever heard.

CHAPTER 32

INTO THE BELLY OF THE BEAST

"Come on, Gameknight, lead the way," Stitcher said. "Let's get going. I want to see whatever it is that this Entity303 has waiting for us."

She was pacing back and forth across the dark passageway like a predatory cat anxious to pounce on an unsuspecting mouse.

The User-that-is-not-a-user placed a moonworm on the ground and stepped forward. The green glow from the worm lit the dark gray deadrock walls.

"Careful what you wish for, child," Empech said in an almost grandmotherly voice. Something about it reminded Gameknight of the Oracle. He looked at the tiny gnome and wondered. . . .

They continued to weave their way through the next dungeon level, past countless cells with creatures of all types trapped within the glowing walls. Gameknight continued to place the squirming, glowing worms on the ground as they moved forward, but it seemed like the tiny insects writhed as if in pain when they touched the deadrock. Behind them, he saw some of the worms flickering in the distance, those farthest away already perishing from the prolonged touch of the lifeless stone.

"We need to hurry," Gameknight warned. "I don't know how long these worms are gonna survive. If they die and stop giving off light, we'll be trapped down here in the darkness."

"Then let's get moving!" Stitcher exclaimed. Gameknight ran through the passage, placing the glowing worms as far apart as possible.

"Hurry," Gameknight encouraged.

They ran through the rune dungeon, weaving past blue and green and yellow glowing cells until Crafter spotted a pink one in the distance. They sprinted toward that glowing chamber and found the door on the side. Once it opened, they moved in and built a stone barrier, blocking the entrance.

In the middle of the pink cell was another set of stairs, but this time, they were not the pristine white of the castle, but the gray color of deadrock.

Gameknight and his friends moved down the stairs, placing the worms on the walls as he went. As they descended, a strange rumbling filled the air. It was like the deep-throated purring of a cat . . . a gigantic cat. But the sound was not pleasant, like the purrs of Gameknight's cat at home, Tiger. No, this sounded as if it came from something angry and hateful. The rumbling grew louder as they descended, the sound reverberating in the stairs and walls.

"What's making that sound?" Digger asked, his voice shaking.

"Something unnatural," the pech said. "Empech has never heard that sound in Minecraft. All must be careful."

"Pffft, it's just a monster, and all monsters can be destroyed," Stitcher growled.

"Perhaps, child, but perhaps not," the pech replied sagely. "Humility and caution may serve you better."

Stitcher gave the little gnome a scowl, then continued down the stairs. Finally, they reached the end of the passage, where the stairway ended in a large chamber with an ominous hole in its center. The hole was like a dark circle of nothingness, the space beyond its opening cloaked in absolute darkness. The sounds of monsters could easily be heard below, but it was not the angry growls they were used to hearing. Instead, the monsters sounded scared, which was strange.

Then an earsplitting roar thundered through the very fabric of Minecraft. The beating of heavy, leathery wings filled the air as something big flew past the opening, then smashed into the floor from underneath, making the entire castle shake. A blast of foul-smelling air shot out of the opening as something gigantic exhaled and snorted, then growled in frustration.

Gameknight teetered on the edge of the hole when the creature smashed its wings against the floor again, almost causing him to fall in. Digger reached out quickly and grabbed his armor, pulling him back from the precipice.

"What was that?" Digger asked.

Squawk, Tux said, the tiny penguin sounding terrified.

"I don't know, but it was big," Woodcutter said.

"Even bigger than a dragon, that's for sure," Herder added. "My wolves can take care of any normal Minecraft monster, but not something that big." He took a step backward, away from the hole, his wolves moving with him.

"Come on . . . it's just a monster like any other," Stitcher said.

Another roar filled the chamber, making the walls shake. This one actually hurt Gameknight's ears, causing them to ring after the sound faded.

"At least we didn't have to smell its bad breath that time," Hunter said with a small, hopeful smile, trying to cheer the group up.

No one laughed.

Suddenly, a scream floated from out of the darkness.

"Smithy, it's a . . ." The voice was quickly muffled.

"That was Weaver's voice!" Gameknight said. "We have to go down there. If we can just save Weaver and put him back into the past again, we can restore the timeline and heal Minecraft."

The rest of the party stared at the User-that-is-not-a-user as if he were insane.

"Don't you get it? If we save Weaver, then it all goes back the way it's supposed to be," Gameknight said, his voice shaking slightly with fear.

No one said anything.

The User-that-is-not-a-user shot a moonworm onto the deadrock floor. The creature writhed as it struggled to survive, its normally bright yellow body flickering with an unsteady glow as the deadrock slowly drained its HP.

"Look . . . the very fabric of Minecraft is dying," Gameknight said. "If we don't get Weaver back into the past, then nothing will survive."

"You have a plan?" Hunter asked.

"Well . . ." Gameknight couldn't look at her. He lowered his head in shame.

"That thing down there sounds gigantic," Hunter said. "We need a plan."

She's right; I don't even have a plan, he thought. *How can I ask them to have faith in me when I don't have any faith in myself?*

Gameknight shuddered as waves of fear and uncertainty crashed down upon him, washing away the last vestiges of his courage. He glanced at his companions. They wouldn't look him in the eye, their faith in him shattered by the monster's roar and his own lack of confidence.

But then his eyes fell upon Empech. The gnome's two gem-like blue eyes reflected his image, and he didn't like what he saw. The multi-faceted orbs showed Gameknight what he thought of himself: he resembled a hunched-over, pathetic, weak, cowering child. His skin appeared to droop off his diminutive frame like a suit three sizes too big. But the worst part was his eyes. They seemed to be filled not just with defeat, but with an acceptance of defeat, as if trying wasn't even an option.

You can do only what you believe you can do, the high-pitched voice echoed in his head. *You can be what you choose to be, and do what you choose to do, but only if you believe in yourself.*

How can I believe in this? Gameknight replied in his mind. *That monster down there is huge and will likely tear us to pieces.*

"Empech has memories he does not understand," the gnome said, his squeaky voice piercing the momentary silence. "Empech can see Gameknight999 battling a spider with purple eyes, and standing before four horsemen, and facing a dark creature with glowing eyes. That Gameknight999 from Empech's memories stands here now, yes, yes."

"No, that was different," the User-that-is-not-a-user snapped.

"Oh?" the little gray creature asked.

"Was it really any different?" Crafter asked. He stepped forward and stood at Gameknight's side. "I remember when you faced the spider queen. We all said you were completely crazy, but you did it anyway, because you were brave."

"But that was a long time ago," the User-that-is-not-a-user replied.

"And remember when you faced Herobrine's four horsemen of the apocalypse?" Hunter added. "You stood before them, totally unafraid, and dared them to attack. Those cowardly monster kings ran away because of the courage you showed in the face of those overwhelming odds." She too moved closer, her hand settling gently on his shoulder.

"You even faced an entire army of zombies, just to save me," Herder said. One of the wolves barked in agreement. The lanky boy reached down and petted the animal. "You didn't really have much of a plan then, and you were still successful."

"I had a plan," Gameknight insisted.

"Yeah, well, I was there, and your plan was terrible," Stitcher said.

"Stitcher, be nice," Hunter chided.

"I'm just saying, his plan was terrible, and he just made it up as he went," the younger sister replied. She turned and faced him. "Your ability to react to new situations, and change battle plans on the fly, that's what made it possible to defeat all those monsters. No one can predict what the King of the Griefers will do."

She laughed, causing Gameknight to smile just a bit.

Digger stepped forward and said nothing, just laid his strong hand on Gameknight's other shoulder. Gameknight looked up at him, and could see the fear in the stocky NPC's eyes, but he could see faith as well.

The User-that-is-not-a-user glanced back at Empech and gazed again at his pathetic, wretched image in the gnome's eyes, but the stooped form was beginning to grow straight and tall as Gameknight999 began to believe. Memories of Herobrine's defeat and the destruction of Reaper, the skeleton king, filled his mind.

His reflected image in Empech's deep blue eyes grew stronger and more confident.

Thoughts of when he'd saved Hunter in his own timeline from the wither skeletons came to him as if he were reliving the experience. They hadn't cared about the odds or the danger. All that mattered was that their friend was in trouble . . . just like now.

The User-that-is-not-a-user's icy blue reflection grew stronger and taller in the gnome's eyes until he it was that of a warrior . . . like a mythical hero . . . like Gameknight999.

"Gameknight999 believed back then," Empech said. He took a step closer to the User-that-is-not-a-user. "Believe now."

He glanced around at his friends and saw newfound courage, not because they now believed in him, but because Gameknight finally believed in himself. And as his confidence and strength blossomed, they naturally spread to the others until the whole group was brimming with courage.

Another roar punched through the air, shaking the ground.

"I'm getting pretty tired of that," Stitcher growled.

"Me too," Gameknight agreed.

Squawk, squawk, Tux shouted, her tiny features bristling with courage.

"I think it's about time we go down there and find out what's making all that noise," Crafter said.

"Absolutely," the User-that-is-not-a-user said resolutely.

Reaching into his inventory, he pulled out a pail of water and poured the contents over the edge of the dark hole, Hunter and Stitcher doing the same. Gameknight glanced down at the hole and imagined it was the mouth of some kind of gigantic creature, and he was about to jump into the belly of the beast.

He glanced at Empech and smiled.

"I believe we can do this," Gameknight said, his confident voice booming off the cold stone walls, then jumped into the watery flow and fell into darkness, his friends following.

CHAPTER 33

MANTICORE

As Gameknight floated down the watery column, the sounds of monsters penetrated the liquid. Growls and snarls and the snapping of sharp teeth filled his ears, but they were not as loud as the bellowing roar from the great beast hidden in the shadows.

As soon as he touched the ground, the User-that-is-not-a-user quickly placed moonworms all around the flowing pool. The worms squirmed and writhed at the touch of the deadrock, their glowing bodies flickering; they weren't going to last long. The great beast roared again. It was even louder from down on the ground, and the stench of the creature's breath wafted throughout the chamber.

The sounds of monsters surrounded them, but none of the creatures charged; there was something keeping them hidden in the darkness. Gameknight moved farther into the darkness, placing additional worms on the ground. The glowing creatures revealed more of the chamber; deadrock stretched out in all directions, with dark obsidian pillars standing here and there, the walls of the impossibly huge chamber still hidden within the shadows.

Suddenly, a vile, malicious laugh echoed through the chamber. The User-that-is-not-a-user instantly knew the mocking voice to be that of Entity303.

"So, you finally made it here, Gameknight999," Entity303 said from the darkness.

"Come out and show yourself, coward," the User-that-is-not-a-user snapped.

"Coward . . . ha!"

Three flaming arrows streaked through the darkness. Each burning shaft hit a piece of netherrack that stood atop the tall obsidian columns. The unquenchable fire of the burning netherrack cast a flickering yellow light, unveiling more of the chamber. Another flight of arrows came out of the darkness, lighting more trios of the flaming pillars. Slowly, the burning netherrack pushed back the shadows, revealing a massive chamber built from the gloomy deadrock stone, the dull, gray walls merging with the floors in the distance.

Along the edge of the huge cavern were monsters of every kind, some they'd seen incarcerated in the glowing prison cells of the rune dungeon above, and others that were still unrecognizable. They hugged the walls as if deathly afraid to venture out into the center of the room. Glowing balls of XP, skeleton bones and pieces of zombie flesh showed that some of the monsters had tried to move away from the perimeter, but unsuccessfully.

On the far side of the room stood Entity303, holding a rope that was wrapped around Weaver, a terrified expression on the young NPC's face. They stood on a mound of deadrock that seemed as if it had oozed out of the wall, creating a gently sloping pile that spread across the floor. Next to the mound sat a small enclosure glowing a sickly yellow, the sides of the box made of force fields like in the rune dungeons. Trapped within the pale sheets of light was a chest that sparkled with magical energy. Entity303 stared down at the chest, a look of crazed desire in his eyes.

He wants that chest, that's why we're here, Gameknight thought. *He can't get past the force fields on his own.*

ROAR!!!

A massive creature glided in from the dark side of the cavern and settled at the user's side. It had the body of a lion, with a thick, bushy brown mane ringing its face. The furry cowl stood out against the short-cropped tan fur that covered the rest of its body. It looked strong—really strong—with clawed front and back paws and legs rippling with muscles. From its back jutted two large, bat-like wings, their leathery skin as dark as the deadstone that surrounded them. At the tips of the wings, Gameknight could see what looked like razor-sharp horns that could probably tear through iron armor as if it were paper. This was a creature built for destruction.

"What is that thing?" Digger hissed.

Before anyone could answer, the monster moved, revealing its tail. Instead of seeing a lion's tail, the monster extended a segmented thing that was similar to the tail of a scorpion. The thick, scaly thing writhed in the air, snake-like, showing a deadly scorpion's stinger at the end.

"We studied mythological creatures in school last year," Gameknight mumbled, his fear barely held in check.

"What is it?" Hunter asked, her voice actually shaking with fear.

"That thing is called a manticore, and it was considered a creature of incredible strength and ferocity," Gameknight whispered as he slowly put away the Moonworm Queen and drew his iron sword with his left hand. "In our textbook, it said these creatures were capable of destroying entire armies."

"Good thing we brought an army with us," Stitcher said with a smile.

No one found it funny.

The monster turned its massive head and faced the intruders. Gameknight was shocked to see its face; it was not that of a lion. Rather, the manticore had the face of a villager, with a large, bulbous nose and deep-set eyes that glowed red with anger. Large white teeth jutted from the side of the creature's mouth, the sharp tips gleaming in the light of the burning netherrack.

The villagers around Gameknight999 gasped in shock when they saw the monster's face.

"I can see you noticed my little pet manticore," Entity303 shouted from across the chamber. His voice echoed off the walls and mixed with the growls and snarls of the monsters that ringed the chamber. "They are very loyal creatures, and since I saved this one from certain death, it is now mine to command." The crazed user took a step forward and patted the mighty beast on the side. "The mindless brute doesn't know that it was I who put it in mortal danger in the first place. Ha ha ha. That's what you get for not having much of a brain."

"Just give us Weaver and we'll let you leave, unharmed," Gameknight shouted.

Entity303 smiled and shook his head. "You must earn your little prize." He patted the manticore on the side again. "First, I want to do a little experiment. Let's see how many monsters you can battle at once." He pointed at the monsters along the wall. "Manticore, send the monsters into battle!"

The huge beast sprung into the air, its dark wings flinging ash from the burning netherrack into the air. It streaked along the sides of the room, dragging the horn at the end of one wing against the dark wall. The scraping sound scared the monsters into action. They scattered away from the walls and into the center of the chamber. When the myriad of growling creatures realized they would not be slain for standing out into the open, they turned and glared at the intruders, their snarling voices growing loud.

"Everyone stand with your backs to the water," Gameknight said. "We need to stay close and watch out for each other. Remember . . ."

Before he could finish, Stitcher yelled a vicious battle cry and charged toward the monsters, her bowstring singing its song of violence.

"Stitcher . . . come back!" Gameknight shouted, but the young girl was lost to the fury of battle.

"We have to protect her," Hunter said and ran after her sister, her own bow twanging away.

"This is bad, yes, yes, very bad," Empech said as he pulled out a potion of something and threw it at Gameknight999.

Instantly, sparkling purple swirls floated around this head. The User-that-is-not-a-user stared at the gnome, confused..

"Potion of swiftness, yes, yes."

Gameknight smiled, then turned and sprinted after the sisters. "Come on, everyone, we need to protect our friends!" he yelled to the others.

He streaked forward, zipping past Hunter and quickly catching Stitcher. He found the girl on one knee, firing at some kind of icy sparkling creature. It reminded Gameknight of a blaze, only without the wreath of flames and smoke around it. Instead of being a bright yellow, it was the color of snow and ice. The monster fired something at the young girl. Gameknight batted the frosty projectile back at the creature. It hit the monster in the head, making it flash red and expire, a loud clanking sound filling the air.

"One down!" Stitcher giggled.

By now, Hunter had reached her side and was also firing at the monsters, an expression of grim determination on her face. Gameknight could see they were completely outnumbered, and being out here in the open was not ideal. Putting away his sword, he pulled a stack of dirt blocks from his inventory. Using his swiftness, he ran around his friends, placing the blocks on the ground, building some defenses. Quickly, he constructed a wall two blocks high, then placed cubes of dirt behind the wall for his friends to stand upon.

Something streaked overhead; it was one of the short-winged demons. The monster's claws reached down at Gameknight at it approached. He shoved the block of dirt he had in his hand at the monster, pushing it away. Then, with a quick, fluid motion, he drew his swords and swung at the next one that swooped down on them.

Suddenly, Crafter was at his side, his bow buzzing. Woodcutter appeared off to the left with Digger at his side. The stocky NPC put Tux safely on the ground behind him, then exchanged his pickaxe for a bow and added his arrows to the fray.

Herder moved up next to Gameknight999, then put his fingers to his mouth and made a shrill whistling sound. The lanky boy pointed at a group of zombies. Instantly, his wolves dashed across the ground and fell on the monsters, tearing into their decaying legs and snapping at their sharp claws. Some of them yelped in pain, but they refused to retreat until their attack was completed.

"Call them back, Herder." Gameknight grabbed the lanky boy's shoulders and turned him so they were face to face. "The wolves are outnumbered and are getting hurt."

A look of crazed violence filled the boy's eyes. Herder too was lost to the fever of battle.

Gameknight shook him. "Call the wolves back!"

Another yelp filled the air, then a great, sad howl echoed through the chamber and was suddenly silenced. This snapped the boy out of the violent trance. He whistled again, bringing the now-smaller pack to him. As soon as the wolves were at his side, he whistled and pointed again, this time to a group of creepers.

More monsters charged toward them, creatures never before seen in Minecraft, and all of them angry and lethal-looking. The mixture of all their growls and snarls and cries of rage filled the chamber with a cacophony that was both terrifying and painful to hear.

"We're completely outnumbered," Crafter said. "We can't keep this up."

"Crafter's right," Hunter said as she fired three quick shots at a creature made of ice that floated in the air, razor-sharp crystals of frozen death slowly revolving around its core. The creature flashed red, then shattered in a spray of ice-covered shards. "We have to do something different, fast, or . . ." She paused to shoot down one of the flying demons, then ducked as a skeleton arrow streaked over her shoulder. "Gameknight, do something," she pleaded.

A group of short blue monsters came at them from the right, followed by a squad of creatures that spun spiked balls over their heads, the deadly weapons held at the end of whirling chains. The ball-and-chain monsters charged at them, each one howling like a crazed animal. In front, green hobgoblins, each with a vicious golden spear, approached the defenders. Their group was at least twenty strong, and the tips of their spears gleamed like a field of shining stalks of corn. More creatures, all stranger than the next, poured out of the shadows, each intent on their destruction.

"Gameknight, we do we do?" Digger asked, his voice soft and shaking with fear.

Squawk, squawk!

Fear and doubt crashed down upon him like an endless monsoon, drenching him with uncertainty. But when he glanced at Empech, he found the little gnome smiling.

"The Lich King, yes, yes. Use that which you took from the Lich King."

Gameknight thought for a moment, then with sudden clarity he laughed as the storm of fear suddenly evaporated.

I know what to do, he thought. *I believe!*

And then he reached into his inventory and pulled out either the weapon that would either be their salvation or their destruction.

CHAPTER 34

ZOMBIES

The bone handle of the Zombie Scepter felt cold in his hand, but the green jewel at the end glowed bright with magical energy. Gameknight moved to the dirt wall and climbed to the top.

"Everyone get back," the User-that-is-not-a-user said.

"Gameknight, we really don't know what that thing will do," Crafter said. "The zombies that it creates may turn on us and make the situation worse."

"Worse? Can it . . ." Hunter stopped speaking to shoot at another of the flying demons. "Can it get any worse?"

"Well . . ." Crafter said.

"Here goes," Gameknight said, then flicked his wrist just as he remembered the Lich King doing. The green gem flashed bright, blinding him for just an instant. When his sight returned, there were nine zombies standing before him. They stared up at the User-that-is-not-a-user as if waiting for instructions.

"Protect us!" he shouted, the cold feeling of fear slowly growing from within.

The zombies growled and moaned, then turned and shuffled toward the approaching monsters.

"It worked!" Stitcher squealed. "I never thought I'd be glad to see one of those stinking monsters."

"Send some over here!" Woodcutter shouted.

A group of kobolds were about to reach the defenses, their bright blue skin standing out against the dreary deadrock floor. Woodcutter put away his bow and drew his axe. He began cleaving away at the tiny creatures as they slashed at him with their sharp claws. Gameknight saw Digger look down at Tux, then pulled out the glowing battle axe that had once been the Lich King's. It shook in his hands, but as he swung the massive weapon, it tore through the blue demons, causing them to burst into flames.

Gameknight flicked the wand in their directions. The zombies that suddenly appeared fell on the kobolds, then moved out and attacked other monsters. Flicking the wand all around their position, he made more squads of zombies, each one willing to battle the monsters of the Twilight Forest to protect the wielder of the Zombie Scepter.

But eventually, the green gem on the end of the scepter grew dark.

"It doesn't work anymore?" Gameknight asked.

"It has served its purpose, yes, yes," Empech said.

"What now?" Crafter asked.

"We fight!" Gameknight shouted.

Leaping over the dirt wall, the User-that-is-not-a-user charged at a group of monsters, his blades swinging through the air in a blur. Suddenly, Digger was at his side, the glowing axe cleaving through skeletons and destroying ice-shard creatures that had likely belonged to the Snow Queen.

Flaming arrows shot past them and struck more demon-like creatures, causing them to burst into flames. Before they could reach them with their swords, the tiny red monsters disappeared with a pop.

Gameknight saw no more monsters before him. He turned and rushed to Crafter, who was battling a group of fire beetles. Herder's wolves bit at the insects from behind, careful to avoid the sheet of flames that came from the insects' mouths. A group of zombies also fell on the monsters, tearing into the beetles with their razor-sharp claws.

Slowly, the snarls and growls of the different monsters began to be drowned out by the sorrowful moans of zombies . . . which meant they were winning.

"Hunter, Stitcher, look for more netherrack blocks and light them with your bows," Gameknight shouted.

With the potion of swiftness fading, the User-that-is-not-a-user streaked across the battlefield, the Moonworm Queen now in his left hand. The royal insect seemed to glow bright on his wrist; it must have recharged its energy somehow. He placed glowing, squirming worms on the ground as he searched for the small pockets of creatures that now tried to hide in the darkness. As soon as they were found, zombies shuffled toward the creatures.

More blocks of netherrack burst into fiery life as Hunter and Stitcher found the remaining obsidian columns that held the rusty blocks on top. With their flames and the surviving moonworms, the massive chamber was now completely lit. Across the floor, maybe fifty of their zombies still survived, all of them milling about in the center of the huge cave. The attacking monsters were all destroyed.

Gameknight ran back to his friends, then glared up at Entity303.

"We passed your test, now give us our friend," Gameknight growled at him, pointing at the user with his diamond sword.

"Passed my test . . . ha!" Entity303 reached out and petted the manticore, which had settled itself again at his side during the fighting. "That was just the opening act. If you want your little villager back, you must defeat my pet here." He patted the monster on the side, then glanced down at the radiant enclosure that sat near his feet, his eyes focused on the sparkling chest trapped within.

"You would sacrifice your companion, just to test us?" Crafter asked.

"My companion? Ha! You are a fool, villager. This isn't a companion; it is a servant to be ordered about . . . it is a tool to be used and then discarded when no longer useful . . . it is a weapon to point at a target, and when the target is destroyed, the weapon is useless. This creature is not important. Do what you can to protect yourself, though most of you will certainly perish. Say hello to your destruction."

Entity303 patted the beast firmly on the back, then spoke in a clear, angry voice.

"Manticore . . . destroy!"

The beast bellowed a great roar that made the walls of the chamber shake, then leapt into the air. Its massive, leathery wings lifted the creature higher and higher. It streaked to the small hole in the ceiling and smashed into it as if trying to escape, splashing steams of water in all directions, then turned in a great arc, its eyes focused on its prey far below. With another roar, the monster pivoted and dove straight at the User-that-is-not-a-user and his friends, its razor-sharp claws extended, a snarling expression on its vile, NPC-like face.

Gameknight999 stared up at the manticore as chilling fingers of terror instantly wrapped themselves around his body, making it impossible for him to move. All he could do was watch as his destruction descended down upon them.

CHAPTER 35

STITCHER

The monster dove at Gameknight999 and the other NPCs, but banked away at the last second and attacked the remaining zombies. The manticore landed amidst the decaying green bodies, swiping at them with its massive paws, the sharp claws tearing at the monsters' HP. Its scorpion tail darted from one creature to another, skewering the helpless zombies with its long, poisonous stinger.

Wails of pain and sorrow came from the rotting creatures as the manticore quickly destroyed one after another. Gameknight wanted to go out and help them, but he knew there was nothing he could do; Entity303's monster would easily overpower him.

"You have any ideas?" Crafter said as he watched the slaughter.

The User-that-is-not-a-user didn't reply. His mind was trying to find a solution to this puzzle, but he'd never seen a creature in Minecraft as strong as the Manticore. It made the Hydra and the Naga seem like playful little puppies in comparison.

This creature was like three monsters in one. The manticore's scorpion tail stabbed at the zombies, while its claws tore into the HP of the zombies closest to it and its sharp, clawed wingtips sliced at those farther away. It was impossible to fight it up close and impossible to fight it from far away. This was the perfect machine of destruction; it had no weakness to exploit.

"Gameknight . . . you're thinking of something, right?" Crafter asked again, his voice shaking.

Again, Gameknight did not reply. Every thought going through his head was focused on the monster before them, but he wasn't coming up with anything.

"Well, *I* have an idea," Stitcher said fearlessly.

"What is it?" Crafter asked.

The young girl didn't reply. Instead, she marched forward, her arrows streaking through the air, striking the creature in the side and shoulder and leg. They flaming arrows continued to burn as they embedded themselves into the manticore's thick hide, but the monster did not flash red. The arrows were doing no damage at all. In fact, the huge monster didn't even seem to notice them until one of the arrows bounced off one of its huge, protruding teeth.

After bringing its thick, poisonous stinger down upon the last of the zombies, the monster turned and faced Stitcher. Gameknight and Hunter ran forward, trying to reach the young girl's side before the monster pounced. Suddenly a wave of furry wolves shot past them, barking and growling at the monster. One of the wolves ran up to the manticore and bit at the creature's leg, but the massive giant didn't even notice.

As Gameknight and Hunter closed in on the manticore, arrows streaked over their heads; Woodcutter and Crafter were following, each of them firing their bows as they ran. The manticore glared down at its attackers and growled, then swung a clawed fist at Gameknight and Hunter. To Gameknight, it felt as if a speeding bus had hit him. He flew through the air, landing a dozen blocks away, his head ringing. Hunter landed next to him, flashing red with damage.

Woodcutter and Crafter landed in the pile shortly after. Wolves yelped and flew in all directions as the beast flicked its barbed tail like a whip, knocking the animals through the air.

"That creature is unstoppable," Hunter said. "What do we do?"

"We go protect Stitcher," Gameknight said.

The young NPC was still standing before the monster, firing her arrows at the creature, but now the manticore was beating its wings, knocking the projectiles out of the air. With a great roar, it stomped its huge paws on the ground, making the entire chamber shake, then slowly approached Stitcher, its scorpion tail ready to strike.

"Stitcher, the arrows aren't working!" Gameknight shouted. "Get out of there, please . . . RUN!"

She glanced at Gameknight, and he could see she was consumed with anger and violent rage. But then she gave him a strange, knowing smile and calmly put away her bow.

"What are you doing?" Hunter screamed. "Run away!"

Stitcher pulled out Empech's magical fishing pole.

The manticore took a step closer, its growls growing louder and louder, the stench from its foul breath washing over them.

Stitcher glared at the monster and held the fishing pole out in front of her. Seeing the harmless tool in the girl's hand, the manticore's eyes grew wide with surprise, then it crouched and prepared to pounce.

"Stitcher . . . run!" Hunter begged, but her younger sister stood her ground.

Time seemed to slow as Gameknight watched the great beast leap into the air, heading straight for Stitcher. But at the same time, the NPC flicked the fishing pole at her target. The shining golden hook embedded itself in the monster's thick hide. Instantly, bolts of magical energy ran down the fishing line and enveloped the great beast. Its roar became a cry of pain as it stopped in midair, then fell to the ground, writhing in agony. At the same time, Stitcher screamed, as if she too were being tortured.

"Yes!" Entity303 shouted with sick glee.

Gameknight glanced at the evil user. He was standing next to the yellow enclosure. Cracks were beginning to spread across its glowing surface.

Suddenly, the cries of pain stopped. Stitcher had lost her grip on the fishing rod and it fell to the ground, just out of reach. The manticore shook its large, furry head, then stared down at the young girl and wagged its horrific barbed tail. Stitcher glanced up, then reached out and grabbed the wooden pole before the mighty giant could move. She flicked the hook toward the creature, and more waves of magical fire shot down the line, causing both the wielder and target to cry out in anguish.

Stitcher screamed as the waves of magic shot down the fishing line and slammed into the manticore. The gigantic beast flashed red as it took damage.

"Hunter, fire your bow," Gameknight shouted as he drew his enchanted bow. He advanced across the chamber, joining his companions as he fired.

Pulling back an arrow, he aimed at the monster and fired. The arrow streaked through the sparkling envelope that surrounded the manticore, then struck it in the side. The beast howled in pain, as did Stitcher. Hunter fired her arrows as well, and with each strike, both beast and girl screamed in anguish.

The winged nightmare's HP was gradually being blasted away by the waves of magic. Slowly, the manticore fell to the ground, its muscular legs no longer able to support its own weight.

"She's doing it!" Woodcutter shouted. "Go Stitcher!"

Both monster and girl screamed again, but then Stitcher flicked the fishing pole, pulling the hook from the creature's hide.

"What are you doing?" Hunter asked. "It's almost destroyed."

"No more . . . I can't bear it," Stitcher said as tears flowed down her face.

"Go on, kill the beast," Entity303 shouted. "Kill it or it will destroy you!"

Gameknight glanced at the terrible user. The enclosure before him was cracked even more, light from the glowing chest leaking through the fissures. Entity303's eyes were lit with a cruel joy. Behind him, Weaver struggled with his bonds, but the rope around his body held him firmly, its free end still in the user's hand.

"I refuse to destroy this creature," Stitcher moaned as she struggled to stand. "It is too special, too rare . . . too alive."

The manticore raised its massive head and looked at Stitcher, its eyes filled with sorrow and fear. Stitcher stepped forward and placed a hand on the creature's furry mane. It closed its eyes, as if waiting for the end to come with cold, heartless finality. Instead, Stitcher looked up at the small hole in the deadrock ceiling high overhead, streams of water still falling from the opening. Extending her arm, she sent the fishing pole's hook high into the air, where it snagged the opening and held firm.

Bolts of magical lightning shot up the taught line and smashed into the ceiling, tearing huge chunks out of the deadrock. Blocks flew in all directions as the magical energy carved a massive hole overhead. She threw the line again and again, sculpting an opening that was getting bigger and bigger. As she did this, the manticore moved to her side and just watched, its massive head tilted upward.

"What do we do?" Digger asked. "The monster is right next to her!"

"Do nothing," Empech said. "Stay perfectly still. Stitcher has learned what the manticore needs. Relax and watch."

Stitcher finished carving the hole, then lowered the fishing rod and gazed into the beast's face. With tears in her eyes, she reached out and placed a hand on the creature's cheek, then stroked its thick, furry mane.

A grumbling sound came from the monster, filling the air. Gameknight drew his sword, but a small, gray-skinned hand settled onto his arm.

"It is not a growl," Empech said. "It is a purr, yes, yes."

The rumbling grew louder, and gradually Stitcher's tears stopped. She reached into her inventory, pulled out a piece of cooked steak, and offered it to the manticore. The creature carefully took the meat from her hand and ate it, replenishing its health. It leaned forward and rubbed its mane against Stitcher's face, then it beat its huge leathery wings and took to the air. It soared around the chamber, getting higher and higher until it was near the ceiling. The huge manticore then shot out of the opening overhead, and was gone.

Stitcher turned, looked at the others, and then collapsed, her limp body landing on the dark floor, laying deathly still.

CHAPTER 36

WEAVER

"What did you do?!" Entity303 shouted. "You were supposed to destroy the beast, not set it free."

The user yanked on the rope, pulling Weaver nearer to him, then moved closer to the yellow force fields and began swinging at the cracked sides with his pickaxe. After three swings, the surface shattered. The user tossed the pick aside and lifted the chest with one hand, placing it on the ground and opening it. Magical light leaked from the open box and illuminated the area as the enchanted items in the chest gave off waves of iridescent light.

Entity303 smiled, then turned and faced his prisoner.

"Looks like I don't need you anymore," he said with an evil smile.

Reaching into his inventory, Entity303 pulled out his glowing infused sword and raised it high in the air.

"NO!"

A booming voice filled the chamber. Entity303 turned toward the sound and found Digger approaching, the glowing battle axe in his hand.

"Ahhh, the coward has something to say?" the user asked.

"No more killing, no more killing, NO MORE KILLING!"

Digger's voice filled the chamber with thunder as his anger overwhelmed his fear. With both hands gripping the handle of the enchanted weapon, Digger raised the battle axe high over his head and threw it straight toward Entity303. The user saw it coming and easily took a step backward to avoid the attack.

Digger just smiled.

The axe spun end-over-end, its sharp, glowing edge leaving a faint orange trail across the chamber as the enchanted weapon cleaved through the air. It hit the rope connecting Weaver to the user, cutting the boy free. Entity303 fell backward as the tension on the rope suddenly went to zero.

Weaver stumbled for a moment, then wormed his way out of the ropes and ran.

"Come on, everyone . . . let's get him!" Hunter shouted.

Digger pulled out his pickaxe and ran toward the evil user, the rest of his companions following. A wave of white fur passed the stocky NPC as the wolves streaked toward their target, ready to attack, their growling voices echoing off the chamber walls.

Entity303 saw the creatures charging at him and acted quickly. He pulled something out of the chest, then placed it on the ground. It was a pedestal.

The wolves were getting closer. Gameknight was sprinting toward the user, hoping to get there before he could try to hurt Weaver.

The terrible user pulled out a book from the chest. It had a brown cover and seemed ancient, as if it had been trapped within the yellow force field for eons. He set it on the pedestal, then turned and faced the wolves as the vicious animals rushed toward him.

The wolf pack leader charged up the pile of deadrock, its jaws snapping together, sounding like a metal vise slamming open and shut. Entity303 glared down at the animal and smiled, then leaned toward the book. Instantly, he was enveloped in a cloud of purple and silver, then disappeared just as the animal tried to clamp down on his leg, the blast of magical energy knocking the wolf aside, throwing Weaver to the ground with a thud. The boy and wolf both landed hard on the deadrock ground and didn't move.

Entity303 was gone.

"Stitcher," Gameknight said, then turned and sprinted to where the young girl still lay on the ground.

He dropped his swords, and knelt at her side.

"Stitcher, are you all right . . . Stitcher, please be all right." Gameknight was so scared he began to weep. "You have to be OK, Stitcher . . . come back to us."

The girl opened her eyes and the User-that-is-not-a-user breathed a sigh of relief.

"You're OK?"

"I'll be better if you let me stand up," she said with a sarcastic smile.

She climbed to her feet slowly, then bent over and picked up the magical fishing pole. The others were gathering around her, each of them asking questions at the same time. With a hand raised, Stitcher silenced them all, then stepped up to Empech.

"You were right, the price for this power was too much," she said as she handed the fishing pole back to the little gnome. "I will never touch that thing again. You keep it."

"Thank you, child," the gnome replied as he put the magical weapon back into his inventory.

"Stitcher, what happened?" Gameknight asked.

"Empech's magical weapon is incredibly powerful, but it makes the wielder feel what they are doing to their target," Stitcher said, wiping the tears from her cheeks. "I could feel everything that was happening to the manticore, all the arrows hitting it, all of that magical energy stabbing at its body . . . it was terrible.

"But not only did I feel its pain, I also saw inside the creature's mind, and it saw inside me as well. That majestic creature was trapped down here by

Entity303. Closed spaces terrify it beyond all rational thought. The manticore, her name is Growlarra, and she is extremely proud of her growl . . . anyway, she was trapped down here and was nearly driven insane. Entity303 tortured her with the darkness and all the other creatures until she would do his bidding, but she is a thoughtful, intelligent creature that cares for others . . . even us."

Stitcher turned to Empech and took one of his hands in hers.

"Your weapon taught me I should think about other people; my actions have repercussions for others." She turned to Gameknight999. "And Growlarra taught me to always be proud of myself and my actions. She asked me if I felt I was doing the right thing . . . and I didn't. She was willing to accept her death at my hands, but pitied me, for I knew I was doing wrong. She taught me to consider what I was doing, and that if I wasn't sure it was right, then it probably wasn't."

A tear trickled from her eye.

"All Growlarra wants to do is fly through the clouds and enjoy the wind. She doesn't want to fight . . . it's not her way, just as it isn't our way. I think Growlarra brought me back from the brink of losing myself to my anger and hatred. She saved me, just like you all did."

And then she wept. Hunter rushed forward and wrapped her arms around Stitcher. Crafter came forward and hugged the sisters, then the rest of the party did as well, the wolves howling loud.

Suddenly Stitcher pushed them all away. "Weaver . . . where's Weaver?"

Just then, Digger walked up, carrying the unconscious Weaver. His small arms hung down, swinging from side to side like limp noodles. Carefully, the stocky NPC placed the boy on the ground.

Gameknight quickly knelt at his side and cradled his head in his arms.

"Weaver, are you OK?" Gameknight said, his voice weak with fear. He shook the boy gently, but his eyes did not open. "Why won't he wake up?"

Gameknight looked up just in time to see a bucket of water tip and the blue liquid fall onto him and Weaver.

"Hunter," Stitcher chided her sister.

"It's always worked so well in the past," the older sister said with a smile.

Weaver coughed, spitting water from his mouth. He opened his eyes and peered up at Gameknight999.

"Smithy, is that you?" Weaver said in a weak, hopeful voice.

"Quick, someone give him some food," Gameknight said.

"Wait," Empech said.

He set his pack on the ground and reached in, pulling out a shimmering golden apple.

"A Notch apple," Crafter said in a low, awed voice.

Empech nodded his oversized head. He handed it to the boy as Weaver's eyes widened with surprise. He took a bite of the shining fruit. Instantly, color began to flow back into his skin, his blue eyes growing bright. He gobbled the rest of the apple, then sat up.

"Where's Entity303?" the boy asked.

"Gone," Gameknight said. "He opened some kind of book and disappeared. But we have you back, and that's all that matters. Now we need to get you back to your own time and fix everything."

"What?" Weaver asked, confused.

"Do you remember the diamond portal in the Nether?" the User-that-is-not-a-user asked. "You know, the one that Entity303 used to kidnap you?"

The boy nodded his head.

"Where did you come out?" Gameknight asked. "Where is the other end of the portal?" he asked. "I know there was a portal in the Nether when we were fighting Herobrine in the past, at the end of the Great Zombie

Invasion, but where is the other end in this timeline? Do you remember?"

"All I know is that it was in a desert," Weaver said. He stood and looked at all the people around him, his eyes lingering on Herder longer than the rest. "After Entity303 brought me through, he put something over my head so I couldn't see, then led me out of the desert. I don't know what happened next."

"Do you think you could find that desert?" Crafter asked.

Weaver shook his head. "I have no idea where it was."

Gameknight started to pace back and forth. "We must get Weaver back into the past to repair the damage Entity303 has done to Minecraft. He is the key, and he must be returned."

"But how? We don't know where the portal is located that will take him back," Crafter said.

"What do we do?" Stitcher asked.

Gameknight considered all the puzzle pieces before him.

"You know what you must do, child," Empech said. "You just need to come to terms with the decision you've already made, yes, yes."

Gameknight nodded, then stopped pacing and turned to face his companions.

"You're right, Empech," Gameknight said. "You are wise even beyond your years."

"What are we gonna do?" Stitcher asked, her eyes bright with hope and kindness for the first time in a long time.

"We're going after Entity303."

CHAPTER 37

INTO THE AGES

Gameknight led the group to the chest, which still sat open, iridescent purple light spilling out and creating an oasis of color in the dull deadrock chamber.

"This was what Entity303 was after all along," Gameknight said. "Somehow, the manticore and the enclosure were linked. As the animal, her name was . . ."

"Growlarra," Stitcher filled in.

"Right, Growlarra," Gameknight continued. "As she became wounded, cracks formed across the force fields. I bet if we'd killed her, the force fields would have been extinguished. But Stitcher freed her before her HP was exhausted, even though enough damage had already been done that Entity303 was able to break the walls and pull out the chest."

"What's in it?" Crafter asked.

The User-that-is-not-a-user walked to the chest and stepped around to the open side. He peered into the glowing wooden box and instantly recognized many of the items: books, sheets of blank paper, bottles of ink, and some furniture. Pulling the furniture out of the chest, he set them on the ground. One seemed like the writing desk that his dad had in their office at home, and the other was a brown box with grooves carved in all the surfaces.

"The chest is filled with items to write books," Gameknight said. "Very special books."

"Why would Entity303 want a bunch of books?" Crafter asked.

"Because they will take him to different dimensions within Minecraft," he replied, a knowing smile spreading across his face.

"How is that possible?" Digger asked with a shaking voice, his self-doubt returning after the battle.

"You see, a long time ago, some programmers made a computer game that was incredibly popular," Gameknight explained. "It was called Myst, and it redefined computer gaming."

"That's really interesting, professor," Hunter said. "But get to the point."

"I'm getting there," he replied with a scowl. "In that game, you used books to go to different universes, or multi-verses, as they're called today. Fast-forward about twenty years, and a programmer came out with a mod to Minecraft called Mystcraft. In that mod, you used books to jump to new worlds, called Ages, like in the original Myst game." He reached into the chest and lifted up a large, brown, box-like thing. "You use things like book binders and writing tables and rune-covered pages to create these special books."

Gameknight placed the items on the ground. He then bent over and picked up the book Entity303 had used to escape.

"This is where our enemy went . . . into this book," Gameknight said.

"You mean Entity303's in that book?" Digger asked.

"No, this book is a gateway to another universe, like a portal, and that parallel universe is where our enemy fled."

"But why would he want to do this?" Crafter asked. "It doesn't make sense."

"One time, I heard him mumble about something he'd lost in an Age," Weaver explained. "I thought he meant it was lost a long time ago, but now I'm not so sure."

"He must have messed something up when he added all these mods to Minecraft; something he needed to complete his plan must have become stuck inside Mystcraft," Gameknight said. "Entity303 must be looking for the right Age so he can carry out the next part of his plan."

"We need to get there first, before he does," Herder said as he patted the wolves gathered around him. "And if Entity303 is the only person who knows the location of the portal that will take Weaver back, then we need to catch him."

The others nodded their agreement.

Weaver glanced at the lanky boy and gave him a scowl, then looked back at Gameknight999. "So what are we gonna do?"

"We're gonna follow him through the ages until we catch him," Gameknight said. "But first, we need to make some books of our own, and the first one we need is a linking book."

He quickly assembled the book, thinking back to a long ago when he'd first played the Mystcraft mod. The User-that-is-not-a-user combined some leather and sheets of paper, then placed it on the ground and concentrated on right-clicking on it with his mouse, back in the physical world. Suddenly the book changed from gray to green. He held it up for all to see.

"This is our linking book, and it will allow us to return here, to the Twilight Forest, after we've caught Entity303," Gameknight999 said. "We'll then go back to the Overworld, where we'll find that diamond portal in the desert."

He glanced at Weaver and gave him a confident smile, then tucked the green tome into his inventory.

"But how do we know where that user went?" Crafter asked.

"We'll use his book here," Gameknight said, gesturing to the book on the pedestal. "After that it'll be more difficult, but for now, we just follow the trail of breadcrumbs."

"Trail of breadcrumbs?" Hunter asked, confused.

"He's so weird sometimes," Stitcher added with a friendly smile.

Hunter tousled her sister's hair, then smiled back.

Gameknight broke the writing table and book press with an axe and allowed them to flow into his inventory. He then emptied the chest of its contents and stepped up to the book on the pedestal.

"All of you come close and hold onto me, so we'll all be transported to the next age," the User-that-is-not-a-user said.

His companions moved up close and held hands, the wolves in the center of the circle, each with either a paw or tail touching someone.

Empech glanced up at Gameknight from the center of the circle and gave him a smile. He could sense the little gnome was proud of him for leading the party to this point. It was as if the pech was giving him some kind of parental approval.

Gameknight looked at his companions.

"You know, there were times I wasn't sure we were gonna make it," he said.

"Like when we were battling the giant snake," Hunter offered.

"Or fighting with that skeleton king," Stitcher added.

"Maybe it was when you took us to visit the Hydra," Woodcutter said with a smile.

"Yeah, pretty much all of those things," Gameknight replied. "I was so afraid of failing all of you, that I started becoming afraid to try."

"That's crazy," Hunter said.

"Well . . . I started doubting myself when I was terrified. But the faith all of you had in me kept me going."

Gameknight took his hand off the book and wiped away a grateful tear.

"Do you still doubt yourself now?" Crafter asked.

"Not when I have all of you around me."

"Then you just better keep us around," Digger added.

Gameknight nodded his head, then reached out and touched the book again.

"Everyone ready?" the User-that-is-not-a-user asked.

They nodded, some of them appearing a little scared. He flashed them all a smile.

"Entity303, we're coming for you," Gameknight said in a loud voice. Then he imagined himself right-clicking on the book in the physical world.

A cloud of purple and silver mist seemed to wrap around the party, clouding their vision, and then they disappeared, on their way to a new dimension, fast on Entity303's trail.

MINECRAFT SEEDS

As I'm sure you are all aware now, this book involved a modded version of Minecraft. When I play mods, I like to use mod installers like Feed-the-Beast, sometimes referred to as FTB, or the Curse Client. These mod installers will load various mod-packs into the correct versions of Minecraft, making them much easier to play. In the past, I've had difficulties finding mods that would work with my version of Minecraft, and it's always important to be extra cautious about which mods you use and where they are coming from, as they could have viruses inside them or could cause instabilities in computer performance. As a result, I now only use FTB or the Curse Client, both of which come with mods that have been already screened. I've found this to be a much better way to play and experiment with mods.

Keep in mind, when you are playing modded Minecraft, you'll be running many mods, simultaneously. These mods have been tested for compatibility with each other and should function properly, but some of the modpacks will cause your Minecraft to crash unexpectedly. I've found that I like using the Direwolf20 modpack, and I've had very few crashes when using it. However, there are a lot of mods in that modpack, and it strains my computer a lot! I get lag issues because my computer is old, and that can be frustrating for me sometimes. But the modpack is so incredible that I'm willing to put up with a bit of lag. Wait until you go to the Ur-ghast's castle and see how incredible it is; you'll forgive a little lag in exchange for a great gaming experience.

To download Feed-the-Beast or the Curse Client, first talk with your parents and tell them what you are doing. These programs might cause problems on your computer and may cause difficulties for others, so always get your parents' permission beforehand.

(When I downloaded FTB, even I called my mom first and asked her permission. She's eighty years old, and she said "Mine-what?" I took that as her agreement.)

Certainly, the safest way to see the things I was writing about is to go to YouTube—again, only with your parents' permission—and watch some of the mod showcase videos from Direwolf20. He has a great mod showcase on the Twilight Forest that is definitely worth watching.

You may need to make an account on feed-the-beast. com or curse.com, so ask your parents first. I went to https://www.feed-the-beast.com/ and downloaded it from that site. You can also find it at https://www. curse.com/games/minecraft, but anywhere else is risky. Direwolf20 has a great video, showing you how to load the Curse Client, and how to load different modpacks. It's at https://youtu.be/lf2y1D8wMdU and is worth watching.

You can find instructions on how to install FTB on their wiki page, https://ftbwiki.org/Tutorial:Installing_ Feed_The_Beast_on_PC, or http://ftb.gamepedia.com/ Getting_Started_(Main). There are also numerous videos on YouTube that show how to load FTB and how to install modpacks. There are many great resources there to help you install this software successfully, if you do your research and are careful.

Once you have FTB or the Curse Client and your modded Minecraft is working, you can create a world with the seeds below, and go to the coordinates I've listed to check out what I was seeing when I was doing my "Research" for this book. I was using the Direwolf20 modpack with these seeds.

Lastly, I want to apologize in advance . . . you won't be able to see any of these biomes on the Gameknight999 Minecraft Network, because the Twilight Forest mod will not run there.

Enjoy!

FTB – Direwolf20 mod, seed: -7068356819993160018

Overworld
Chapter 2 – Crafter's village: x=176, y=65, z=-13
             or x=-2720, y=68, z=1885

Build a portal to the Twilight forest – 2x2 hole, fill with water, put flowers around the edge and throw in a diamond.

Twilight Forest
Chapter 7 – Mushroom Kingdom: x=-1199, y=32, z=-300
Chapter 8 – Alpha Yeti: x=-16, y=32, z=-1292
Chapter 10 – Naga: x=-492, y=32, z=-955
Chapter 14 – The Lich King: x=-1058, y=37, z=-257
Chapter 20 – The Hydra: x=671, y=34, z=-2320
Chapter 24 – Snow Queen's Glacier: x=346, y=68, z=-1316
Chapter 26 – The White Castle: x=-332, y=122, z=-294

AVAILABLE NOW FROM MARK CHEVERTON AND SKY PONY PRESS

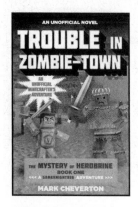  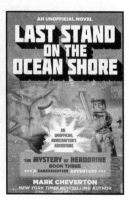

THE MYSTERY OF HEROBRINE SERIES
Gameknight999 must save his friends from an evil virus intent on destroying all of Minecraft!

Gameknight999 was sucked into the world of Minecraft when one of his father's inventions went haywire. Trapped inside the game, the former griefer learned the error of his ways, transforming into a heroic warrior and defeating powerful Endermen, ghasts, and dragons to save the world of Minecraft and his NPC friends who live in it.

Gameknight swore he'd never go inside Minecraft again. But that was before Herobrine, a malicious virus infecting the very fabric of the game, threatened to destroy the entire Overworld and escape into the real world. To outsmart an enemy much more powerful than any he's ever faced, the User-that-is-not-a-user will need to go back into the game, where real danger lies around every corner. From zombie villages and jungle temples to a secret hidden at the bottom of a deep ocean, the action-packed adventures of Gameknight999 and his friends (and, now, family) continue in this thrilling follow-up series for Minecraft fans of all ages.

Trouble in Zombie-town (Book One):
$9.99 paperback • 978-1-63450-094-4

The Jungle Temple Oracle (Book Two):
$9.99 paperback • 978-1-63450-096-8

Last Stand on the Ocean Shore (Book Three):
$9.99 paperback • 978-1-63450-098-2

 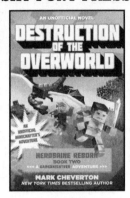 

AVAILABLE NOW FROM MARK CHEVERTON AND SKY PONY PRESS

HEROBRINE'S REVENGE SERIES
From beyond the digital grave, Herobrine has crafted some evil games for Gameknight999 to play!

Gameknight999, a former Minecraft griefer, got a big dose of virtual reality when his father's invention teleported him into the game. Living out a dangerous adventure inside a digital world, he trekked all over Minecraft, with the help of some villager friends, in order to finally defeat a terrible virus, Herobrine, who was trying escape into the real world.

Gameknight thought that Herobrine was gone for good. But as one last precaution before his death, the heinous villain laid traps for the User-that-is-not-a-user that would threaten all of the Overworld, even if the virus was no longer alive. Now Gameknight is racing the clock, trying to stop Herobrine from having one last diabolical laugh.

The Phantom Virus (Book One):
$9.99 paperback • 978-1-5107-0683-5

Overworld in Flames (Book Two):
$9.99 paperback • 978-1-5107-0681-1

System Overload (Book Three):
$9.99 paperback • 978-1-5107-0682-8

EXCERPT FROM
MONSTERS IN THE MIST

The cobblestone platform was surrounded by columns of ice that stretched high into the air like the ice spikes of the Overworld. But these frozen structures were much taller than anything his companions had ever seen, stretching up thirty blocks, if not more. To Gameknight999 they looked like some mythical giant had thrust them up through the snowy landscape from deep underground. The bright sun overhead sent rays through the crystalline structures, breaking the light up into rainbow colors that splashed down across the snowy terrain. Red and greens and blues and yellows stretched across the ground, coloring the snow like sheets of multi-flavored cotton candy. It was like standing inside a kaleidoscope . . . it was fantastic.

"What is this place?" Digger asked as he set Tux on the ground.

Instantly, the little penguin flopped down on her side and rolled around on the ground, the cold, frozen carpet of snow caressing her skin. She squawked and squeaked with delight. Stitcher sat down next to the penguin, picking up balls of snow and rubbing them against her black and white body. Tux purred contentedly.

Gameknight moved to a small hill and climbed to the top. Carefully, he surveyed the landscape, searching for any of the purple taint that was slowly infecting the last world. This Age was covered with snow and ice, the white terrain only broken by the occasional dark trunks of trees, the normally green-shaded leaves frozen to a glacial blue. Strange jagged shafts of translucent ice stuck up into the air, forming complex crystalline structures in every shape and size. It was as if the giant forms had been moving, dancing in every way possible, then were suddenly frozen in place, their waltz violently stilled. Though Gameknight found the shapes beautiful, they were also disturbing.

"Pretty incredible landscape." Crafter moved to his side and gazed out across the biome.

"Sure, if you like freezing," Hunter added as she crunched her way to the top of the hill.

Gameknight glanced at each and smiled. "It's fantastic the way the sunlight goes through those icy pillars and the . . ."

"Village," Hunter snapped suddenly.

"The what?" the User-that-is-not-a-user asked, confused.

"I said village," the girl replied, her curly red hair looking unusually bright against the frozen landscape. "There's a village over there." She pointed with her enchanted bow.

Gameknight turned and peered in the direction she pointed. In the distance, a village was visible, the houses made of snow and packed ice, blending in with the background. A tower made of light blue ice loomed over the village, the top covered with snow. It reminded Gameknight of a frosted blueberry popsicle. He smiled.

"This land is in pain, like the last, yes, yes," Empech said in his high-pitched voice.

Gameknight turned and glanced down at the little gnome. The pech shook, but not from the cold. The User-that-is-not-a-user could see a look of fear in his deep blue, gem-like eyes. Something wasn't right.

"What's happening here?" he asked.

"It is not clear, but something is wrong, yes, yes."

"We should check the village," Crafter said. "Make sure everyone there is okay."

"Maybe you're right," Gameknight replied.

One of the wolves barked, then gave off a loud howl.

"My wolves found Entity303's scent," Herder said. "He went that way." The boy pointed in the direction opposite from the village. "We should follow."

"I think we need to check the village first," Gameknight said.

"But the trail . . ." Herder said.

"Sometimes people are more important than animals," Weaver interrupted, his voice ringing with anger.

A wolf next to Herder growled, his fur bristling.

"It's all right, Weaver," Gameknight said. "Herder just wants to keep the wolves on a fresh scent."

Herder nodded, his long, tangled hair falling across his face.

Weaver smirked.

"I'm going to the village to check it out," the User-that-is-not-a-user continued. "All of you can stay here if you want."

Squawk, squawk! Tux said, then scurried up the hill and stood at Gameknight's side.

"I have to agree with Tux," Hunter said. "Let's follow Gameknight999."

"Everyone get your bows out and keep your eyes open," the User-that-is-not-a-user said. "We need to be ready just in case Entity303 left some kind of surprise here for us."

They moved out, following Gameknight999 as he ran toward the village. His breath created a billowing cloud of mist as he exhaled, his nose and lips growing cold and getting slightly numb. His fingers ached as he squeezed his bow, but Gameknight didn't want to put it away; an itch at the back of his neck was telling him something was amiss.

A growl sounded off to the left. It was a polar bear with two of her cubs. The huge animal stood up on her back feet and snarled at the party, her eyes and nose dark as charcoal. The creature extended sharp, black claws for the end of her front paws and waved them in the air. Instantly, Gameknight veered to the right, wanting to keep as much distance between them and the massive animal as possible; it was never a good idea to tangle with a polar bear while her cubs were near. The wolves growled back at the bear, but happily moved away from the huge predator as well.

"Anyone there?" Crafter yelled as they neared the village.

The only sound was the crunching of their boots through the frozen crust of snow. The ever-present wind blew from the east, causing a jingling sort of sound to fill the air. Gameknight thought it sounded like delicate crystalline wind chimes, but he'd never heard those before in Minecraft.

"Looks like they're all gone," Hunter said.

"Come on," Gameknight said, sprinting forward.

The party ran across the frozen plane, the sound of tinkling wind chimes slowly getting louder. When they entered the village, the companions split up, searching the homes. Herder's wolves circled the cluster of buildings, smelling the ground for traces of NPCs, but quickly returned; they found nothing.

Gameknight stood next to the village well and waited, nervously shifting his bow from one hand to the other.

Squawk! Tux said.

Kneeling, the User-that-is-not-a-user patted his friend on her soft head. "I don't know where everyone is either. But if they're gone . . . where did they go?"

The penguin squawked again, then flopped over on her side and rolled about in the snow.

Hunter suddenly appeared at Gameknight's side, her brow furled in confusion.

"Anything?" he asked.

She shook her head, her curls bouncing about like crimson springs. "I didn't find anyone, but I found items from people's inventories discarded all over the place."

"That doesn't sound good," Gameknight replied. "Show me."

She led him to the nearest house. Right in front of the door, a pile of tools hovered just off the ground, bobbing up and down as if riding the gentle swells of an unseen ocean. The pickaxe, shovel, and sword were all covered with a thick layer of snow, making them difficult to see against the snowy ground.

"What are these?" he asked, pointing to the wall.

The wind chimes grew louder.

Thin shards of ice were stuck against the door of the house. Each looked like a tiny dagger and was plunged deep into the wood. Gameknight reached out and touched the keen edge of the frozen spike; it was razor sharp. He glanced over his shoulder and found Crafter and Empech standing near the village well, talking. He motioned them to come near. Digger and Woodcutter saw the gesture and came as well.

"Anyone ever see anything like this before?" Gameknight asked, pointing to the door.

"Oh no," a high-pitched voice said. "Ice cores, yes, yes."

Gameknight turned and found Empech staring at the door, a scared expression on his oversized, gray face.

"What?" Hunter asked. "Are these frozen spikey-things called ice cores?"

The pech shook his head, then glanced around nervously. The sound of the wind chimes grew louder, coming from south of the village. This drew the little gnome's attention away from the door and toward the jingling sound.

"They're coming," Empech screeched. He shifted nervously from foot to foot as if he were standing on blazing hot coals. "Ice cores are coming. Can't you hear them?"

The wind chimes grew even louder, as if the source was now in the village.

"You mean those bell-like sounds?" Crafter said.

"Yes, yes, ice cores," the pech said, his deep blue eyes filled with fear. "They're coming. We must flee."

"Flee from what? A bunch of icicles clinking together?" Hunter asked.

Just then, a handful of razor sharp daggers of ice streaked through the air and thudded against the wall of the home, one of them striking Gameknight in the shoulder. He flashed red, taking damage.

Turning, he drew his diamond sword to face the threat. Expecting skeletons or zombies or bears; Gameknight999 was shocked at what he saw. Weaving between the buildings were creatures he'd never seen before. Their heads seemed as if they were made of packed snow and ice, a speckled blue and white texture to their faces, with black soulless eyes that stared right at Gameknight and his friends. Around the disembodied head, blue, crystalline spikes revolved, each one faceted with razor-sharp edges and pointed tips, some of the icy shafts clinking together, making the wind chime sound.

The frozen spikes began spinning faster around one of the creatures, then it leaned forward and shot them at the company. Out of instinct, Gameknight reached into his inventory and drew his shield. Holding it before him, he felt the icy shards embed themselves into the shield, some of them going all the way through and protruding out the back.

"I'm thinking we should get out of here," Hunter said as she pulled a spike from her leg, grunting in pain.

"I think you're right," Gameknight replied.

The group turned to escape, but the sound of more wind chimes filled the air as another group of ice cores approached from the other side of the village. Mixed in with the floating terrors were creatures that looked like armored guards, but as they neared, Gameknight saw they had no legs; they floated across the frozen ground just like the ice cores, frozen clouds of snow streaming out from beneath their breastplates. A loud growl filled the air as a squat creature with white fur and frozen blue flesh ringing its mouth and eyes approached, a toothy snarl showing on its square face. Long, sharp teeth filled the creature's mouth as it bellowed.

"Yeti!" Empech exclaimed, "and aurora guards. We are in trouble, yes, yes."

They were surrounded, with their backs against the building. Gameknight knew if they tried to run through the crowd of approaching monsters, they would be doomed.

"Gameknight, what do we do?" Hunter asked, "You have any plan that doesn't involve us being destroyed?"

But the User-that-is-not-a-user was paralyzed with fear. He couldn't move. It felt as if he feet were frozen in the ground and the blood in his veins had turned to ice. All Gameknight999 could do was stand there and wait for their destruction to crash down upon them.

COMING SOON:
MONSTERS IN THE MIST
THE MYSTERY OF ENTITY303 BOOK TWO